A Future Hollywood

The Time Chronicles

Book 4

A Future Hollywood

A Novel by

P. J. Hatton

The Time Chronicles, Book 4 - A Future Hollywood

To my daughter Emma, DC, who loves the movies even more that I do

Introduction:

Hollywood and the Digital Age

Hollywood, the glamour, the glitz, the nightlife, the stars. All of it real, but also strangely surreal. A world of fantasy, adventure and excitement. From cowboys to "Star Trek", Hollywood has been fascinating us from when the first black and white moving pictures were shown up on the screen, bringing the human race into a new world of marvelous, unparalleled entertainment.

It was back in 1895 when the world received its first glance at these novel 'moving pictures', shown to a packed theater, by the Lumière Brothers in France. The revolutionary and stirring images conjured up in their short, silent film, "*L'Arrivée d'un Train en Gare de la Ciotat*" (translated as, "the arrival of a train at La Ciotat"), had an immediate effect on its virgin viewing audience. It was a relatively simple, black and white film showing a steam locomotive pulling to a stop at a train station platform. Of course, for most of us today something so basic would be a very modest example of historic modern film. However, for those unfamiliar very unsuspecting spectators of the time, this seemingly everyday occurrence, now displayed in front of them on a large overhead screen, had a chilling effect. Some say its portrayal caused the patrons to stampede out of the theater when the larger than life, steam train came barreling out of the screen towards them.

This was the very first time the realism and effect of the motion picture was recognized, marking the beginning of a new era of memorable entertainment. It was only onward and upward from there, the possibilities endless. The consumers wanted more, and the Lumière brothers, and others, were only happy to oblige.

Over on our side of the water, a man by the name of Charlie Chaplin, in the orange groves of southern California, constructed and opened the first American studio, beginning to make silent films shortly thereafter. In 1910, the first movie, "In Old California", was officially released. Filmed in a new place called Hollywood, the area continued to build in both notoriety and size. People of all ages flocked to the new industry and more and more studios and films began to develop, rising out of obscurity, to meet the building demand of theater goers.

Photography, acting and scripts also improved, however, silent, black and white films dominated the budding industry. Movie makers made do using makeshift subtitles to signify speech and hired live piano musicians for the theaters to accompany their offerings. But as the studio's sizes increased and the shows became packed with eager patrons wanting more, money started to flow. And with this capital came fame and fortune for both the stars, but more importantly, the studios.

With their newly acquired wealth, the technology of film was able to develop in leaps and bounds. Soon, in 1927 "The Jazz Singer", the first film release to be developed with integrated sound, was released and the final piece was in place. The transformation now complete. Films could now be realized to duplicate life in all forms and the industry skyrocketed. Big filmmaker names like Cecil B. DeMille, John Houston, David Lean, John Ford and Alfred Hitchcock joined Charlie Chaplin to build up the thriving industry. Stars like Douglas Fairbanks, Buster Keaton, Lillian Gish, Mary Pickford, John Gilbert, Harold Lloyd, Gloria Swanson, and Marion Davies, to name only a few, eagerly joining them. Hollywood was on its way, and there was no stopping it.

In 1918, the first film shot entirely in colour, "Cupid Angling" was made. But it was unrefined, not yet perfect and the popularity of the treasured 'black and whites' had not yet worn thin. So, the process of filming in colour did not take off in Hollywood until decades after, when in 1939, a new process called Technicolor was introduced. Many great films arose in this new medium, like Victor Flemings's "Gone with the Wind" and how could we forget the wonderful "The Wizard of Oz" that combined both colour and black and white for the first time. It meant a new age for the industry and a very literal end to black and white as a production standard. But not before such great films as John Ford's "Stagecoach" and "Grapes of Wrath" and of course Orson Wells most famous "Citizen Kane", were released to extremely appreciative theater goers.

Some filmmakers, so set in their ways, unfortunately shunned the new technology, sticking with black and white until the bitter end. Frank Capra's "It's a Wonderful Life" being an example of a 1946 film, shot entirely in black and white, while all the productions completed around it sported the new Technicolor format. In fact, the new colour presentation was so impressive that the great filmmaker Cecil B. DeMille re-shot his 1927 silent, black and white movie classic, "The Ten Commandments", over again in 1954. This time with new actors, surround sound and Technicolor images to salivating public scrutiny, resulting in several prestigious industry awards.

Movies of the later 40's and 50's became more refined and lavish in their appointments, and numerous masterful works were generated, receiving their just rewards at the Hollywood party of the year; the Academy Awards. Put on annually, each

March, by the Academy of Motion Pictures Arts and Sciences. A truly apt name, for not only were the studios producing a new art form, with excellent writing, photography and acting, they were also developing different levels of sophistication in the technological and scientific aspects of the business, special effects, sound effects and editing.

New genres of film also emerged during this time of almost unparalleled advancement. While studios continued working the historical, western, mystery and city dramas, they added new and exciting realms such as fantasy and science fiction to their vast repertoires. Providing the audience with many truly new and different cinematic experiences. While Fritz Lang's widely popular 1927, black and white, classic "Metropolis" introduced the audience to science fiction as a genre, it was not until later that films like Roberts Wise's, "The Day the Earth Stood Still", elevated science fiction as a truly accepted medium within the industry. However, for the majority of studios, science fiction and fantasy films remained in the "B" category for most of the 50's and 60's, staring lower rated actors and sporting poor special effects, delegating themselves to a cult status enjoyed by only the younger generations.

Still, the genre did produce a clear star in Steve McQueen, who rose from his role in the 1958 science fiction horror, "The Blob", to become one of greatest known stars in Hollywood history. The 50's and 60's also gave rise to many other Hollywood legends as they would be referred to in later years; Marylin Monroe, Paul Neuman, Anne Bancroft, Charlton Heston, John Wayne, Audrey Hepburn, Cary Grant, James Stewart and the always infamous, Marlon Brando.

As movie technology developed and acting improved, so did the writing and directing. All leading to an increase in the cost of doing business. The cost of people.

For it was human individuals that made the movies, wrote the films, and starred in the productions. Good writers became very expensive, good directors similarly so and A list actors, well, they were hard to find, and when they could be found, demanded enormous sums of money to complete a picture. Some of the smaller studios just could not afford the continually mounting price tags and, not being able to keep up, closed their doors. Making movies had become a rich man's game.

The later part of the 20th century saw Hollywood advance in both amazing ways and in different directions. Finally coming to a head in the 1970's with ground-breaking films of yet a new genre, that of the disaster film. With such movies as "Earthquake", "The Towering Inferno" and "The Poseidon Adventure", huge films with 'A' list actors and the most sophisticated special effects Hollywood had ever conceived were now offered to the eagerly awaiting public. The audience now wanted a different style of film, one that would combine all the crucial cinematic elements including, acting, writing, directing, music and special effects.

"Jaws" was another example of a movie with it all, when in the summer of 1975, its horrifyingly good story, from a novel by Peter Benchley, swam on to the screen. Using modern film techniques, perfect direction from a young upstart director, Steven Spielberg and music from the maestro of Hollywood, John Williams, it was the first movie of its kind to affect the general public in a way no film had ever done before. After seeing the engrossing, perfectly acted and very memorable picture, people refused to get in the water that summer, suddenly afraid that the deep baritone notes signaling the approach of a man-eating, great white shark would be there to meet them. Hollywood never had it so good!

The late 70's, however, saw another new pioneering film come to light. One written and directed by a young local California boy, from up state. A movie combining good story, acting and as well as revolutionary special effects from a relatively obscure studio called 20Th Century Fox. The man's name was George Lucas and of course his movie was "Star Wars". Star Wars went on to be the highest grossing film of the summer of 1977 and opened up the realm of science fiction in a completely new way, elevating the genre to top tier status for the first time in Hollywood, generating a swath of copycat movies. Some which did extremely well, others that put the category to shame.

Star Wars also went on to generate a new, hither to unheard of occurrence in Hollywood, the sequel. Up to now the only sequels were in westerns, utilizing the same characters in different films, but the Star Wars Saga, with Star Wars, "Empire Strikes Back" and "Return of the Jedi" really brought home the notion of sequels in modern film. Star Wars was also so progressive, it was the first film to finally, and rightly, recognize *all* the workers on the film. From the producer, director and actors, right down to the effect's modelers and painters, even to the caterer on the set, all of whom were included in its end credits! It was an amazing change and its pioneering precedence set a new requirement for film credits throughout the industry.

But the main thing Star Wars and its sequels developed was the use of cutting-edge technology in sound and special effects. Never before had a series of movies accomplished a previously unattainable level of sophistication in this regard, and as the 80's continued, other films began to further the technology in hither to unheard of ways. From "Raiders of the Lost Ark", to Star Trek, from "Superman" to "Back to the Future", special effects were now a staple of every film and were getting better with each year.

The 90's saw the movie industry and the computer industry ultimately collide and meld into one. With the many advancements in processing technology, the continuation of the Star Wars Saga, "The Lord of the Rings" Trilogy and others, came the further advancement of digital special effects. 1995 also saw the first film to be completely generated within the computer using digital technology; Pixar's "Toy Story". A phenomenal example of advancement in computer artistry, combining film and computer technology seamlessly. The digital world was taking Hollywood by storm.

With this rise in sophisticated computer-generated imagery, it was not surprising that, eventually, attempts would be made to incorporate digital images into live action pictures, and this began in the late 1990's. Most of the created images were of imaginary characters and digital recreations of set pieces now felt too expensive to build. So instead of using carpenters and painters, the directors chose instead, to film scenes on a green screen set and later, using computer graphic technicians, filled in the digital environments in post-production. There were several scenes in the last Star Wars film that were filmed entirely in a green soundstage, including the green suits for actor's costumes, all of which were later added, long after principal photography had wrapped.

It was therefore inevitable that within this ever improving, digitally enhanced world, a human character would be finally replaced with their digital counterpart. That happed most successfully in, yes, another Star Wars film, entitled "Rogue One, a Star Wars Story". Shot in 2015 as a prequel to the 1977 original Star Wars, the story required resurrecting a character from the original film as portrayed by the late, great Peter Cushing.

During principal photography, an actor indeed performed the role on the set. He was of similar build and height and wearing a reproduction of Mr. Cushing's original costume. But instead of his face being visible, he wore a green hood, effectively screening him out. Using the latest advancements in computer technology, imaging and scanning, a digital road map of the actor's movements was created. In post-production, a computer reproduction of the Peter Cushing's face was digitally placed within each frame of film creating the first successful, computer-generated human actor. For some it was still unreal, not yet perfect, but for most, they could not tell the difference.

So began the movie industry's first step into the creation of digital actors. Through the intervening years, the technology continued to advance, studios even making younger versions of older actors, that were digitized on screen, a good example of this being, Disney's "Tron Legacy" where we were able to see the wonderful Jeff Bridges in both his real and not so real aged forms. This was soon continued through other studios as well, the idea now having caught on. Writers now able to produce scripts for more seasoned professionals acting roles as they might have looked when they were younger. It was quite an achievement.

And it was within this continually evolving matrix that in 2019, an obscure science fiction film called "Alita: Battle Angel" was released. This was the first movie to combine a fully digitally created human character interacting with other 'real' human actors in the film. A stand-in actress was used for the role during principal photography, but after completion of the film, she was digitally removed and replaced with the computer's creation for the final product.

A fully computer-generated actor working with other actors on the set. What would be next for Hollywood, its actors and its technicians? What interesting developments will digital computer technology, imagery and scanning provide in the years to come, as the technology, science and machines get even more and more sophisticated. Will there really come a time when actors eventually become obsolete?

Only the future can tell.

Prologue: Time for Something Different

Well there it was, three trips ahead and three strikes and I let me say I was thoroughly put out. I had experienced futures with insane, power hungry, mind controllers, insatiable human androids, and a third world war on a devastated planet earth. How much worse could it get!

My time travelling experiences to date had really not been very pleasant. Although, when considering it further, despite the pitfalls, I had met some very courageous youngsters, some good friends, and most importantly, a few brave souls working hard for a better world in which they could live. But on my next trip, I really hoped for a future that could be experienced without too much hassle and preferably one in which I didn't have to use a weapon and wasn't running for my life!

Each time I returned to my own past, the dials of time were reset, to begin anew. So, no matter how bad my previous travels had been, there was still a good chance the next one might be different. One compelling feature of my previous visits was that I had remained in my hometown for each successive voyage. This time, in order to shake things up a bit, and hopefully experience an enjoyable future, I was determined to try something a little different. This time I would venture further out.

My son was constantly bugging me to take him on a trip to California to visit his cousins and so I thought it only prudent to agree. The only difference was I planned to take my machine along with us. As you will remember, my device travels in time, but not in space, so wherever I depart physically on the globe, is where I will arrive in the selected future.

Southern California, Los Angeles, Hollywood! All seemed as good a place as any to me and would provide a different location as a send-off point. I had been a movie buff for years, always taking time to enjoy a good film whenever I got the chance and was quite interested to see what might be happening in the movies many years from now. So, it was time to pack up the van, and get on the road, for what was sure to be a very inspiring, if not enlightening, father and son road trip.

Originally, my son was all for a trip to the Golden State, but when he learned we would be driving, he hummed and hawed about all the long hours on the road. I eventually talked him into coming, explaining that using our own vehicle, we would be much more mobile and could go anywhere we wished upon our arrival. The beach, Hollywood boulevard, the Griffith's Observatory, Long Beach even Disneyland. He eventually warmed up to the concept and, still excited to see his family, we were soon on our way.

Taking our time to get there was the key. It was a long way and seeing as I was the only driver, I did not want to get too tired on the trip. Making the journey in short stints would also help with the boredom of the road that sometimes develops when one spends too much time in a car. The two of us wanted to be sure we enjoyed every minute of our excursion, so would visit a few stops on the way. Because as they say, "getting there is half the fun!" Indeed!

Chapter One – The Trip South

We made good time on our run south, travelling about 600 km a day, with stops in both Oregon and central California. The passenger cabin of the van was extremely comfortable, plush and well appointed, but that should be expected for a Mercedes-Benz. Especially after making sure when purchasing it, several years previously, that I did not skimp on the options. The air-conditioning was top notch, ensuring the surrounding temperature was always pleasant, no matter where we were or how hot it was outside our vehicle. We also had self-cooling, supple leather seats in which to recline. This was a feature my son took full advantage of, often detecting his soft snores when we came to a long stretch of asphalt, particularly after a heavy meal of burgers and fries! I had to be very careful at times like that not to fall asleep at the wheel myself! Always remembering to pull over and take a walk, or even rest, should the feeling ever arise.

Just east of Grants Pass, Oregon, a small, sleepy little town on the southern end of Oregon's Interstate 5, was where we turned off the main highway, taking our first side trip to beautiful Crater Lake. It was pleasing driving down its wafer-thin, 2 lane approach road, through the spindly pine trees, the early afternoon sun beating heavily down on us from above. The marvelous view of the sunbeams arching through the tall trees, creating strange shadows with every turn. But the towering firs provided some welcome shade from the blistering heat, making the entry to the natural wonder even more spectacular.

Losing track of time, we soon passed the ranger station at the National Park's entrance, taking a short rest stop at the gift shop and information center. Then it was off to ride the switchbacks ascending to the lake's incredible rock lined, perimeter roadway. As we drove this scenic byway around the rim of this environmental spectacle and gazing down at the incredibly beautiful blue water, I felt an extreme sense of belonging, a calmness not felt in ages. It was deeply relaxing and soothing, rejuvenating my very soul.

Stopping at one of the pullouts, we left the van in the shade and hiked up to the nearby overlook. This particular lookout presenting us with a rather spectacular view of 'Phantom Rock', rising like a ghostly pirate ship, out of the lake's sparkling, turquoise waters. The air was fresh and clean, with an underlying fragrance of pine, and apart from the occasional young child showing their enthusiasm for the view, it was quiet and serene. After a short break, we continued on, experiencing the sheer magnificence of the local monarch butterflies, flying around us in droves. They were everywhere! Across the road, in the trees and above the mounds of melting snow, liberally powdered with dirt, still found along the roadside. It was a truly gorgeous sight, but in another way also quite sad. For the sheer number of the dark brown, yellow and black fluttering creatures flying around us was so excessive, that at times they appeared to have a suicidal need for escape, ending up soaring directly in front of our van. We, therefore, couldn't help but plaster the hood and bumper of our cruising vehicle with their dusty, fluttering carcasses.

It was another fine day, and we spent the evening in a local restaurant, feasting on tangy, tasty barbeque before finding a quiet motel just off the freeway to rest our heads. Going to bed early, we managed a good respite, but were up even earlier the next day, still having a long way to go. In under an hour od setting off we were mounting the incline into the mountains, followed by some very steep hills dropping across the state line and onward into California.

Then it was through the great redwood forest, seeing the oldest and tallest trees in the USA, their majestic presence captivating and awe inspiring. As a lark, we drove our van to one of the many available tourist traps, barely making it through a tunnel cut in the massive bulk of yet another huge redwood's trunk. After that, it was back to the highway running through the tall ancient trees mostly in shade, the towering forest creating mottled, dark green shadows everywhere we drove. A very pleasant, worthwhile and memorable experience.

Soon after experiencing this beautifully primeval forest and working our way back on to the main freeway, the majestic form of Mt. Shasta greeted us as we travelled further south through the northern part of the state. The soaring edifice rose out of the treeline resembling a snow capped, rocky sentinel guarding the occupants of the unforgiving interstate highway winding around its wide base like a coiling serpent. Over rivers and streams, the roaring white water creating a lullaby of sound as we ventured further on.

At one rest stop, we sheltered next to one of these small rivers, and while sitting in the shade sharing a sandwich we listened, watching intently as the churning waters energetically made their way onward to their eventual destination in the Pacific Ocean. It was pleasant rest, a good break in what was certain to be a very tiring day. After the brief respite, we left the higher elevations, passing down into the hot desert valley, through the seemingly endless walnut and fig tree plantations. The straight, unnatural parallel lines of abundant fruit trees standing row upon row, in the various fields along the roadside, being carefully tended to by proud growers. Or sometimes, not nearly as proud, hired hands.

At last it was time for us to head west, out of the sun-soaked valley towards the coastal mountains and the bay area, which was always the favourite part of the trip for me. So, after experiencing some more blistering central California heat, we soon arrived in the cooler, slightly moister climes of wine country and the vineyards of Napa and Sonoma. After visiting a few of the more traditional estates and acquiring their selected vintages, we stopped again for a late afternoon rest. Later, as we unloaded our suitcases from the van, my son and I watched the sun setting out west, the sky turning a burnt orange on the horizon.

That evening, while I sat patiently watching in a deck chair enjoying some of the areas fine tasting wine, my son frolicked about in the glittering clear waters of our motel swimming pool. He was a good lad, putting up with his dad and all his quirks, especially on our long ride. I felt happy for him, as after my first time-travelling adventure, it was good to see him enjoying some of life's more simple pursuits, rather than spending his time, face affixed to a handheld device. Forever surfing the net, draining his brain of all of its energy, squandering his hours away on useless games and mindless entertainment. I would be even more delighted to be able to have him join his cousins for some well-earned fun when we reached Los Angeles.

His new hobby of photography had, so far, been well put to the test during our trip, as he had taken some of the nicest photographs I had seen in ages. John had captured the beauty of Crater Lake and the majesty of Mt. Shasta certainly better than I could ever hope to do, and all with a smart phone, no less. But thankfully, it appeared that was all he was using the device for. We would definitely be making prints of some of the better ones.

The evening remained cool and fair, the two of us appreciating our chance for relaxation, just as one should when on vacation. It had been a good time for us and so far, we were thoroughly enjoying each other's company.

"Hey dad," he shouted, his voice wavering slightly as his body shivered in the cool water, "I'm hungry. Can we go get something to eat when I'm done?"

"Sure, whatever you want," I replied, "let me know when you've had enough of that water and then we'll see what we can rustle up." I smiled, sitting back to relax, knowing he would be at least another hour, the boy not yet willing to extricate his thin form from the cool water until he was all well and 'pruney.'

Later that night, and two extremely large hamburgers later, my boy was safely tucked in one of our rooms two double beds, his light snores rumbling beside me in the half-lit chamber. Knowing he was fast asleep after his long tiring day, I thought at first about joining him but then decided, it was a good time for a walk. So, I left him lying there, being careful to ensure the door was locked, exiting the motel for a much-needed twilight stroll.

The evening was warm, but a light breeze blew in from the nearby Pacific, lending a pleasant coolness to the fresh smelling air. I wandered down the local street at a leisurely pace, marveling at the bright neon and bustling restaurants along the road. Certainly, Napa had come a long way from its early days, now with its 5-star eateries, serving dinner jacketed and evening gowned guests, all paying through the nose for a small morsel of elegant, but no doubt, tasty food. With wine of course. There was no way I would be able to take my son to any of those stylish establishments, so instead, just marveled at the decadence of it all, grateful not to have to drain my own wallet for their measly offerings, then leaving with an appetite unsatisfied.

Finding a small park, off the beaten path, I walked through the well-manicured, landscaped area until a comfortable bench presented itself and sat, staring up at the clear and cloudless sky. By now the dark night was in full bloom and the scattering of silver stars smiled down at me, sparkling like small pinpricks in a vast swath of backlit, navy blue felt. It was a very agreeable time of the day, the traffic noises from the nearby highway had diminished at nightfall, and the air smelled crisp and clean. With the subtle taste the fine wine still detectable on the back of my tongue, I thought life just couldn't be better.

My warm thoughts were smoothly interrupted with a recollection of my time machine, sitting there in the back of the van with our suitcases, sandals and swim trunks. What on earth was I doing? Was I really going to travel through time when we reached Hollywood? Would a trip into the future there be any different than the ones I had already experienced back home? Would it finally be the utopia I expected, or just another perilous adventure? Would it even be worth it?

I cut myself off. Sure, it would. It had to be. Because I was fed up with what had gone before and felt certain I had enough bad trips to last a lifetime. I was thoroughly looking forward to a positive experience, a truly favourable future, one that I would remember because I wanted to, not because I was forced to.

This road trip and all the beautiful places we had visited had indeed cleared my mind, removing those horrible experiences personally witnessed in 2114, at the hands of the Rulers, and my so-called friend Doc. I could still remember the awful smell and the sound of his piercing screams as his body burned and melted away before my eyes. Very real and very nasty, certainly no Hollywood movie special effect. Also recalling how glad I was to be rid of the Micro Docs that had invaded my body. While the tiny, devious medical parasites had helped to keep me alive during my adventure, it was good to be rid of the little buggers once and for all.

As my thoughts continued further back to my time in 2114, it also brought back to mind Erica, poor emotionally and bodily scarred Erica. Her and small Jasmine, hoping the two of them had strengthened their bonds of faith, each supporting one other in their new lives as only a mother and daughter could. Finally, I remembered my good friends, Joker, Nimbus and JP, but mostly my best friend, Tyco and what he went through. I only hoped the send-off I gave him was good enough, painfully recalling the dried blood stains on his nametag and insignia in my desk drawer. Then, my mind fully drifted away as I felt the fatigue of the day's journey taking hold.

I could only have fallen asleep thinking of my past friends and adventures, for I awoke shivering to a very chilling breeze. Goose bumps had arisen on my arms and leg, being simply clad in a light tee shirt and shorts. The night sky was inky black and only the noise of the prevailing wind provided any company. To warm up, I jogged carefully back through the empty park and along the abandoned sidewalk to the motel, noticing now that most of the fancy establishments along the road were quite deserted, their lights extinguished, the town having gone to bed hours ago.

The hotel was equally quiet as I opened the outside door with my key card and negotiated the short walk down the dimly lit corridor to my room. The prevailing scent was vaguely musty with a hint of lemon, my soft soled shoes padding inaudibly on the patterned rug. Entering our small home away from home, all was rightly as it should be, my son still safely in his bed. Although the covers were now in complete disarray and one of his spindly white legs poked out from under the sheets. After putting the dead bolt on the door, and brushing my teeth, I slowly undressed, placing my dusty clothes on an available chair before sliding under the cool covers of the second bed. The pillows were soft, the sheets cozy, but like in most motels, the mattress was tad too firm. Nonetheless, I settled in nicely, now very ready for sleep.

The curtains were partially open, allowing the filtered, blue moonlight to shine in, illuminating the far wall of the small chamber, and the ugly, black framed print hung there. But the moon beam was like an old friend, welcoming me, guiding me into my renewed slumber. I smiled, content, falling asleep happy, my mind clear, looking forward to another day on the road, our last driving day on our trip to Hollywood, 2020.

Chapter Two – Hollywood 2020

We left Napa early in the morning and headed west towards the Pacific. One of the most thrilling parts of travelling through California by car was a chance to motor down Highway 101, down the hill and around the blind corner to eventually reveal the glistening, bright orange towers of the Golden Gate Bridge. Crossing the bay from Sausalito to San Francisco, the magnificent, 6-lane, cable stay bridge welcomed visitors from Marin County in the north into the famous city with all the hills. As we crossed, I looked up to view the soaring towers and huge, braided steel restraints supporting the bridge deck, imagining the feat of engineering to produce such an enduring landmark. Sure, there were longer and wider suspension bridges in the world, but none could surpass the timeless beauty of this iconic structure. Opened in 1937, it was now almost 100 years old, and had surely stood the test of time. A truly unforgettable architectural masterpiece.

As we approached the south end of the crossing, we passed the now abandoned toll booths, long since automated, welcoming us into the city by the bay. My son took one longing look behind as we turned east, heading through the Presidio and then up Lombard Street. Riding up Russian Hill, instead of turning right at Van Ness Avenue, I headed through the intersection, over the cable car tracks and down the celebrated, single most, crookedest street in North America. Its eight hairpin turns heading down the hill directly into the heart of downtown. Upon reaching the foot of Lombard Street, we turned right through the city. First passing the TransAmerica pyramid, then reaching Union Square and shortly thereafter, turning left onto highway 80 across the Bay Bridge.

Now the Bay Bridge was not nearly as famous as its Golden Gate cousin but nonetheless provided spectacular views of the bay area and Alcatraz Island. As we made our way through the old cable supported, double decker section, or west portion of the bridge, we saw how its tall green towers and sturdy lines mimicked the elegant orange ones of our first crossing. Then it was on to the eastern section and across the brand new, cable supported potion, taking us from Treasure Island to Oakland on the far side of the inlet. This new bridge structure, built in 2017 as a seismic upgrade, replaced the old outdated truss style bridge that collapsed in the earthquake of 1989. In place since 1936, the ancient edifice was in desperate need of change and the new suspension bridge now did the crossing justice. It too was indeed a sight to behold, but its modern lines did not hold the iconic flare of the Golden Gate. My son did not agree, his camera snapping several, magazine quality pictures as we crossed.

Once past this extremely long crossing, it was through the coastal mountains and back to Interstate 5, then south to our final destination, Los Angeles. The lower part of the state saw further climatic changes and more desert style flora and fauna than we had witnessed previously. And the temperatures soared as we travelled further south. While the air-conditioning kept us nice and cool, putting your hand on the dashboard under the wide windshield, one could feel the searing heat beating unrelentingly on your skin. I did not relish the thought of what we might do if the A/C failed, and as we drove, seeing some older local cars scream by with their windows wide open, made me pity those surely, very toasty occupants.

After a quick stop for fuel, both for the van and ourselves, we made it back to the San Gabriel Mountains and the long climb into the hills, north of Los Angeles. It always amazed me how some cars would race up the steep incline, racing onward, burning fuel, only to have to ride their brakes all the way down the other side. I, on the other hand, maintained a reasonable speed on the way up, then used my engine and a lower gear to slow us on the long ride down. As we made our way into the Hollywood hills, we passed 6 Flags, Magic Mountain, its multi-coloured steel rollercoaster tracks rising into the sky like so many twisted skeletal spines of some ancient fallen giant.

"Hey, wouldn't you like to try some of those stomach teasers?" I asked my boy sitting next to me, staring at the swirling metal tracks curving into the late afternoon sky, "They look like pretty fancy rides."

"Oh no way, Pop," he replied, "I don't like those get sick rides. I like the ones with a bit of character. Something to look at, as well as thrill you."

I had just learned something new that afternoon. My son apparently had taste.

We continued on south towards Burbank, finally turning off I-5 and onto highway 170, before joining back on to the 101 towards Hollywood proper. But instead of heading up to our hotel at Universal City, we decided to detour south onto Hollywood Boulevard to get a good look at downtown Tinseltown.

We passed the Capitol Records building, still standing after all these years, its round cylindrical shape looking like a tall stack of old LP's. Then it was past the Pantages theater, the Hollywood Wax Museum and the Musso & Frank Grill, serving Hollywood patrons savory delights since 1919. Finally, we saw the ancient pagoda designs of one of the most famous landmarks of all, the TCL Chinese Theater, formally known as Grauman's Chinese. Displayed directly in front, of course, was the forecourt of the stars, where the world's most celebrated actors and actresses had placed their hands and feet, immemorial in concrete. Quite a place, the stars of Hollywood's Walk of Fame all terminating at this historic theater, where even today most of the largest film premiere events were still celebrated.

It was indeed a grand place, but also a bit unlucky, as the famous building did not look nearly as majestic as it had once done in the past, now being sandwiched between two, much taller buildings. Even worse, one being the modern glass and steel structure of Madame Tussaud's Wax Museum, complete with its own Starbucks. This had the unfortunate effect of relegating this classic and celebrated place to the background, diminishing its grandeur, taking away from its dignified history.

The hideously dressed and costumed Mickey Mouse, The Hulk, Spiderman and others out front, all offering themselves for cheap photos in exchange for $20, did not help either. Not one bit. All the garishness amounting to a bit of a disappointment for my son who, although not resisting a photo of the splendid palace itself, refused to take even one other shot along the now, somewhat tasteless, Hollywood strip. When prompted, he was not even interested in stopping, instead asking to head out and see some more of the other sites around the area.

We turned around at the next set of lights and, travelling back the way we had come, headed east under the highway, turning left on Fern Dell Drive. Up the switchbacks and windy road onto Mt. Hollywood, through a short tunnel and out onto the lavish promenade that was the entry to the Griffith's Observatory. A white stone, art deco structure mounted on the side of the mountain, the famous observatory demonstrated some of the area's most spectacular views.

It turns out, a group of cars had just left, presenting us with the lucky find of a premium parking spot close by, providing the chance to finally exit the van for a much-needed stretch.

As we walked up the green grass verged walkway on approach to the famous tri-topped building, we had an excellent view of its primary, aquamarine patinaed dome over the entrance way. We also stopped to stare at the large figures carved into and surrounding the bright white iconic entry pillar, topped with a blue tinged copper planet, rising high in the center of the building's front courtyard. It was a welcoming sight and the two of us felt secure and content, as we sauntered around this very agreeable and relaxing location.

Moving forward nearer the main complex, rather than enter the observatory itself, we went around to the right side of the building, mounting the circular staircase up to the roof. Our climb was rewarded with access to the entire perimeter wall encircling the front of the structure, allowing us to take in the stunning views of downtown Los Angeles to the far west and Hollywood far below. Off to the right and just behind, was of course the most notable landmark of all, the famed Hollywood sign, sitting like a tall, white clad guardian high up on the hill.

The day was clear, and the warm sun beat down on us from above, but despite the heat, the vast yellow orb was invisible, the sky and city itself still misted over in a cloud of smog. This ever-prevalent haze blurred the sharp edges of the various downtown buildings; like the Wilshire Grand Center and US Bank tower. The lack of clarity did not deter my son at all, however, his camera taking pictures of everything from the city, to the sign and even the observatory rooftop itself. He even took some pictures of the two of us, the famous city as a backdrop. It was a peaceful and enjoyable afternoon, but we had one last stop to make on our way back to the hotel.

We left the observatory, leaving our parking space, to a very enthusiastic and thankful tourist from Canada, and headed west, cutting across the mountain roads to Franklin Ave and up to Deronda Drive. The street was not very wide, and we had to watch for traffic coming down, pulling to the side when we ran into an opposing vehicle. Then we parked the van, being careful to make sure we weren't in a residence only spot, before hiking up old Mt. Lee Drive to the top of the hill and the Hollywood sign itself.

It was a long tiring walk, and I knew that later that night my hips and thighs would regret it. But the closer we got, the more energy we seemed to muster, both of us anxious to see the sign up close. We ended our walk just above it, but to our dismay were forced to take pictures through tall, black chain link fence, the larger than life logo safely guarded and surrounded in security cameras.

The sign was huge! Each gleaming massive letter sat on its own towering metal frame, painted bright white, glistening in the late afternoon sun. It was a bit disappointing not being able to touch the famous symbol of opulence but being that close, really made our day. We stood there for an hour waiting, while the sun went down behind the horizon, staring over the giant missive and down, watching intently as the lights came on all over the sprawling city. It was truly a magical moment. A masterful Hollywood moment.

We hiked back down the hill at a leisurely pace, in the twilight, the paved road providing sure footing and a relaxed gait. Upon reaching the van, it was then an easy drive back down the mountain through the various residences and then back on to highway 101 for the short hop to the exit for Universal City. We passed by the main entrance of Universal Studios, turning left and then down, beside the large concrete parkade and into the forecourt of the Sheraton. I dropped my son off at the front desk with the luggage and proceeded into the multi-level garage, making sure to choose an end spot on the first level for my relatively large van. Before leaving, locking it up tight and setting the alarm, forever mindful that my priceless time machine rested inside. It would not be pleasant to have any prying eyes or slippery fingers spoil my potential ride into Hollywood's future.

The room in the Sheraton was modern chic, and very spacious and clean. It had all the amenities one could ask for even robes for after the shower. And all the mirrors! There was mirrored glass all over the place with a full mirrored wall over the bathroom sink. It was very different from some of the very somber motels we had stayed in and my son felt immediately at home. Considering it was about three times the cost of those places, I wasn't surprised. But the nice soft pillows and mattress made up for the difference and that night, as I cuddled under the

Egyptian cotton sheets, I sighed in comfort knowing it was all well worth it!

The next day, we made our way to the main entrance and took a round through the Universal theme park, packing in all of the major attractions including the Wizarding World of Harry Potter, The Simpsons play park, and the three E-Ticket rides at the bottom of the world's largest escalator; Jurassic World, Transformers and The Mummy. These attractions were right up my son's alley, both of us thoroughly enjoying the cross between complex mechanical apparatus and computer-generated special effects, prevalent throughout. Quite a show and well worth it.

I've learned over the years that it's tough to have a staple diet with a pre-teen in tow, particularly when all they eat are burgers and fries, so after a brief lunch of more fast food, we headed back up the escalators, past the Simpsons and onward to the Studio Tour trams.

As it was later in the day, the lines were not as long, nonetheless we still had to stand with the rest of the many rows of holiday goers, moving in switchbacks back and forth, to-and-fro in the heat of the falling sun. Mercifully, at the end of every second aisle, a fan and misting system blew cool water droplets at us from above, making the wait just a tad more bearable. Most of the area was thankfully undercover and production posters of famous Universal pictures greeted us from all sides. Myself remembering each and every film, but for my son it was a little harder, not being one for "classic movies".

Once we made it to the tram, and were contentedly secure on the comfortable bench seats, we motored through the backlot, a light breeze blowing in our faces, making the tour more enjoyable. First up was a run through the sound stages and picture car row, containing vehicles from many of the latest as well as some much older films. A few of the souped-up cars from Fast and Furious were in evidence, including several vehicles from Jurassic Park also acknowledging us from the side lines. Then it was through the Central American village to experience the 'Flash Flood', an effect still in use at the park from the early days of my childhood remembrances. Once secure from any further surging waters, we cruised through the old western town, before passing under the defunct collapsing bridge, now vine covered and derelict.

Beside this old classic and through a black, skull encrusted archway, was the new 3D experience of King Kong. Our perilous tram first being waylaid and attacked by a roaring tyrannosaurus rex, before the big ape decided to make his heroic debut, coming to save our poor hides. This last-minute rescue, unfortunately not in time to save the rear tram car as it was brutally "thrown" into a bottomless chasm. Hope those folks purchased vacation health insurance!

Following that, it was on to the streets of New York, or Chicago or Philadelphia, whichever the particular downtown location the movie of the day happened to be. Both old and new streets backing on to one another at just the right angles, providing the studio endless possibilities for uninterrupted filming, without any of the hassles of location shooting. Next, was a drive by of the immense outdoor effects pool, with a massive lightly clouded blue-sky backdrop used for large, open water shots. The clear water glistening in the sun as we drove by, remnants of a film shoot still being tidied up.

Then it was on to Martha's Vineyard, Cabot Cove and a surprizing great white shark attack, in which my son was splashed and so frightened, he could not help but laugh hysterically for the rest of the ride. Afterward, motoring up a rise, we passed the 'Bates Motel' and the infamous 'Psycho House'. A real 'Norman Bates' sat pacing the dusty forecourt, patiently waiting for our tram to arrive, then began to run determinedly after us, a knife poised to strike, many patrons screaming in enjoyable fright as he did so.

Leaving this maniac killer safely behind us, we proceeded up the hill past the old house and through the diorama of a crashed 747 aircraft, from the movie 'War of the Worlds'. Apparently, the film's director, Steven Spielberg, so concerned about getting the shot *just right*, and with digital affects not yet quite up to muster at the time, purchased a real Boeing Jumbo aircraft, breaking it up, and stratifying the pieces all over the Universal backlot in an attempt at ultimate realism. A costly endeavor, yes, but now a very impressive display for any future theme park visitor.

The tram had two more stops. First, it was past the residential street, representing the best of little town America, various craftsman house designs all in one cute, well maintained lane. And lastly, it was on to another new building housing yet another 3D attraction, the Fast and The Furious. A blisteringly fast, digital picture show displaying alternate action on both sides of the tram, expertly fooling the riders into thinking they were travelling much faster than they really were. A spectacular version of movie special effects made to wow the unenlightened.

Upon our arrival back at the station, fond remembrances brought me back to when I was my sons' age and the old tram tour back in the day. At that time Universal was not a Theme Park with rides galore, it was a working studio with just the tram tour to entertain the guests, displaying the greatest effects of the time. Along with the Flash Flood, I distinctly recall the submarine torpedo sinking the warship, the 'parting of the red sea', the 'collapsing bridge', the avalanche of Styrofoam rocks and everyone's favorite, the spinning, ice tunnel. I, however, will always affectionately remembering it as 'the Six Million Dollar Man' sasquatch tunnel!

Ah, the good old days! Universal certainly had come a long way from its somewhat humble beginnings.

Disembarking the tram car, evening was now upon us and so we ascended back up the escalator to the upper level for the nighttime light show on Hogwarts castle, before finally heading out of the park and the short hike back to our room. My son had enjoyed himself and was looking forward to doing it all over again with his cousins the next day.

Previously, I had arranged to meet our family at the hotel and, taking advantage of my brothers' exceptional hospitality, would be leaving my boy with him and his cousins for the entire following day. That would allow me some time alone, to go for a drive with my machine and see what the future had in store for us here in glitzy Hollywood. I was now quite excited about my next adventure in time and looking forward to it. Hoping that finally I would be welcomed into a new time that would be pleasant for once, instead of another trial, as I had experienced on my several previous trips out.

But I was not naïve, being no stranger to the art of time travel. I knew, there was no guarantee for anything different, good or bad. As it would be the future, a completely new future and, as they say, who knows what the future might bring. I was destined to find out, though, in exactly 12 hours' time.

We went to bed exhausted from all the walking, but both equally excited for the upcoming morning. My son looking forward to visiting and exploring with his cousins, and I looking forward to doing the exact same, but in the future. The unknown distant future.

Our rest was comfortable and dreamless.

Chapter Three – Hollywood 2065

My brother and his boys met us early, eagerly taking my son right off with them for breakfast. I waved goodbye as the group headed off to the "City Walk" for food, agreeing to meet them for dinner back at the hotel later that evening. Although I had enjoyed my time at the park the previous day, I did not want to see it again, at least not as it was in 2020.

They left laughing and smiling, my son instantly forgetting his old Pop, enjoying the moment with his cousins, relating some of his preferences from the day before. His first words to his cousins being that he would especially like to see the Special Effects Stage and Water World Stunt Show that he had missed on our previous visit. It was good to see him happy and enjoying himself, I smiled knowing he would be safe and secure with my family. That left me now content to go and participate in some very different explorations of my own.

After a quick breakfast in the hotel dining room, I returned to my room to dress in my regular gear, making sure my pack was fully ready, assembling my various weapons, in preparation for my voyage forward. I had made a decision to test a theory of mine and selected the future year 2065, the exact same year in which I had encountered not only the Kanusan Empire, but my own son in his most unwelcome, future form. I wanted to prove to myself that the clock did do a full and complete reset after each return from the future. Also, to settle once and for all, that my son did not end up leading a company of mind controlling villains. The van was easy to drive around the city, as long as one stayed off the main highways. I had already chosen an appropriate departure point, one that would ensure my machine would land in an undisturbed location. Selecting the hills near the Griffith's Observatory, on the road towards the Hollywood sign, I was certain that 45 years hence, after having totally rebuilt the iconic monument in 1978, the city would, no doubt, still want it undisturbed and retained for future generations. Thus, without hesitation, I made my way to the same neighborhood on Mt. Lee that we had visited the day before last. There was never any intention to lug my heavy apparatus all the way up the mountain, but only to take it far enough up the trail to insure it would not be discovered.

Pulling the van into roughly the same spot on Deronda Drive, it was easy to see that, due to it being a workday, the neighbourhood was deserted and quiet. After disembarking and removing the device, I literally rolled my machine next to me up the gradual slope near the trailhead for Mt Lee. It was relatively easy going and being still early, the sun was not that hot, making the trek stress-free. The swelling smog, however, was like a heavy mask over the city and from my highly elevated vantage point, only the silhouettes of the tall downtown buildings could be detected through its thick ambivalence. The Hollywood sign above, however, was clear as day, its brilliant white lettering standing tall, reflecting the diffused light provided by the partially blocked sun.

After setting the machine down on a secure ledge amongst some scrub pines, I activated the mechanism, enlarging its hourglass form, exposing the magnetic rods. The slow lifting of the upper shell on the silver spindles was like a phoenix rising from the ashes in the heat of the day, lifting its head to welcome the glowing sun, eager for its warmth and rejuvenation. I stood there marvelling at its elegant beauty for a moment, but really just cementing my nerve for another trip.

Without any second thoughts, or further hesitation and before I changed my mind, I stepped onto the transport pad and reached up to activate the machine. Within seconds the magnetic arms began their quick counter current rotation and the panel beeped once, the rods spinning readily to full speed. Almost as soon as it began, they started to slow, coming to a complete stop to reveal a blisteringly, bright spring day, the sky completely clear, the sun beaming down with its full intensity. Knowing at once I had arrived in 2065 and that indeed the whole world had changed.

There was no smog! Not one ounce of smog coated the city, in fact it was so clear you could see far out to the Pacific, past the tall gleaming spires of the downtown core. Amongst the buildings I had witnessed two days ago, were several new towering structures, all of different design, but still glass and steel reaching high up into the sky. The strange glass, however, was different, gleaming in the early daylight, reflecting multi-coloured beams in all directions. Unbelievably, equally as bright as a nighttime laser show, even in the morning sun. The truly unique phenomenon held my gaze for several minutes, intrigued as I was by the look and sensation the spectacular view provided and wondering how it was accomplished. Impatient to experience more, I exited my machine stepping onto the rocky earth, appearing almost unchanged from my past. Finally, I took my eyes off the wonderous spectacle of the downtown core's colour palette and turned around to look upward, my mouth falling open in disbelief.

For up above me, as before, was the Hollywood sign, but it was not the sign I had just left. The 45 intervening years had obviously not been kind to the landmark logo, for it sat dark and derelict, looking broken, diseased and rotten. Wanting a closer look, I shut down my machine, retracting the rods, hurriedly covering it with some scrub materials and branches for camouflage. Looking again at the sad sign above me, however, it was doubtful anyone had even hiked this path in over 20 years.

The brisk walk was good for me, the clear, pollution free air refreshing in my lungs, allowing me to make excellent progress arriving at the exact same spot my son and I had shared two days previously. It allowed me to get a better view of the totally destroyed, landmark icon.

The letters were no longer white but grey and dingy, the discoloured paint peeling off in great strips like sagging wallpaper. Graffiti was etched on some of the letters, the excessively bright tints of each tag further defacing the already disappointing visage. Some of the massive panels had come loose off their frames and had plunged to the ground, further distorting the now ancient letters. One top arm of the H was missing, the belly of the D gone as well as some of W and O's now converted to U's. The worst damage was the Y that had fallen over completely. The sign no longer read 'HOLLYWOOD' but instead, 'hUL1_VUOl'. It was most a most distressing soul-destroying picture.

In further contrast to its condition, when reaching the pinnacle of Mt. Lee Drive, I discovered that behind the sign, the protective chain link fence, once surrounding the massive billboard, was gone. Completely collapsed in most places, the posts were twisted, the mesh all torn. Unlike before, I was now able to clamber down right down to the base of what remained of the letters, maneuvering the treacherous path from behind, then walking right up to the supporting frames and missive fragments. I reached out to touch one of the broken-down O's, feeling the forlorn surface, the cracking paint, the rusted metal. The once iconic Hollywood sign was now an abandoned mess, an eyesore on the hills of Los Angeles, forgotten by all, ignored by the world. Indeed, I was heartbroken, but then immediately fearful to have once again stepped into yet another horrifying future.

After a long tour around the derelict sight, I returned to the mountain path and made my way back down towards the awaiting residential street. The asphalt of the lane, once pristine, was cracked and broken, alligatored all over, several large potholes dominating its surface. One would have required a large wheeled 4 by 4 to even think of climbing this sad excuse for a road.

As I rounded the final corner near to where my van used to be, all that greeted me was a burnt-out hulk of what must have been my trusty transport, lying askew in the ditch. The wheels were all missing, the engine and hood completely gone, all the doors had been removed, and the glass smashed, the particles scattered over the shattered remains of the charred vehicle, like rice thrown at a wedding. There would be no use for that sorry excuse for a transport anymore. At least not in this time. I would have to wait until returning to my own time to see it safely and assuredly, resurrected.

I sincerely hoped that things might improve further down, being not yet ready to throw in the towel on this future visit. I was not to be disappointed.

With no other option plausible, I began the long hike down the hill. While the sign and my van were in complete disarray, the residential houses appeared fairly well attended to. Most of the lawns were still kept up, the houses in excellent repair and the gardens clean. It was strange to see such well-manicured landscapes and dwellings below the devastated lettering of the giant billboard staring forlornly off the mountain peak. Other than the sign then, with the residences obviously well cared for, indications were very positive that this future was indeed in at least reasonable shape. But what had occurred to make the people of Los Angles neglect one of their most famous landmarks? What had transpired to warrant such abuse? It was one of the many things I wished to find out before travelling home.

Suddenly, I was almost run over from behind, as a silent electric vehicle made its way down the mountain road behind me. My mind had wandered, and I had as well, right into the center of the street, the driver having made no sign to indicate that he was coming. I remembered the electrical cars from my own time and how silently they travelled on the asphalt, tire noise the only signal of their approach. Jumping to the side just as the car passed, I was able to notice its design. Certainly, it was no Aircar, but it was very well rounded and sleek, maneuvering quite easily around the hairpin turns as it sped happily on its way down the hill. Definitely nothing I had seen the like of before.

The driver had also been invisible on account of the vehicles completely blacked out windows, that included both the front and back windscreens. Its black shape disappeared almost as fast as it had appeared, easily and smoothly negotiating a turn past a set of fancy manicured hedges lining the side of the road. All in all, a very interesting development.

Continuing down the residential street, this time more carefully, I made sure to stay to the side on a constant look-out for any more electric vehicles. Several thoughts swirled around in my mind as I walked. A potential explanation then struck me as to why there was no longer any smog here in the Los Angeles of the future. Perhaps all the cars were now electric and fossil fuel vehicles were a thing of the past, finally shunned to the automobile graveyard. It would be curious to find out if this was the case in my continuing adventures into this so far very conflicting, but interesting future.

Eventually, after the long walk downhill, I made it back to Hollywood Boulevard, and in doing so confirmed several things about this particular future. My initial hypothesis regarding transportation in this time was correct. There were no longer any petroleum-based automobiles, all the cars and trucks on the road being electric, the light smell of Ozone permeating the otherwise fresh air. The complete lack of gas stations visible along the road also confirmed this. Each car looked very similar to the rest, with round streamlined shapes, and hardly any colour variation, all of them seemingly either black, white or a silver shade, in-between. And all with completely blacked out windows.

Second, the exteriors of the various shops and conveniences visible, did not appear to have changed much. It was as if I was back on the Hollywood strip, very similar to the one I had driven down in my own van, 45 years previously.

Third, I apparently needed new clothes, for clearly everyone within close proximity to me, both male and female, were dressed in such unique ways and palettes. And with such weird kinds of unfamiliar fabrics! Clearly standing out a bit in my stone washed jeans and leather jacket, vowing to change into something more 'local' at the earliest possible convenience.

Lastly, as any good time traveler would be after a long sojourn through time, I was famished.

All this meant only one thing. Local currency was required and needed soon.

This, fortunately, would not be difficult. With the street in front of me so similar to the one back in 2020, I knew just where to go. Contrary to popular belief, Hollywood Boulevard is not really the nicest strip of road in Los Angeles. Sure, it has some memorable buildings and the walk of fame, but mostly, at least in my time, it was a mixed bag of restaurants, souvenir stores and pawnshops. As the strip had not appeared to have changed much, one of the later would be my first stop.

The nearest one was easy to spot, and luckily for me, it appeared devoid of any significant activity. Before entering, I reached into my satchel and grabbing my velvet pouch, extracted a few of my sparkling, white diamonds. The store was full of the typical kinds of knickknacks found in any pawnshop, jewelry, sporting goods, small furniture, musical instruments, some of which were unrecognizable, and of course weapons. The interior atmosphere was warmer than the outside, the buildings air conditioning clearly in a state of disrepair, immediately causing me to sweat profusely. This was rather awkward as I was in no position to take my coat off because of the large weapon safely strapped around my middle. As doing so might have created all other kinds of problems for me. I just hoped my visit would be a brief one.

Walking right up to the occupied service counter, I waited anxiously to be served. After patiently standing for several minutes, I felt compelled to tug on the stained sleeve of the distracted proprietor, his eyes glued to the screen on the wall, showing some sort of action film. It displayed two seemingly beautiful leads, the man and woman actors almost too good looking for a simple action movie. I put it aside.

The clerk was a very obese man, with jiggling, stubbly jowls and saggy arms, his massive gut overhanging his belted trousers, exposing an excessively hairy belly underneath his, one size too small, sweat-stained cotton shirt. He was smoking from a metallic mouthpiece, connected by a clear tube, to an unfamiliar countertop device which bubbled loudly, emitting a strange buzzing noise. With his every exhale, I became enveloped in another vaporous steam cloud, each time detecting the familiar scent of hot chocolate. After he turned towards me, I noticed his left eye was fogged over and milky white, under a wide, dark unibrow, giving him a very unfriendly countenance, some might even say scary looking.

Not one to let something so trivial deter me, I proceeded to request the exchange of a few of my diamonds into some of the local currency. Contrary to his horrifying visage, the clerk gave a deep and hearty laugh, instantly agreeing most enthusiastically with the trade, offering quite a fair sum in trade for my few precious stones. After the transaction, he greedily took them from me, carefully placing the gems in a lock box under the counter and then, as if nothing had happened, returned his full attention back to the movie on display. Once again, he completely ignored me, as I walked out of the musty, sweet smelling establishment. Back in the street, it was interesting to note that, finally, the US had begun to use coloured bills, each of them all of different shapes and sizes, made of some transparent, futuristic material, completely waterproof and tear resistant.

I placed the wad of used bills securely in my pocket and continued down the street. With only one thing on my mind, food.

Chapter Four – Denny's 2065

It was an interesting walk along the Hollywood Boulevard of 2065. I saw all kinds of strangely familiar things but in addition to that all sorts of not so comfortable ones. And despite the electrical cars, the complete lack of smog, the endless sunshine and the bright and interesting clothing, this was certainly no perfect utopia.

This was proven on my approach to a shop that appeared to be one of those fancy adventure tourism outlets, advertising all method of fantastic undertakings for the brave traveller. However, when I found myself a bit closer and read some of the offerings on its advertising board, it revealed a gruesome twist on the exploration theme. Shockingly displaying an apparent lack of risk tolerance of this future society:

'Cordless Bungee Jumping – great views before you check right out!'

'Skydiving in Your Birthday Suit – fine way to end your last flight!'

'Waterfall Surfing – like riding an elevator straight down!'

'White Water Swimming – the best way in life to drown!'

It appeared these California folks still had a lot to learn about appreciating God's greatest gift and how to make the best of things when one has so little. But in reality, life is like that, always full of surprises and ups and downs. Some of us can handle a higher threshold than others, but eventually we just have to learn to take the good with the bad. Because no matter how awful things get, there's usually a silver lining waiting around the corner somewhere. Obviously, the folks of this future did not yet understand that. If life give you lemons, make lemonade, isn't that what your mom always used to say? Cordless bungee jumping, indeed!

My stomach was calling, so not having time to stop in any more of what were sure to be very interesting establishments, I soldiered on. Thankfully, it was not long before the tall, rotating sign of a very familiar family restaurant called out to me from up ahead. The red lettering on its yellow background, more flowery than in my time but still reading the seemingly immortal word, Denny's. Swiftly approaching the eatery with only one thing on my mind; quelling the building hunger that arose from my midsection. The faint hints of fried food emanating from the vents on the rooftop, as I neared the restaurant, caused me to salivate in eager anticipation.

Determinedly making my way through the glass doors and into the café, the most agreeable thing was that finally, on my fourth trip into the future, an almost normal, healthy and vibrant population of patrons was there to greet me. Passing into the humid, but very well air-conditioned environs of the restaurant, revealed various booths and tables sprinkled with all manner and mix of old, middle aged and young people. There were large people, slim people, children, grey hairs and raven hairs, octogenarians to babies. Finally, somewhere where I might feel completely at home.

What differed in this Denny's of the future, however, was the décor. Unlike similar restaurants of my time, harboring a very basic family style, fit and finish, the elegance in this establishment was clearly upper crust. All the silver and chrome features, exotic lighting, and even rich lavish carpets and wallpaper told me this was not your normal, family, Sunday outing. Evidently the Denny's chain had come a long way in my 45 years away. A very long way.

This was first most evident in the working staff. One of the most beautiful hostesses' I had seen in a long time, met me at the kiosk. Sporting a ballet style bun and superb make-up, she appeared closer to a model or actress than a homely greeter at your neighborhood eatery. She even touted a "little black dress" found more often in higher class venues, its high cut skirt and off the shoulder top, not leaving much to the imagination.

Tracy, as I read from her extremely prominent, electrical Denny's nametag, was also wearing high-heeled patent leather shoes and dark stockings that had a shimmer to them that glittered in the room's overhead LED lighting. The overall effect was quite impressive, all be it a little too seductive, for a plain luncheon offering.

Her voice was very pleasant, almost sultry, as she asked, "Just you?"

"Yes," I replied, "It's just me." still taken in by her beauty, I stood motionless, gawking.

"Are you okay, sir?" she asked, concern now evident in her voice.

"Oh yeah, no, I'm good, please lead on," and after she had retrieved a menu, I followed her further into the busy restaurant.

"Would here be okay?" Tracy pointed to a table in the middle of the open area.

"I would prefer a booth if possible," pointing to an open booth for two, over in the corner.

"Sure, no problem." she stated it quickly and sauntered over to the booth gesturing first for me to get seated before placing a menu in front of me on the table. I had changed seats because of my rule to always be able to see the entire area of any unfamiliar location, not only allowing me to see who was coming and going, but also permitting a great view of the entire scene and the various patrons. Enabling me to observe their actions in this strange new time.

"Christine will be your waitress today," Tracy added, "she'll be along shortly. Enjoy your lunch."

Then she was gone, back to her station, her hips swaying, as she left to meet the next arriving guest.

Admittedly, as I watched her go, my thoughts began wandering into realms best left undisturbed, but then Christine walked up to my table and all pleasant thoughts of cute young Tracy disappeared, my mouth falling open in shock.

My new waitress was barely clothed at all! Her "little black dress" was not even a dress, consisting only of a single, shoulder strapped crop top and an extremely truncated mini skirt barely covering anything. Her well-tanned, very muscular belly looked almost as if it had been carved from stone, a true Aphrodite if ever one existed. She was of a mixed ethnicity, which was difficult to place, perhaps having some Mexican in her blood, but nonetheless appearing very exotic. She too wore a ballet style bun in her dark hair, and like Tracy, was heavily made up, clearly sporting false eyelashes and wearing the same shimmery tights. But really it was her shoes that took the prize. I had never seen high heels that tall before. It was amazing she could even stay upright, let alone walk.

Her voice was melodic, almost musical in its tones, softly but assertively requesting, "Can I get you something to drink while you review the menu?"

"Sure," I hesitated, unbelieving the outfit and perfection poised before me, my mouth going dry, eventually replying, "I'll have a coffee, uh, please."

In the heat of the moment, perspiration forming on my brow, I could only think of my last future visit and the recommendations from that time, sticking with what was familiar.

"Coffee? You mean Café, don't you?" Christine squished her brow up as she asked.

"Uh… sure, Café then, Yeah! That'll be just fine," I said it almost stupidly.

Christine gave me another interesting look saying, "Comin' right up," and then she was gone, stalking away on those towering high heels, back the way she had come. I stared at her lithe, departing form, her calve muscles trembling, then took a deep refreshing breath, sitting back thinking, boy, what more was in store for me in this bizarre, future Hollywood.

Carefully, I took the intervening time to look around me at some of the other patrons, interested to know if customs had changed, and if so, how. Obviously, the clothing styles had transformed, that much was certain, but it would be interesting to see if anything else was vastly different. While my eyes moved about the room, I spotted a cute couple sipping obviously cool, brightly colored drinks in tall crystal glasses, unmistakably wet with condensation. Instantly, beginning to regret my previous decision to order coffee, or Café, whatever that was, instead of deciding on a cold beverage that might have been a much better choice with the rising heat outside. Supposedly, one could still change their mind later. It would give me an excuse to begin a conversation with my new friend, Christine.

Amid my flowing observations, another very attractive couple, sitting close by, figured prominently, noticing at once the strange resemblance the two young ladies had between them. In fact, the two women sitting across from one other, looked exactly alike, like identical twins, but with a difference. The facial features of each of the girls was exactly equal, there were no subtle differences, not a blemish out of place, not a facial mole, no variance at all. As it was, the only thing that did distinguish the two apart, was the colouring of their hair, one clearly having a darker tone to her locks, and one having more blond highlights than her companion. So, they could not possibly be sisters.

This was a most interesting revelation, and on top of that there was something else. Thinking back to my experience at the pawn shop, and the movie the fat clerk was so busy watching, I remembered the perfect looking actress playing the heroine. These girls, although it was impossible, looked very similar to that woman on the silver screen. It was quite an odd coincidence, but I put it aside thinking I must have been mistaken, only having had such a brief glance at the screen during my visit.

My review of the stunning duplicates and the strange happenstance, was interrupted by the return of my equally stunning waitress Christine, returning for my decision on what I would like to eat.

"Haven't decided yet, have you?" the vague teasing in her tune like voice, music to my ears.

"No, not quite yet," I answered. Then seeing an opening, pointed to the two women at the opposing table, "Hey, what's up with those two?"

"Oh," was her simple answer, "they've been to the slicer."

"Slicer?" was my immediate, almost uncontrollable response.

"You know. The alternating surgeon," Christine said it like it was obvious, making me feel ashamed for asking. Then she added, "They've permanently changed their appearance to emulate their favorite screen stars, you know the artificial ones. I think those two are modeled off on Susie Shine, but I'm not sure." concluding, "It's all the rage, everyone wants to do it. While, I agree you should look your best, hey, even I've done it. But bottom line is you really should stay yourself, you know? Don't you think?"

"Absolutely." was all I could say. At least now I had my answer, and I had not been mistaken. This Slicer person must be a master artist to have created something so real. So perfcct.

"You must be on your way to the rally?" Christine asked me directly, changing the subject.

"The rally?" there it was, happening again.

"Yeah. The way you're dressed, one would think your about 40 years out of date." Christine commented, "That's a real nice costume by the way. I kind of like the old times, things were much simpler then, or at least that's what my mom always used to tell me. Wearing these outfits," pointing to herself, "sometimes makes one feel a bit… cheap."

Then she turned on her heel and was gone, leaving me alone to look at the menu and contemplate what she had said.

My further review of the various diner's exposed several other youngsters that had apparently, like Christine, met the "slicer" and had some work done. It was interesting, glancing around to see who was real and who was sliced. After a while it became easy to pick out, the sliced patrons looking just a little too perfect to be their real selves. I wondered if this was just a phase the young people were going through or a permanent sign of the times. Perhaps Christine could tell me more, after all she had admitted to being to one of these slicer characters herself. Although, she appeared quite normal compared to some of these fancy Susie Shine lookalikes.

While eating my meal and managing a few conversations here and there as she worked her way around her tables, I found out from Christine, that this new type of plastic surgery, while still expensive, was fast and painless. Some patients getting in and out of the treatment centers in under a few hours. I was amazed at the advancements of this style of medical technology, but more about the exactness in which it was applied. Looking again at the two identical women, I really could not see one skin follicle out of place between the two. Truly astonishing! I promised myself I would visit one of these "slicer transformation clinics" before heading home.

The café drink turned out to be a variant of hot coffee, tasting okay, but certainly not the coffee of my time. It was more a facsimile, an attempted copy but just not quite meeting spec. Christine informed me that real coffee had become virtually unavailable decades earlier, when the Caribbean nations, becoming the mecca of retirees, had all of the once thriving coffee plantations torn down to make way for condos and high-rises. Hawaii had also apparently stopped making coffee, or really anything else, when it had become overrun by the ever growing, floating plastic island of the Pacific. The formally beautiful chain of Pacific islands now only an abandoned land of homeless, drug dealers and pimps.

As an after I ordered the ice cream, interested to try something cool on this warm day. The ice cream of this future was very tasty, but I was not quite certain it was actually made of ice milk. After my experiences in 2114, I decided it was probably not a good idea to ask. As I ate desert, I did, however, have one more question for Christine.

"Hey, I really enjoyed our chats. I'm Ryan by the way."

"Nice to meet you, Ryan," and she held her small hand out for me to shake. I did so but with only three fingers, not wanting to be too forward.

To break the awkward moment, I said, "Earlier, you mentioned a rally. I ran out of the house this morning and forgot to bring the details. Can you tell me when it starts and point me in the right direction?"

"Boy, you really are out of it, aren't you, Ryan?" she commented, "Have you be vaping up that new cannabis fluid their touting these days?" her probing question hung in the air a few moments.

After receiving no response, she exhaled loudly and stated, "You're right there, on the right street and," glancing at her flat screen wrist unit, "you have just about 20 minutes before it starts. It's just up the block at The Google Chinese Theater."

Then one could almost sense the inner workings of her mind churning furiously, "Hey, if you can wait a few minutes, my shifts almost over and I get off in 15. We could go together." she smiled at me, obviously feeling a bit sorry for me, almost as if she wanted to be sure I would make it there safely, "That's if you don't mind a waitress for company? I know how you actors sometimes get."

It was an interesting statement, and the fact she had connected me to acting was most intriguing.

"Of course, I don't mind," thinking of something to quell her uncertainty, "I'm not your regular run of the mill actor. I'm a bit more open and accepting," adding further, "You'll find I'm not as stuck up as the rest of my type."

"That's good to know." prompting her to smile again, while pulling a small tape from the device mounted on her wrist, "Here's your bill. Pay Tracy up front. I'll meet you outside in 10 minutes, after I change, of course." Christine bounded away, balancing precariously on her towering heels.

"Of course." I mouthed as she faded away into the bustling room, disappearing into the kitchen.

Wiping my mouth, I stood up, and taking the small tape printout, began waking to the front of the café. Looking down at the check, I finally understood why the burly man at the Pawn Shop had been smiling. What I believed to be a good trade for the diamonds, he knew was even better. The cost of the food was immense, revealing that I had, unmistakably, as one might say in my time, been royally *ripped off* in the exchange. I would have to be more careful on any further currency/diamond interactions.

Back at the entry kiosk, Tracy took my money with a smile and not wanting to appear cheap, with my new friend Christine, I attempted to leave a healthy tip. Tracy looked shocked and quickly handed me back the superfluous currency stating, "You need only pay what's on the bill, sir. We don't accept any more than that! It's against the law, you know!"

She said this rather loudly as if defending herself, so, not wanting to generate any further attention, I quickly withdrew the additional funds, placing the bills in my pocket, making a beeline for the exit.

Well, just one more lesson learned about this world that I could file away. Before the day was out there would, undoubtedly, be many more of these key remembrances here in this Hollywood of 2065.

Pushing the vestibule doors open, I stepped out into the heat of the late morning. The stifling temperature, hit me like a knock-out punch, affecting my body instantly, the gentle coolness of the restaurant's A/C no longer in play. The sky was cloudless, and the sun shone mercilessly down, its rays stinging my unadjusted eyes, after the somewhat darkened atmosphere of the diner. I immediately began to sweat, opening my heavy jacket wide for some relief, being careful not to expose my knife in its shoulder holster.

I wandered aimlessly around the parking area for a few moments, when suddenly a short, Hispanic girl walked right up to me, coming from around the rear of the restaurant. She was dressed in similar clothing to other females of the day, with multi-coloured leggings, a flowing white skirt and loose, open blouse, all made of materials unfamiliar to me. Her rather unruly, very curly hair fell somewhat gracefully down her back as far as her shoulder blades, their wavy wisps gathering about her face in the light early afternoon wind. Her face was plain, but extremely pretty and sparkled with a residue glitter of some kind. She had big eyes and generous lips, a well-formed figure, and was wearing flat style, white pumps on her feet.

She walked right up to me as if she knew me and stated, "Well here I am, Ryan. Let's go!" her most familiar melodic voice waking me from my momentary stupor.

"Christine?" I asked stupidly, "Is that you?" the girl must have been almost a full foot shorter. Then, I remembered the shoes.

"Of course, it's me, numbskull!" Christine looked a little ashamed at my loss of recognition, "See, I told you the so called 'uniforms' we wear are a bit too much. You didn't even recognize me."

"Well I…" I didn't know how to respond, being a venerable jerk not to notice it was her.

She put it aside, cutting me off, "Well, no matter, let's just go."

And turning around she headed up the street.

Boy, Ryan, I mumbled to myself, you certainly have a lot to learn about women and 2065! I turned and followed her petite form up the sidewalk.

Chapter Five – The Rally and the Riot

Resolutely following Christine up the street, I raced to catch up. She was in very good shape and her rapid walk, now in flat shoes, was quick and determined. Her pace was almost calculated, and she had a look of expectation on her face as we headed west on the south side of the block. Ultimately, upon reaching North Highland Ave, I did catch up with her, the two of us standing in front of what was the derelict façade of the old Ripley's Believe it or Not! Museum. Evidently, in my 45 years away, folks had grown tired of Mr. Ripley's bizarre form of entertainment, the facility clearly having been abandoned many years previously. The large sign, however, was still up, but by the obvious marks of neglect, it had not been lit or used for some time. As the venue had not yet been taken over by anything else, the windows and entry vestibule were all boarded up, the decades old plywood sheeting well greyed in the southern California sun. Poster boards, advertising today's noon rally, and other upcoming events, were plastered all over their sagging wood faces.

"Wait up!" I commented, "I said I was sorry. Really, I just didn't recognize you."

"You guys are all the same!" was her very vibrant and incensed reply, "Always staring, when you see us in the sexy uniforms, but not really seeing us at all? I know the owners do it for that very reason, to bring in the patrons. I know we're just considered eye candy, but it hurts just the same. Especially when coming from someone like you. I was hoping you were different from most of the others, but it fits. You are an actor after all."

"I am different!" I said blubbering, "I'm definitely different than anyone you've met before. You can be sure of that!" laughing to myself, at my own joke, "It's just your shoes, they're what threw me off." making nothing but pitiful excuses, I knew, but having to say something, "You appeared so much taller in them at the restaurant. You really look much better now. Way more natural."

"You're just saying that." moving her arms about, flustered, as if shooing me away.

"No, I'm not kidding! You're beautiful, much better now than in that silly costume! You look so much more genuine, more real!" That appeared to strike home.

"Well, I gotta' admit, those damn shoes do make me way taller. I know that. And I guess we did only meet today." she stated demurely, "Are you sure you're not just saying that?"

"Absolutely." I replied, honestly, "And I'm really glad you agreed to come with me to the rally," now being doubly honest, "I really would not have even known about it without you."

Christine looked at me with a bright smile, sealing the deal. Our friendship now restored, we looked across the street.

At the corner, we noticed the police barricades that had been raised over the driving lanes to isolate Hollywood Boulevard in front of the businesses, including the Chinese Theater, between North Orange Drive and North Highland. At each end of the roadblock were two, City of Los Angeles squad cars parked nose to nose, their black and white sleek shapes very prominent, the red and blue flashing lights on top, creating a strobe effect throughout the street. The vehicles were of an interesting design, clearly like the other automobiles of this time, electric in function, but uniquely equipped with large tires and rims, almost too large for the sheet metal surrounding them. The bumpers, fenders and windows were of one common form and shape, the only dividing lines visible being the edges of each door, several of which were propped open, revealing a reclining policeman in each driver's seat. The officers appeared tired, almost board, not really paying too much attention to the movement of concerned citizenry around them. They seemed only to be there for show, and to make sure no one carelessly drove down the asphalt lanes now teaming with protesters.

We crossed the road, and through the barricade, passing the ambivalent policemen, unimpeded, into the rapidly growing throng of brightly attired people. Moving off the curb into the enclosed thoroughfare, now clogged with participants, we moved still further west in an attempt at getting closer to the theater. This enabled us a much better view of the raised dais that had been erected in front of the towering, red and green pagoda. Once the angle improved, I had a better look at the old facility still sandwiched between two imposing structures built closer to the road. Unfortunately, nothing had changed, the old oriental palace remained well back from the street, as if hiding, spoiling its grandeur, reducing the effect of its earlier Golden Days glory. An ancient now relegated into obscure shadow. The structure itself was still in relatively good shape, its new owners Google Inc. having plenty of money to keep it up, the bright reds, green and yellow filigree very prominent in the bright noon day sun. Its courtyard still sporting the cherished hand and footprints of the Hollywood stars of yesteryear providing a very welcome and historic aspect to the square.

As we were still pushing through the building mass, in order to stay together in the crowds, I suggested we hold hands. Christine readily agreed, immediately grabbing my wrist with such gusto, I instantly regretted the suggested request. We moved on, Christine with her very determined gait, pushing and pulling me relentlessly through the mob. Then, as we approached what I believed a better viewing position of the speaker's platform, amidst the ever-growing mass of humanity, she took us just past the dais, very close to the temporary barriers on Orange Drive, before coming to a stop. Now believing we were suitably located, her grip loosened somewhat, our contact becoming much more tolerable, almost friendly in its feel.

We stood still together like that for several more minutes, the noise building around us, the protesters getting restless, wanting something to happen. There was a vibrant energy to the crowd, as yet very unclear in its focus, but just mounting and ready to burst. It was either going to be a very energetic and peaceful rally or fall heavily on the opposite side of the scale, dissolving into something much more sinister.

As we had finally stopped moving, I was now better able look around, take in the surroundings then view and read some of the various placards mounted on crude shafts of wood that some of the attendees enthusiastically waved up and down in the in the air. 'Save Our Industry' read one, 'Down with the Computer' on another, 'Don't Let the Studio's Win', and a much more enlightening one, 'Eliminate the Fake Voices – Give Us Back Our Jobs'. Clearly this had something to do with actors, voices and computers in film. What exactly, would be revealed shortly.

With the crowd building to a frenzy, precisely at noon, a tall, well dressed and very good-looking gentleman made his way up the stairs and across the stage to the small podium. Jet black, wind-swept hair covered his head, and his striking face retained a cleft on his chin so deep, it looked unreal. His shoulders were wide, and he wore a bright white, open necked shirt under a multi-coloured suit, his brightly polished shoes sparkling vividly in the sunshine. Very large hands gripped the microphone stand as he began to speak, the dull murmur of the crowd dying down almost instantly. His deep, resonating voice shook the street, through the many electronically enhanced speakers, efficiently set up along the face of the Chinese Theater and around the courtyard.

"Fellow actors, voice actors and fans. Many years ago, at this very time, we discussed the chilling, if not unprecedented assault on our industry. We have gathered here today to discuss an unwelcome follow-up to that very shameful calamity. An unfathomable, unparalleled tragedy and the final disturbing turn for what is sure to be the demise of the future of film and television. In fact, the entire world of entertainment."

His voice boomed, deep emotion laden within its message, "Last week, the studios announced a most unacceptable decision." he hesitated for effect, "Voice actors will no longer be required!"

Huge yells, boos and hisses arose for the uptight assembly, the cacophony of noise temporarily drowning out the speaker. He paused and raised his arms for silence, his hands wide open, pleading for quiet, for calm. The crowd eventually began settling down so that he might continue, but the pent-up energy remained at the breaking point.

"Thank you all for your support. I and all of my fellow voice actors share your concern." he continued with his diatribe, "Now the studios have confirmed it. They not only wish to create film actors using the computer, but their voices as well!"

The crowd went wild again, their cries louder than before, some of such high-pitched screaming, I was forced to let go of Christine's hand to hold my palms against my head, blocking out the ear shattering din. Once more, after a short while, the speaker held up his hands for quiet.

"Well, we are not going to take this persecution any longer. We are not going to take this latest decision lying down. We are going to fight and fight hard for our livelihood!" he paused again for emphasis, "We ask all residents of Hollywood, and fans worldwide, to boycott all movies and TV for the next week in protest of this most disturbing and industry shattering decision."

The crowd now burst into massive applause, screaming, catcalls and whistling, in apparent support of the well-spoken gentlemen's request.

Continuing, before he was cut off again, he shouted above the commotion, "We will not be forced out! Humanity should not and will not be removed from film! Who's with us?"

His final question set the crowds on fire. The screams cheering and support now reached a crescendo and the good-looking man smiled widely at the encouragement. He only stood for a few moments more, gazing out amongst the throng, waving and smiling and then was gone. Where he suddenly disappeared to, I did not notice, perhaps into the theater or behind it, but upon his departure the mob went wild.

Shortly thereafter, and not unexpectedly, the riot began.

With the speaker's departure it was as if a bomb exploded, energy that had been patiently restrained for the last half hour finally unleashed. Store windows were smashed, the dais swarmed, the microphone and podium toppled. What had been a relatively peaceful demonstration, becoming complete and utter anarchy in a matter of seconds. Garbage cans were lifted high and thrown over the heads of the rioting actors. Several cars that had not made it out of the street before it was blocked off, their windows, head and taillights already broken, were now set afire. Hoodlums climbed the streetlamp poles, breaking off the heads and raining shattered glass down upon the screaming hoard.

Christine grabbed my arm hard again and we headed out of the intensifying disturbance, west to the closet barricade, at North Orange Drive, near the south entrance to Madam Tussaud's Hollywood Wax Museum, to the left of the theater. But the awaiting police, poised for action, had already closed the gap. We turned around looking for another way out, finding ourselves pummeled with garbage, being screamed at by passersby. It was bedlam and we had nowhere to go.

Then quite surprisingly, a group of thugs appeared outside the containment, wanting to get in, looking for a piece of the action. Armed to the teeth with baseball bats, looking mean and determined, deliberately pushed the police aside, jumping the barrier. This disrupted the guarding forces at the barricade just long enough to provide Christine and I the cover we needed to squeeze our way out and away.

Without looking back, we ran north up Orange, just as the main riot troops, called in for suppression of the uprising arrived, immediately entering the controlled area. Halfway up the street, we paused a moment to look back, watching as the squads moved in with riot clubs and tear gas, in their attempts to overpower the exploding crowds, who were now fighting back in earnest. This stalemate carried on for a while, the police taking the abuse, some of the public retreating, but most just beating at the Lexan riot shields, making the situation even worse.

Then it became ugly, the police batons came out, rubber bullets started flying, and slowly, very patiently the police moved forward and subdued the crowd. Unfortunately, with heavy hits to various unprotected skulls of the protesters, and unrelenting physical force.

The rowdy group of thugs, that had done us the unexpected favour, initially had their way, felling one of two officers with their bats, breaking a few limbs, and having their fun. You could see the joy in their vicious faces as they very expertly dispatched several of the well-equipped troops. But soon, due to the sheer numbers being against them, the tables turned and one by one, they became overwhelmed, the police staff showing no mercy, knocking them rather brutally down to the ground with the rest.

Some of the bystanders had been lucky and like us, were able to make it out behind the advancing forces. But most, were left to fight for themselves, literally hammered down by the merciless actions of the adrenalin frenzied police personnel. Carnage was everywhere, bodies strewn throughout the square and in the street. In some cases, what were now certainly corpses, lay sprawled on the ground, gelatinous grey matter drooling from their broken skulls. Plasma could be seen running in the gutters, and the famous hands and feet of the stars began filling with blood, dark crimson pools shining like oil. It was a complete massacre.

We could stand it no longer and accelerating, ran further away, north up the street to Franklin, then turning west, continued to flee trying to forget the mayhem and bloodbath we had just witnessed. Eventually, stopping for breath, at the welcome sight of Dorothy and Benjamin Smith Park, (now called West Hollywood Retreat). We entered the park, at a slow pace, still glancing behind now and again for any pursuing authorities. Finding none and seeing as we were alone and had miraculously survived, we searched for an empty bench, in a nice secluded area under the shade of a large oak tree.

We sat down to give our weary bodies a rest and gather some much-deserved repose. By now, both of us were spent, perspiration dripping from our brows. Running so hard in the extreme heat of the day had been unwise, draining most of our available energy and strength. Christine reached into her large purse and angelically pulled out some bottled drink. It was not water and was lukewarm, but nevertheless, its wetness provided a perfect solution to sooth our parched throats, and quiet our spent nerves. For a moment, it also gave us something else to keep us occupied, taking our minds away from the obscene violence we had just witnessed. Finally, when we had both calmed down sufficiently, it was time for me to ask some rather pointed questions.

"Christine, what the hell happened back there?" taking a depth breath, "What was that all about? What made the police so incensed, the felt they had to use such a violent means to quell that riot? Is there something more going on here?" I was so scared at what we had witnessed the questions flew freely from me, like automatic machine gun fire, as if draining the nervous tension from my body. Christine, at first, did not appear to be very empathetic to my horror.

"Well, you heard it as well as I did." Christine replied defiantly, "The idiot studios now want to fully replace humans in film, using the computer. It's a disgrace."

"Of course, I heard that. But what on earth was he taking about before that?" I questioned again.

"What do you mean?" she answered me with a question. I really hate it when people do that.

"I'm referring to what that guy said before he got into the voice stuff. Did they really already replace actors with computer generated ones?" my question hung out there.

"Well of course they did, dummy. Where have you been?" she gave me another one of her weird looks, "That's old news. That happened about 15 years ago, just like he said."

"So, they don't use physical actors in movies anymore, just computer models?" I was flabbergasted.

"Yes, I keep saying it, but you keep asking it."

You could tell Christine was flustered but when she saw the look I gave, she first frowned, then settled down and instead chose to elaborate.

"One day, almost overnight, computer technology became so good the studios were able to replace entire characters, using animators and data bases to create them. The technology let these computer actors meld with backgrounds and other facsimiles seamlessly and perfectly, looking every bit as human as the real thing. Of course, it first started with fantasy characters and only evolved into human ones. With the convenience of the computer-generated characters blending flawlessly with the already computer-generated backgrounds, it was only natural things had to progress."

"At the time, actors were still very highly paid, and their schedules were always interrupting or delaying filming. With the new available technology, smaller studios began making films with completely computer rendered characters, using unknowns for motion capture work and voice acting. Soon these films became faultless and looked just as good as the ones the big studios were producing with real people. The unknowing public couldn't tell the difference."

"Movie goers even started emulating these fake actors, just as they used to do for the mainstream ones. Like those girls you saw this morning! After that began to occur, the big studios began to investigate the benefits of the computer-generated images. They realized creating their characters in the computer would eliminate the ego's so prevalent in the Hollywood actor and enable films to be made without the huge salaries or working schedule boundaries the big-name actors demanded."

Christine continued, "That was the turning point. That's when it all changed. As I said, originally, about 25 years ago, it was just a few small studios making the changes and at the time no one in the Screen Actors Guild cared. But when the big studios followed suit, a decade later, there was an outcry like you wouldn't believe, leading to uprisings all over. Some of the big-name actors, obviously having plenty of money, arranged for sabotage and other activities, hampering the studios to no end."

"But ultimately, it was all in vain. The studios prevailed and the decision stuck. And what were once famous actors on the screen, were now disgraced. And out of work! Unless, they agreed to be demoted to providing studios with motion capture or just their voices. Actors themselves, however, were now a thing of the past. Or so it was thought, because no matter how good the graphics were, they always needed the voices. They were having too many issues with computer simulations and so luckily, most name actors maintained their jobs as voice actors." she hesitated before she went on.

"Now apparently, the studios appear to have solved the problem with the computer-generated voices and have taken the last step. They have decided to remove actors from those roles too. Ending, once and for all, acting as a profession. This is what had the actors so up in arms, because anyone can be used for motion capture. You don't have to be a famous actor to be a motion capture drone. Therefore, the studios have now eliminated the one and only highly paid acting job remaining on the planet. Of course, the actors aren't happy."

"Okay, that makes sense. I understand now why they're upset, but that certainly doesn't explain the carnage we witnessed out there? What's up with that?" I asked with my face flushed, so many thoughts buzzing around my skull.

Christine continued, her breath returned, some of that fiery determination back in her quivering voice, "When the character actors were eliminated, 15 years ago, the resulting melee caught the LA Police woefully unprepared. There were so many innocents killed during those earlier uprisings, the authorities were determined not to let anything similar happen again. So, based on those previous experiences, they had resolved to quell this new one immediately, should anything occur."

"Those officers in the cars we saw entering looking so relaxed. It was all a ruse. They had clearly been tense from the first moment they closed off the streets. That's also why the riot squad arrived so fast. And that's why they were so harsh on the protesters. I'm telling you, Ryan, we were lucky to have gotten away with our lives. I knew they would be more prepared, but I didn't think it would be as bad as all that, otherwise we would have stayed away for sure!"

She concluded, nervously, now all emotion visible, her mind distraught, "You know, if it hadn't been for that party of thugs wanting to mix it up with the Police, I don't know what would have happened?"

"Well, were safe now." I calmed her, still somewhat jumpy myself. "It's going to be alright."

Christine collapsed finally, her spent emotions on overload, and whimpering she began to cry, placing her head into my shoulder. I gently wrapped my arm around her for consolation as she wept, letting her empty herself of her pent-up anger and fear. She made no move to stop me, so we sat there in the shade of the park, the only sound Christine stifled cry's, the tweeting of the birds, the light breeze blowing the leaves of the trees and the hollow sound of sirens screaming in the distance. Both of us shocked and upset, thinking what to do next.

It had been interesting listening to her narrative and had done so with utmost care and attention. Taking in everything about the story about the change and eventually of the horror created by the decision of the studios. Ultimately, like everything else in this world, is was all for money. What isn't? At least that part of the human psyche hadn't changed much. The executives, however, were immune, and didn't seem, or wish to care who was affected. Or how they were affected. Only how they might save money in order to make even more money. Whatever could be done to increase the coffers of the studio and make life easiest for its administrators, no matter what the cost.

I needed to get into one of these studios and find out for myself what was really going on and what, if anything, I could glean to take back with me so that this would never happen again.

Little did I know, that was going to be a lot easier than I expected.

Chapter Six – Universal Studios – 2065

We remained there in silence, sitting still for a while, enjoying the pleasing shade and light wind, regaining our composure and letting the energy return to our spent bodies. The rally riot had occurred just after noon, so there were still plenty of hours left in the day to make use of the amazing sunshine and brisk Pacific breeze. I thought it best that Christine and I find something to do that would keep our minds off the morning's earlier events, my head swirling with potential activities, both real and imagined of what we might do that would also work with my plans to eventually get a closer look at one of the local studios. Then a much more tangible idea struck home.

"Christine," I stated as she slowly raised herself up off my shoulder wiping her teary eyes, displacing some of her make-up, "is Universal Studio's still running their theme park? It might be a good place to go to have some fun so we can forget about what just happened. You know, put it behind us?"

She sniffled and sat up fully, straightening her flyaway hair, putting a lock behind her ear and answering my query with a strange, yet wholly honest answer, "You mean the Universal Studio museum tour?"

This did not sound even remotely familiar to anything the thriving theme park might ever have been referred to in my time, but her reference to Universal was succinct and certain, so I could only go with it.

"Yeah, that's it." she looked satisfied with my answer.

"Don't you think it might be good to get away from here and find a nice way to spend the afternoon?" I followed-up with my proposition, "We could head over there, spend the rest of the day getting to know each other. And if you haven't had enough of me by then, and you're still up to it, we could find a small place to have dinner at City Walk." (Using the term describing the retail restaurant area near Universal itself, in my own time.)

"City Walk? What's that?" Christine asked, a little confused once again.

Oops, I had made another one of my time-travelling faux pas, "Oh, it really doesn't matter where we eat," I back peddled, "you pick where, I'm easy, as long as we can relax and talk. And be together."

She appeared to accept my rather forward proposal, her face brightening, "Sure, sounds good. You've got yourself a date. Let's find a car and head on over." apparently, with a firm goal in mind, her energy had been restored.

What she had said, however, sounded interesting. As her words had not been let's find 'my' car but 'a' car. I could only follow her lead to find out what that might mean.

We walked to the edge of the park, back towards Franklin and along its wide concrete sidewalk. The sun was still bright, with the temperature continuing to be hot and humid. Considering it was early afternoon in northern Los Angeles, the street was not very crowded. Still, several folks, in the now familiar bright coloured clothes, did pass us as we slowly made our way east, the riot seemingly forgotten.

Quite suddenly, Christine stopped. Saying simply, "Here's one, all ready." before proceeding to move towards a car that a couple, heading the opposite way, had just vacated.

I didn't know what to say, so just followed her towards the comfortable four-seater. Opening the door, I took the navigator role while Christine swerved around the trunk, sliding her small hand over its smooth surface, before getting in behind a rather tiny steering wheel. Almost as soon as we were comfortable, using the brightly lit push button, she started the engine, the gauges and lights on the dash winking to life. There was even a heads-up display showing the time and speed, as well as a compass, splashed against the middle of the front windshield. The engine itself made no literally sound as the car, like all the others I had seen that morning, was electric.

Several other interesting events happened at the same time Christine activated the vehicles starter. The seats began to move, self-adjusting to suit their user. My seatback reclining and moving toward the rear, resulting in more leg room, and Christine's, based on her shorter stature, moving slightly forward, placing her in a perfect position for driving. The rear-view mirror also automatically adjusted for Christine's height and proper viewing behind us, at the same time the side mirrors rotated and altered their positions to suit her revised, now custom-tailored, driving position. It was like magic. There was no button to push, no seat memory to activate, all the changes occurring seamlessly on their own, without either of us doing a thing. The final icing on the cake was the automatic release of the seatbelts that expertly curled themselves around our bodies without digging in or pulling too tightly. Both clicking firmly onto their receptacles, securing us comfortably in place. It was an amazing display of fully automated technology.

"This isn't your car by the way is it?" I asked. Again, risking exposure of my lack of local knowledge, "I saw that other couple just leave this one. What's up?"

"What's up? Oh, don't be silly, Ryan. nobody OWNS a car!" Christine answered slightly exasperated, "All cars are free and belong to anyone who wants to use them. If they're there, you can use them. But you already knew that, I know, so don't tease me." she followed through, nicely, "I don't need cheering up that much."

But she smiled as she said it, so my dumb question had served its purpose. One to cheer her up and two to glean some more knowledge of this incredible future. Her answer sure would make getting around town really easy!

Christine was an excellent driver and pulled out into traffic east on Franklin like a pro. But then glancing over towards her and noticing her hands were in her lap, I suddenly realized she wasn't driving at all! I had heard her lightly say something like 'go' but thought she was talking to me. But once out in the road, I distinctly heard her say, 'Universal Studios Museum please', and then it was confirmed. The car was indeed driving itself! Christine just had to tell it where to go!

No wonder the steering wheel was so small! Perhaps it was only to be used on the off chance the guidance system shut down? Or maybe just to give the "driver" a sense that they were still in control, for comfort sake? Maybe it was there just to separate the diver from the passenger? Finally, it could just be somewhere to put your hands. None of that appeared to matter, considering the way we were weaving our way through traffic on that well used road. It didn't seem to be an issue for these fancy auto-cars of the future.

We were soon out of the North Hollywood streets and on to the 101-freeway heading North. The traffic remained light and I was amazed at how fast the automatic vehicle drove us toward our destination. Thinking back, that may have been why I was almost hit earlier that morning up near the Hollywood sign. The car likely being driven by computer probably wasn't expecting me and didn't have time to correct before it was past. Well, at least I knew now what to expect, what a future!

It was not long, and soon the auto-car had us at the Universal City exit. Although, during this time, it was called the Universal Museum exit. I couldn't wait, we were almost there!

"Boy, these Auto-Drive cars are great, aren't they?" I smiled, at Christine, enjoying my free ride.

"There you go again Ryan, you fool," Christine smiled back, "talking like you've never seen a Robi-car before! What will you come up with next?" she emitted a sweet belly laugh, swinging her head back, her dark auburn hair flying and glinting in the sun.

The Robi-car drove past what I remember as the old parkades, nothing like they were, looking more like condominiums. Definitely built up and inhabited, the old parking garages were long gone. After several more turns, we entered a much smaller, two-level parking complex, the self-driving vehicle selecting the first available space and coming to a quick and perfect halt. Wonderful!

We wasted no time in exiting the transport, being careful to make sure we had left nothing inside, before heading towards the nearest staircase. The signage was different than that I had experienced just yesterday, in another time, and it was a strangely eerie feeling to be in the exact same place and have it look so totally different. All within the same 24-hour period!

The elegant stairway exited on to a large plateau surrounded by bright and colourful landscaping and endless green lawns. A bright fountain sparkled in the afternoon sun, the rays of light glinting off the freely cascading droplets. To the right was the highway and behind us were the old towers of the two, 5-star hotels that had once been home to many a theme park guest, the Universal Hilton and the Sheraton Universal. The buildings looked older but had been kept up quite nicely, considering the present state of what we were soon about to see.

A massive glass and steel structure rose above the plaza before us, towering majestically into the sky. The clear roof was supported by extremely long, curved, laminated wood beams, giving the "glass house" a slightly more rustic look, versus the majority of its crystal and stainless-steel architecture. There were two, towering glass doors that had been propped open, welcoming guests the little of whom I could see, into a rectangular, glazed in vestibule connected to the main dome. In addition, there was a wide and ornate ground mounted sign reading, just as Christine had correctly described, 'Universal Studios Museum'. Its hours of operation clearly shown in small black capital letters below.

"Do you like all this fancy glass?" Christine asked, "They only put it up only recently. Folks thought the area was getting a bit run down, so the city put some funds together to protect some of the iconic architecture." she added a footnote, "The Studio bastards were too cheap themselves to even consider protecting its own unique history, so the city stepped in, instead."

I could only nod in reply, at her rather strange comment, particularly the final adjective describing the studio management, which appeared completely out of character coming from this previously prim and proper lady. Based on Christine's odd outburst and the message conveyed by the available signage, it was not a surprise when we entered through the doors and discovered what was housed beneath this enormous, very modern enclosure.

There, in its full glory, sat the main plaza of the old Universal Studios Theme Park! And what a sight it was. Everything was almost exactly as I had recently experienced in the Universal Studios of 2020, except for the fact that it was now safety protected from the wind and rain, by the mammoth greenhouse. The huge gateway arch and the brass Universal globe both welcomed us as they had done my son and I just the day before! But they had clearly seen better days, even with their new, overhead protection.

Putting it bluntly, they were old and decrepit. The old fountain under the globe had expired, and while the new one outside spayed fresh clean fluid into the air, this ancient one did not, some of the concrete crumbling from the side of its very dry and empty circular pool. The welcoming arch was not much better, although it would have been much worse without the protection of the glass atrium. The bright white paint was faded, the plaster had begun to spall away from the columns, and the signage 'Universal Studios" was hanging, very precariously. It was the very same place but, before the recent addition of the protective roof, it looked to have weathered in place for over 30 years!

What more surprises could be expected on our tour? At the welcome kiosk, we were given a self-tour booklet, and told the upper level was fully covered and walk through only, and that the ancient tram system still ran daily at various times, once you reached the lower level. They also had something that looked like a ride of some sort called an AirLift, but I was not clear where or how this might present itself. Just, having been there the day before, I knew the meaning of the upper and lower levels and was very interested to see the state of the various attractions in the now deserted park.

A set walking path ran through the enclosed upper level, which we immediately began to follow. As we wandered, my mind did too, traveling back to my recent experience when all of the attractions were in perfect working order. The comparison was like night and day!

We passed the old 'Waterworld' stunt show, sound stage, most of the seating now gone, only the large empty water tank structure still in place. The faded sign, however, did not read 'Waterworld', however, but 'Sea Kingdom', so at some time, while the Theme Park was still in operation, the show had been changed. But in this future, it was only an abandoned hole, a small amount of tepid green muck visible in the faded blue bottom of the otherwise empty, concrete pond. The set structures were un-recognizable and tattered looking, most having fallen down into the empty pool below. It was a rather depressing sight.

We continued on, walking at an even pace, Christine taking my hand as we passed the Shrek /Kung Fu Panda 4D Theater, its marquee now reading, in badly faded red letters, Star Escape in 5D. This inspired an immediate question as to what the other dimension referred to? The old street and souvenir shops still sported the old Universal signage and logos, and some merchandise still resided in the display cases, although cobwebbed and moldy. Christine made a face at a stuffed dinosaur animal that had broken open, its cotton batten stuffing partially visible erupting from its prone form, now home to some industrious rodent. She grabbed my arm as we continued down the path.

The kid's fun area on the left edge of the upper level was closed down, the attractions in that area completely collapsed and unused, a literal pile of garbage. The new security glass cover did not even extend that far, relegating that portion permanently forgotten and abandoned to the elements. We turned to the right and headed towards what I was really looking forward to seeing in this new future. Although I was hoping otherwise, the results created by the last 45 years of exterior aging, were almost certainly not going to be very pleasant.

Amazingly enough, the new glass protective cover extended over even the mock-up of 'Hogwarts Castle' still rising loftily above 'Hogsmede' village. But the entire magical land was not as it had once been. It too, like the rest of the amusements witnessed so far, was in sorry shape. The main archway welcoming patrons to the 'Wizarding World of Harry Potter' was fortunately intact, although faded and drooping, the faux cast iron signage hanging loosely. The cobble stone streets still retained their shape, even the front of the 'Hogwarts Express' still protruded into the entry as it had done for my son and I just yesterday. But now the decorative crimson and black paint had faded, the mechanics were frozen and not even one pitiful ounce of steam arose from its once, furiously belching, smokestack.

The buildings of the 'Hogsmede' village shopping precinct retained their general shape and decor but the snow-covered roofs had collapsed in several places, making some parts of the site unattainable due to the excessive piles of spilled wood and debris. Several of the smaller arches were destroyed or collapsed, leaving only the two sides still visible, making the entry's look like transom-less doorways. 'Olivander's Wand Shop' and 'Honeydukes' candy store were both partially caved in, several of their elaborately decorative stain-glass windows smashed. The abandoned "Buckbeak" roller coaster, off to one side, sat idle and dark, the rusted track lines and drooping chains appearing as rotting bones in a desert landscape, the flesh eaten away by carrion birds. The absolute worst travesty of all, however, was looking up at the castle on the hill. The miserable sight almost bringing tears to my eyes.

The once majestic towers of 'Hogwarts Castle' that used to bravely fill the open sky, like a 'Grifindor' searcher, were now forsaken, stale looking monstrosities with not a single vestige of their previous grace and splendor remaining. No longer an impressive monument to its filmmakers but instead a forlorn, unkempt and crumbling remnant of another time. The towers were rotten and falling, parts of the tiling of the roofs missing, water damage evident throughout, the dark plaster of its brick wall façade spalling and falling off the structure in numerous places, like large blisters. Festering wounds with no hope of repair.

The only thing left to impress visitors was the soaring glass roof of the enclosure, flying over the disintegrating ruins. All I could think of while staring in disbelief, was that it would take a real, working 'elder wand' to bring the edifice back to its formal glory. It was so sad to see it this way, so I turned away. I could not stomach to look any more.

"Hey, Christine. Could we move on? I would really like to get to the lower section if possible. I'm looking forward to riding that ancient tram system they were talking about." making an excuse just to get out of there.

"Sure, Ryan," she answered, responding to my sad look, "You know, this place looks awful now, but I'm sure it would have been real cool in its day! I wonder what it was like in its heyday?" Christine looked at the decaying structure contemplatively, "And all the rides, decorations, stores. They must have been fun!"

They sure were, my dear, they sure were. I said to myself, pulling again at her arm, anxious for us to leave.

On through the deserted and broken park we trekked, past the broken-down Simpsons land. Amazingly enough, it too had lasted through the decades, but it appeared to be in even worst disrepair than the wizard attraction, the bright paints faded to oblivion, the signage warped the rides broken, several of the frontages completely toppled and spilled on the ground. Then it was a short turn left to the peak of the upper area and the end to the gargantuan atrium.

The exit doors of the massive structure lead into a glass lined vestibule, brimming with newly installed and operating conveniences. Here we grabbed a bite to eat at one of the concessions, offering some interesting food selections I was unfamiliar with. Letting Christine choose for me, she eventually handed me some form of fried pastry, which turned out to be very sweet and delicious. The drink I was offered was a dark cool beverage, but certainly no Coca Cola! It was only lightly sweetened and had a coppery taste that I could not place. But it quenched my thirst, giving us both renewed vigor for what was next instore in this Universal Studios museum!

Apparently, what awaited us was the facilities only other attraction, besides the antique tram ride to which we were ultimately headed. We followed the signage for the "AirLift", some kind of new vehicle that I had seen on the map on our way in. I had thought perhaps, it was possible that one of the ancient rides had been expertly restored to its old operation, as an homage to the past but regrettably, this was not to be.

It was indeed a new ride, something modern and incredibly futuristic. As we waited in line, there were only 10 or so people ahead of us, the lone guide at the amusement's entry told us what to expect. We would be riding the distinctive flying contraption down the hill to the lower area of the lot. If anyone who's been to Universal, Hollywood remembers, the upper lot resides above the main studio backlot at the top of the hill. There is (or was) one of the world's largest escalators that took guests between the upper and lower lots. This AirLift was obviously an alternative transport for getting down the steep hill.

We moved out towards the edge of the picturesque overlook, glancing at the yellow brown Hollywood hills and across into Burbank. The view was magnificent, the vibrant sunlight reflecting off the caramel peaks gracing the afternoon with its splendor. After reveling in the beauty of it all, we looked briefly down at the lower lot area, and Universal's extensive back lot before being directed towards the "ride" entrance and boarding area. The vehicle waiting for us was roughly arrow shaped, bright blue in colour and appeared to *hover* over the ground as it sat next to the loading ramp. There was no visible track installed under this AirLift unit, nor any kind that I could see running down the mountain. There were only two seats per car and even though the vehicle had a dashboard, there were no controls of any kind immediately evident, except for a small covered panel on the passenger compartment's left-hand side. Conceivably, like the self-driving Robi-cars, it housed a back-up, manual control system in case of emergency. But for now, it would be just Christine and I going along on the fully automated trip. This was going to be interesting!

As we stepped into the vehicle to get comfortable, it bobbed up and down, like a cork in a water drum, until we were safely seated and our restraints in place. Every time we moved, however, the car jostled slightly as if in a light wind. There was no delay in starting, right after a small beep, we moved off, away from the platform towards the brink of the cliff. Holding our collective breaths, we smiled at each other and then we were off, swiftly angling down and rapidly descending, roughly flying in tandem beside the wall encasing the old moving stairway system. As we gained speed, we held on tight, the wind blowing in our faces, looking around with much interest. The AirLift vehicle was all on its own, almost hovercraft like in its motion, but much swifter. As we flew down the hill next to the old escalators, I could see they were indeed non-functional, sitting idle and in some places disassembled, probably having been in that sorry condition for many years. Several of the intermediate platforms of the moving stairway were tilted, the piers and columns leaning, the concrete spalling, coppery red rusted reinforcement protruding miserably at various points throughout the structure. No wonder they had alternative transport to the lower level. The old way would have been a hazard to life and limb.

As we cruised west and down, we could just see the remains of the old 'Jurassic Park' attraction. It had just been renamed 'Jurassic World', when I recently rode on it and its water ride format had been a fine solution to a very warm day. Presently, however, no one was traveling back in time and no tyrannosaurs were stalking screaming park goers, nor ever would again. In fact, the system, as to be expected, was not running, no rafts were visible and all of the troughs regularly filled with bright green water were dry, exposing rusted pipes and stripped track components, dismantled chains and twisted metal. It was a bleak looking mess. This area of the Studio had not been included under the so-called protective cover and so had sat outside all this time. Expectedly, this portion of the park showed that much more wear, and the broken Jurassic archway and missing signage left one feeling miserable for the permanent loss of such a thrilling adventure.

The AirLift, however, was operating just fine, its brand new, modern equipment zooming us down the remaining landscape, providing Christine and I with our own, alternate thrilling adventure.

"This is fun!" screamed Christine from beside me, yelling over the blowing wind. "I should have come here before."

"Sure is," I returned, "nothing like a quick drop, and an untethered flight to get one's heart going!" I suddenly thought back to the cordless bungy jumping option at the Hollywood Boulevard adventure shop and shivered.

Swooping and hovering expertly over the well-trimmed landscaping and fencing, the AirLift provided a satisfying dream ride, the trip smooth and uninterrupted. Below us all the vegetation had all been cleared and we rode about a meter off the ground over the undulating surface of the cliff face. This made the speed appear even faster than it was, the trip both exhilarating and unforgettable.

Eventually, as with all good things, the ride came to an end, terminating in the plaza between what used to be the "Transformers" attraction and "the Mummy" indoor rollercoaster. Both rides evidently long abandoned like the rest of their silent brethren, their exterior surfaces, eroded and faded, the attraction entries all boarded up tight.

There was no one waiting to board our AirLift car as we floated to a stop at the lower terminus so, as soon as we had alighted from the swift conveyance, it disappeared again, flying back up the hill to retrieve another guest for their downhill run. It had really been a pleasant ride and I looked forward to the return trip on our way back.

The open canopy ride had blown Christine's unrestrained locks around uncontrollably, leaving her with completely windswept hair, resulting in a very refreshed look that was incredibly attractive in the afternoon sun. The cool air had also triggered a renewed flush into her cheeks. She looked happy and revitalized from the ride and eager to continue, so we looked around for the entry point for what I would always refer to as "The Backlot Tour."

Chapter Seven – The Backlot Tour

Thankfully, we did not have far to go as the boarding area for the tram was just to the right of the AirLift exit, beside the back wall of the old 'Transformers' ride building. Both Christine and I, very excited to continue, headed directly towards the small queue. This presented us with almost no delay, as the single ancient tram car awaiting us had enough seats for over 20 people, and even with the 10 others who had preceded us down the AirLift, we were immediately able to join the next tour.

The slightly corroded aluminum side rails of the tram rose to welcome us, just as they had done for me the day before, but it was clear the ancient vehicle had seen better days. The rubber wheels of the tram were grey, not black, and the sheet metal, beneath the bleached paint, was rusted, even fully perforated in several locations. The seats, however, were still comfortable, having been recently resurfaced and a large viewing screen sat at the head of the car, clearly a more current addition.

As the guard railings dropped in place and we pulled away, I noticed two further, very distinct, differences from my tram ride of the previous day. The engine had undoubtedly been replaced, for instead of the loud diesel rumblings and belching black smoke from the exhaust, the indistinct hum of an electric motor was the only sound. Finally, like the Robi-car we had arrived in that morning, the tour vehicle was completely self-propelled, no driver or other host present. It was a bit disconcerting riding in the old tram, newly converted to robotic movement. For some reason, it just didn't seem natural. I began to miss the old system, nostalgia gripping me in earnest.

And then I thought right away that, besides the old dog train from my previous run into 2065, this was the closest any future had come to recreating my own time. It was almost amazing how this time, while different, was almost similar to my own, and how comfortable I felt in its clutches. It was almost normal, or the same in many respects, but with only subtle differences. One still rode around in cars, one still ate in restaurants, one still bought things with money. Differences yes, some in the extreme, but so far quite close. It was all so, refreshing and welcoming. Little was I to know that would soon change.

As the tram began its circle tour, the two of us were able to sit back and get comfortable. We had a bench to ourselves near the rear of the vehicle and I let Christine sit by the outside edge so that she could see better. As she was short in stature, I had no trouble viewing the moving landscape above her flowing hair. The air was warm, and the bright sun shone down from a virtually cloudless sky. There was a slight freshly scented breeze coming in from the coast, and the canopy above us provided ample shade. The resulting ride was extremely relaxing and enjoyable.

"This looks like it will be a fun ride," I stated blandly, just to fill the silence.

"Sure does," Christine replied, "I've never been on this tour before. Sure, looks like fun. These vehicles are really neat, what a hoot! To think folks actually rode around in these as part of an amusement park! Amazing!"

It was, indeed, I thought to myself, it was indeed.

As we moved past some of the large sound stages on the backlot, the image of a guide appeared on the screen, introducing herself and proceeding to outline the various places we would go. When she first appeared, I did not bother to look up, but when she introduced herself, I was all ears.

"Hi, I'm Suzie Shine, and I'd like to welcome you to the Universal Museum and studio tour."

It was amazing! Here was the same perfect woman from the movie I had seen, and a duplicate of the two girls at the Denny's. Well, I really should say they were her duplicate! Here she was, this Suzie Shine character in real life. But then I realized this was a digital human and construct, one that had been used by the studios to replace their real actors. It was truly amazing the detail and exactness of the woman's likeness, the real action of her movements down to the small subtle movements of her body and her hair. Even her chest rose and fell with each breath! What the studios had done, while fantastic, was still a bit scary and it was something I would definitely have to get used to.

"Oh no, are they really using *HER* on this tour, great!" Christine said, folding her arms.

"What? You don't like Suzie Shine?"

"No, I guess it's just what she represents is all." and then she went quiet.

With clearly nothing more coming from my companion, I sat back to listen to the commentary, gleaning some very revealing information about the use of sound stages in the future.

"While in the past," the fake Suzie guide droned on, "our soundstages were used to film *LIVE* actors portraying a scene, because of our advanced technologies, we no longer have the use for *LIVE* actors."

I hated the way she said and referred to 'Live' actors. Like they were animals!

"Instead, today our stages are filled with our specialist design technicians, creating characters and films in the computer, like all of the rest of our fellow filmmakers." then Suzie the conductor added, "And most recently, we have now been able to manufacture voices generated completely within the computer…like my own!" and she laughed, before continuing, "And so the need for *LIVE* actors had now been completely eliminated." Suzie Shine appeared smug and very pleased with herself.

Then her disembodied voice added as an afterthought, "Although, we do have three smaller stages used for the specialties of motion capture, but this is now a very minor part of our film making process and these stages are not close to this location, but further out on the backlot." Then, thankfully, the computer-generated actress and voice quieted down for a moment.

"That bitch," stated Christine in a supremely hostile way, almost as if what the guide voice had said was a personal attack, "they've already programmed her with the new decision. Didn't take them long did it?"

Not knowing what to say to that, I could not respond, so instead I smiled at her to try to calm her down, "Don't worry too much about that now, try to forget about that and let's just sit back and enjoy the tour."

"Your right, I apologize. It still makes me so mad to think what they are doing to the industry." Christine replied, calming almost too quickly, "But, we are here to have fun. I'm sorry, Ryan." and she settled back in her seat to view what was coming up.

As we entered the studio proper, all I could think of again was the backlot tour of my childhood when it was a much simpler time, before the theme park expansion, when Universal was just a studio, with a backlot tour as an add on, long before it became a thriving theme park.

At that time the tour also included off-tram times like the tour of the costume department, the props department and the special effects show. The more modern version, I had just seen the day before, replacing the old outdated attractions and off-tram times with the likes of, the War of the World's diorama of the crashed 747 and the two 3D shows; King Kong and Fast and Furious. All demonstrating the great advancements in film technology over time. I was looking forward to what we would see on this tour,

45 years into the future, and the even greater advancements. I was to be gravely disappointed.

As before, the backlot tour began with the rows of vehicle storage, housing the picture cars from previous films. Most of the vehicles were similar to the ones I had seen previously, but they were in much worse shape, the sun having completely bleached their surfaces. Remaining out in the elements like that for an additional 45 years had not been kind on them. There were, however, one or two I had not seen before, a globe type spaceship, and a funny triangular shaped automobile. In the back, I also detected a newer version of the "Batmobile" indicating yet another remake had been completed in my time away, to honour that much beloved character. There was also what appeared to be two strangely formed, ocean going vehicles, similar to mini submarines, from some new deep-sea adventure, made well after I had left 2020.

The tram continued on past the vehicle storage and into the backlot proper. We passed right into the Mexican village and right away I recognized this as the flash flood diorama. The adobe rooves of the buildings were still miraculously intact, a few of the ceramic tiles smashed, but everything else appearing in fairly decent shape. I was just preparing myself for the torrent of water when the screen came on once again, the slightly grating voice of Suzie our guide narrating a disappointing addition.

"Here were sit in out Central American village. This used to be our faithful recreation of a flash flood weather effect. But with the extreme water shortages, we are no longer able to cycle the demonstration. If you view the screen you may witness the effect in 5D. The screen then presented the flowing water as it had done for me previously, looking extremely lifelike, while the crowd watched in awe. I had no idea what 5D meant so instead, I stared up the street, imagining the flood of water in my mind, while the cobblestone slew way remained dry, dusty and baked in the hot California sun.

We then continued on past the flash flood and into the western village. The buildings were all roughly the same, except the wood components much greyer. Many of the side boards were loose and some of the windows had been smashed. The signage on the various stores and buildings was so faded it was completely unrecognizable. As we drove through the very dilapidated town, we could see most of the wooden clapboard sidewalks, under the overhanging awnings, were broken in places and rotted away.

Turning out of the Wild West, we headed up the hill towards the old collapsing bridge. Its silhouette still graced the side of the hill, but just barely, as it had been completely overrun with foliage, and its old timber structure rotted away to nothingness. Below that was the entrance to the King Kong cave, but we did not go in. The irritating voice of our guide interrupted us yet again as the tram drew to a halt.

"You see before you the entrance to what once was one of our two major 3D attractions, King Kong, based on several films of the same name, that our studio had produced both in the 20th and again early 21st centuries. This attraction has been out of service for over 25 years, even before the old theme park closed its doors. Unfortunately, the screens used for projecting the outdated images have eroded and are no longer suitable for use. In addition, the outdated effects were no longer thrilling to our viewers, so the attraction has been permanently abandoned for some time."

"3D," stated Christine with a laugh, "that's stuffs been passé forever. No wonder they shut it down!"

Again, I said nothing, preferring to remember it as it was. It had sure freaked out my son, still remembering his nervous laughter as we left the attraction not more than 24 hours previously.

Motoring on through the studio, the tram entered the old backlot sets of Universal, beginning with the New York Street and then on to the old Clock tower square so famous in my time from numerous films, the most significant being "Back to the

Future". This struck me as an apt remembrance, considering the subject matter of that motion picture, time travelling, came so close to the mark, at least for me. And so, it was very nostalgic to drive by the courthouse with the four large pillars. Again, like all the other buildings however, the sets were in bad shape and all had eroded somewhat over time. Clearly none of these "backlot" areas were still used in filmmaking and had just been left as a sad reminder of the olden days of film. I was pleased they had not torn down these monuments to the movies, but at the same time could not but help feeling saddened by their present state of disrepair. Evidently something new was now used for motion picture making, delegating even these well used backlot sets to the film-makers graveyard.

We turned out of the New York Street and on through the lot, approaching what I remembered as the large outdoor shooting set for water work. The reservoir was still there as well as the large backdrop painting of a pale lightly clouded blue sky now faded with age. But the pool was empty of water, the light blue painted side walls exposed the floor of the tank dry and full of plants that had pushed their way through the now cracked and broken concrete, providing a sprinkling of dry wheat coloured vegetation throughout the expanse of the old set. An old poster of one of the last shoots was just visible beside the abandoned lake, reading Sea Kingdom II. Obviously, nothing I had seen, made long after 2020, although I did notice a picture on the sheet matched one of the submarine vehicles in the graveyard of picture cars we had recently passed. Evidently, the last film to use the fabled pool. It was real pity to see it discarded in that way.

Past the large abandoned reservoir and then on to Cabot Cove/Amity Island for a look at the ancient 'Jaws' attraction. We could not even cross the old pier, as it had rotted away, most of the wooden log pile sections and decking having toppled into the empty basin. It too also devoid of fluids, exposing rusted rails and inner workings like all of the rest of the water attractions of this sorry looking museum. As we passed, we could see the stationary figure of 'Bruce' the great white shark, sitting in his elevated position, next to the unstable dock, his grey flexible skin cracked and torn, his wide jaws devoid of teeth, and his dorsal fin sagging. Another pitiful resident of this gallery of misfortune.

"What on earth is that thing?" Christine asked, showing interest in the forlorn form of the shark.

"Why that's 'Bruce' the great white shark, or what's left of him." I answered her. My voice lost in emotion.

"What on earth is a shark?" Christine asked another question, immediately answering herself, "Is that like some kind of sea animal?"

"Of course, it's a sea animal! This of course is a mock-up made to scare you, but it's supposed to be close to the real thing."

"Oh, don't be silly Ryan." Christine returned laughing, "There are no more sea creatures. You know that! There're all extinct. Have been for ages."

"Extinct?" I almost shouted, flabbergasted at her comment, "when did that happen?"

"Alright, be like that." Then seeing my expression, "Fine then! Even though I know, you know," Christine entreated, "They all went extinct when the discarded floating plastic islands in the oceans got so large, they began blocking out the sunlight over the seas. That, and all the untreated human waste that began to be pumped into the oceans after all the third world countries were brought up to first world standard. They just couldn't keep up with the demand for treatment dumping the raw sewage into every ocean on the planet. That killed off all the plankton, leaving the small fish and whales with nothing to eat. As they died off, so did the rest of the sea predators. There have been no major sea animals of any kind for at least a decade now." then she paused, looking at poor 'Bruce'.

With wonder now in her tone, she added, "But if that's truly what one used to look like, they were quite beautiful in their own way. Although, this particular one's obviously seen better days," and then she laughed again, like it was nothing. Like the oceans being void of inhabitants was just another day at the office, no care or concern. Nothing.

I just sat brooding, pouring my heart out to the sad fate of our glorious sea creatures. Yet another lot of victims, destroyed forever by that careless, uncaring hand of mankind. I began to think the world I had entered was not as it first appeared, although the continued carelessness of humanities actions didn't seem to have changed much.

A short drive past Amity, we travelled by the 'Bates Motel' and, up on its neighboring hill, to the 'Psycho House', the two buildings in even more decrepit condition than some of the other buildings we had seen so far. The parking lot of the small motel set had become a wheat-field and one of trees near the front of the fabled house had evidently lost a limb in a windstorm, falling and collapsing part of the roof next to the very familiar form of the front tower window of the famous landmark.

"What an ugly house," Christine stated, "no wonder they've let it rot away."

Evidently Christine had never seen Alfred Hitchcock's suspense classic.

Onward up the hill and right past the front of Norman Bates decrepit dwelling, we entered the full-scale mock-up diorama of the crashed 747 jumbo jet from 'War of the Worlds'. This too had been left to the elements, the small natural gas fed fires, usually burning to inject a vague sense of realism to the horrific crash site, now lay dormant, permanently extinguished, never to burn again.

Still mysteriously absent from this most impressive diorama, as was the case in 2020, were the dead bodies. I always found it odd, that for a studio like Universal to miss what would not only be natural, but expected, was very peculiar. But even in the future it was not to be, for amongst the hundreds of torn and fallen seats, there still was not one body. Apparently, this particular aircraft had been a ghost plane, now crashed, forever alone. Sadly, left to perish on its deathbed.

The natural vegetation had also been left to grow wild around this magnificent set piece, and most of the low areas were now indistinguishable from the surrounding grass and bushes with even the towering cylindrical portions of the airplane's fuselage covered with crawling vines and ivy. Only the lofty, rear tail of the plane had escaped the foliage's unceasing and unrelenting reclamation of the ancient sets' surroundings.

"Is that a real airplane?" again, Christine asking a seemingly stupid question.

"Yes, it was," I replied, fully understanding her ignorance, "the filmmakers apparently used a real Boeing 747, when they initially built that set."

"Wow, a real airplane," Christine continued, almost as if she had not listened to me, "That's why they use so much computer stuff now. This mock-up must have been incredibly expensive for one scene in a movie." she added a mindful conclusion, "Finally, I'm kind of beginning to understand the studios motivations a bit more."

Then Christine dropped a bomb, "Of course, they don't use those airplane things anymore. What, with our teleportation booths readily available, they're completely obsolete. In fact, before today, I have never actually seen one. This is quite cool, even though it's in pieces."

"Teleportation?" there, it happened again. Ryan Scott and his immediate questions. I would have to learn to hold back.

"Sure silly. You must have used one of those yourself to get here. I know most people have." Christine was enjoying this, "There're all the rage. They have one installed in the back of every travel shop. Once you pick your holiday, and pay the invoice, they send you right there. Quick as a wink!" again she smiled at my childishness. "Oh, but of course, it is a tad expensive…Sorry, Ryan, I wasn't thinking. You being an actor and all."

Playing the part, I replied, my voice sheepish, my head turned down, "That's okay, I just haven't had time to try one yet. That's all." And we left it at that.

The last part of the tour went quickly, the two of us sitting in relative silence as we passed through the old residential street, again in a state of disrepair, the quaint neighborhood home frontages, looking more like haunted houses at the end of a poorly illuminated 'Colonial' street. Then it was a quick drive past the equally abandoned 3D 'Fast and Furious' adventure, also ignored for very similar reasons to the other archaic, 3D amusements.

As a finale to our long tour, we had the pleasure of experiencing a full blown, modern, 5D attraction from a recent motion picture called Star Visitors. The tram pulling into a theater like structure and us blasting off into the stars, getting attacked by all sorts of strange looking spacecraft, flying through, and around, planets of every kind and lastly having an all-out heroic battle over the rings of Saturn. You could actually feel the heat and searing jets of the lasers, smell the burning cordite and when an opposing vehicle exploded, feel the blast rock the car and the banging against the sides as the tram made its way through the wreckage. It was most enjoyable, certainly something better than anything I had ever experienced in my own world. And no glasses were required! Christine absolutely loved it!

As we headed back, towards the AirLift and end of the tour, we made two additional stops.

The first one was at one of the larger sound stages, which we had previously been told had been converted into computer design shops. There were two large barn doors at the side of the building that automatically opened as the tram approached. We drove slowly through the darkened airplane hangar sized structure, discretely along one edge. To our right was a wall of glass allowing us to see inward. As our eyes adjusted to the gloomy atmosphere, we were able to see that the entire sound stage had indeed been converted, several intermediate floors added and desk after desk after desk of pimply faced kids sitting at computer terminals forever rendering, backgrounds, characters and other images for the latest Universal offerings.

The room continued on seemingly forever, showing the sheer extents of the number of designers employed at the studio. It was amazing!

"As you can see our design technicians, or 'design artists' as they like to be called, are busy at work on Universals' latest film. This one starts Adam Ace and Sally Storm, both computer-generated actors of course, in a thrilling adventure in the Amazon. It has not yet been titled, but we are very excited to see the outcome of their latest exploits, due out this Christmas." Our Suzie guide's voice actually sounded like she was quite intent on seeing the upcoming film. It was quite unreal.

Upon exiting the far end of the gargantuan computer soundstage, we drove out a little further and deeper into the backlot for our final stop at one of the outer lying motion capture studios. They were relatively small buildings on the outskirts of the studio lot and I initially thought we were just going to drive by or drive through like the soundstage before them. But then the tram came to a halt just outside one of the structures and the aluminum safety bars raised, inviting us to disembark and enter the darkened facility. As we left, we could here Suzie's disembodied voice letting us know we would have 15 minutes to wander around to view the facility and then re-board.

We alighted the tram and both of us had a good stretch. Being seated for almost two hours, we needed to get our blood flowing evenly through our bodies once again. Following the other tourists, we entered through the closest door, Christine and I anxious to get out of the hot sun and into the invitingly cooler temperatures of the Universal Motion Capture facility.

Chapter Eight – Motion Capture: A New Job

The motion capture facility was a wondrous place! There was a long hallway, similar to the tramway in the bigger soundstage, except this one was for clearly for foot traffic only. The lighting was subdued and while it created strange shadows along the extended corridor, the intensity was more than sufficient to enable our small group to progress with little effort. Through the glass partitions again located on our right, we could see several different rooms. Each one of them equipped with jet black coloured floors with a white grid painted on them, almost like a perfect geometrically formed spider's web. The walls of each chamber were bright green, expanding upward into the ceiling and there were several with great sheets of green ready to lay over the floors when required. A classical green screen set up giving me a weird dizzy feeling, almost as if I couldn't tell up from down. Several cameras were visible in each room, mounted at the glass viewport side facing in.

We all stopped and huddled in front of one in particular, gazing in on the action, as it appeared occupied. There was a cameraman dressed in the standard multi-coloured clothes, but in front of the camera were two actors wearing what could only be described as bobble suits. Each person had on a jet-black, skin-tight body suit and helmet, all equipped with a series of white nodules or circular points on both the body and the head.

As the actor moved, the circles moved with them, the cameras picking up all the relative motion. When the selected action had occurred, the recorded signals could then be translated into the computer and rendered together with the actual computer-generated characters to simulate their correct human movements within the computer. All fine stuff, but nothing that I had not seen myself before, in my own time.

Looking for more interesting viewing, I moved off from the main group, further down the hall. It was relatively silent, each room soundproofed against the outside influences and as I approached the end of the hallway it became almost hauntingly quiet. Then I spotted one of the rooms that had its glass entry door propped open and stepped inside. The chamber was larger than any of the others and was clearly set up for shooting, several cameras appearing to be loaded and prepped. As I looked around a voice called out to me.

"Finally! There you are! We've been waiting for you all day! It's about time you showed up, but that's typical for you actors with the shooting day almost over." It was a tall dark gentleman in a very vibrant suit, perhaps the cameraman, but then behind him another person came in the room, this time female, and began fiddling with one of the cameras. OK then, obviously not the cameraman.

"Me?" I said as I pointed to myself, my hands held out in front of me.

"Of course, you!" The tall man continued, "You're the motion capture actor we asked for, aren't you?" he continued, "Although they should have told you, you didn't have to wear a costume, we provide all that through the computer. I've really got to hand it to you though, that costume certainly does look 40 years old, where did you get it?"

"Oh, this? I just pulled it out of my closet" I smiled at the truth.

"Very funny, uh… what's your name?" he was not impressed.

"It's Ryan, Ryan Scott."

"Well Ryan, you're not on the list, but you're obviously here for the filming wearing that getup. Looks like the union fouled up with the names again. You were sent here by the union, weren't you?"

"Of course, yes sir!" I replied falling in step with the lie, hoping this might be a chance to learn more about the movie business of 2065.

"Fortunately, you're in luck. The cameras are having all sorts of issues today and so we couldn't have filmed anyway. But we'll need you to come back tomorrow. Go next door and see Marcia. She'll set you up with all you need, including the correct attire." He pointed me out the door and to the left.

"Remember though, just because we're having equipment issues," he looked back at the camerawoman still fiddling with the camera, "doesn't mean you can show up whenever you feel like it. So, be here all the earlier tomorrow. We'll start shooting first thing in the morning, 8 am sharp." Then he turned his back on me, walking over towards the back of the set.

I quickly retreated the way I had come, quite pleased with the great stroke of luck, and found Christine still watching the antics in the first motion capture studio.

"Hey, Christine something's just come up and I'll not be able to come back in the tram with you." I hesitated, trying to think of what to say, not wanting to upset her, hoping I would not be long with Marcia. "It's most important that I stay here for a short while. I'll meet you back up at the top, in say, an hour." Not able to hold back the excitement in my voice, Christine detected it immediately.

"Ryan you seem so excited. What's happened? Where did you disappear to? I thought we were going to have dinner?" she asked quizzically.

"We are, trust me. I was just in the studio up the hall and it looks like they've mistaken me for one of the motion capture actors." I was out of breath, and continued developing the lie like a pro, "You know the situation I'm in, how desperate I am.

This is a big chance for me, and I can't blow it. You understand, don't you?"

"Well I…" was all she got out.

"Thanks, dear. You're a real peach." holding Christine lightly by the shoulders, I gave her a quick peck on the cheek, "I'll see you in a few hours up near the castle exhibit."

"Okay, but don't leave me hanging there too long, or you can find you own way out!" her tone was very authoritative, but still a tad unsure. Almost as if she had other plans as well.

"Trust me, I'll be there, just please, give me an hour!" smiling widely.

"Okay, Ryan. I'll see you back up top…, in an hour." Christine looked at me with uncertain eyes.

And then I turned and ran back down the hall to meet with Marcia, leaving the open-mouthed Christine staring after me with a look of surprise. I just hoped she would stick around.

This of course was my chance to get access to the studio as an employee and I was not about to pass it up.

Turning into the room to which I'd been directed, there to meet me was a petite, blond, Asian woman. Obviously dyed, her hair was cut in the style of a pixy, but much more severe. Strangely, she had sparkling blue eyes, under her heavy lids, but they looked back at me in a very cold, unfeeling way as I approached the very basic desk behind which she sat. To her credit, Marcia wore an expertly tailored navy-blue suit, distinctively different from the normal colourful get-ups most of the future folks were wearing. Her heavy plastic, black rimmed glasses, with their very large frames, covered most of the top of her face, and her olive skinned, chin and cheek bones were extremely angular, resulting in a very severe countenance, but at the same time providing a very handsome oriental look. I was so excited about the chance to work at the studio, I was not in the least discouraged and quickly sat down in the chair, she offered with her extended right hand.

"Hello, Mr.…?" her voice was distinctly oriental, but with only a slight accent and very clear inflection.

"Scott." I answered.

"Mr. Scott. Thank you for coming." Marcia remained seated, almost completely blocked by the desk, maintaining constant eye contact with every word, "You are a very fortunate man. We are presently in great need of motion capture actors." She hesitated but only slightly, "Many of your fellow acting brethren have abandoned their posts leaving us, to be frank, desperate for good subjects to assist in our films. Most of the time, when we arrange actors to come here through the union, they simply don't show up." her voice remained hard and to the point, but pleasant. It also had a breathy quality giving it a very sultry edge. "You are the first we have had in several days. We are thankful that you did eventually turn up, even as late as you were. As it turns out, we couldn't have shot much today anyway." she stopped, continuing to look at me with varied interest.

"What about the two actors in the studio down the hall?" I inquired, interested.

"That, Mr. Scott is an optical illusion put on for the tourists. It is a 5 D projection of a past film shoot when we used to use two actors interacting together. Now all we need is one."

"You mean there's no one in that studio at all?"

"Yes, exactly." she said this with such finality I knew I should ask no more questions. It was her time to speak.

"That outfit of yours is very unique, very similar to the costumes your avatar will wear in our next film." her oriental voice remained succinct, "You're aware of course that, as a motion capture actor, you don't have to wear a costume, only the motion capture suit?"

"Uh yeah, the fellow next door told me the same thing." I was nervously searching for a response, "I wasn't sure and so wanted to go all out to impress you."

"Well you certainly did that. It's not very often we get MC actors like you showing so much interest. Your attitude is most reassuring." while furring her brow and tilting her head, adding, "And that fellow you referred to, by the way, is the director, Simon Evans! Try not to forget that please!" I gulped.

Then returning back to the subject at hand, "Please take your time reading the contract I'm going to give you. Afterwards, we'll get you set up with some credentials for security," Marcia finished and then slowly stood, moving gracefully across the room to a cabinet against the far wall to retrieve what I assumed was a contract. However, the contract was furthest from my mind at that moment because it was her body, now fully visible, that had me perplexed.

Marcia like most of the others I had met to date was not very old but had obviously had some major work done by one of those slicer characters. Her body was beautifully formed, almost a perfect hourglass shape, fitting flawlessly within her skillfully tailored suit. All of her female proportions appeared as they should, except one. The craziest thing was the size of her waist! Exposed under the cut of her jacket, it could not have been more than about 6" wide! 36"-16"-36" Amazing! There was no way her figure was natural! She also wore very high black heels, similar to the one's Christine had worn as part of her uniform at the restaurant. The artificial height adjustment, combined with Marcia's distorted figure, resulted in a very peculiar, overall look.

Marcia returned quickly to the desk, almost as if self-conscious of her adjusted look, spotting that I had trouble taking my eyes away from her oddly shaped form. Sitting back down and placing the contact in front of me, she said simply, "Read the contract well, Mr. Scott. You will not have another chance to ask questions." then she turned away, becoming absorbed in her own paperwork, leaving me to read mine.

It did not take as long as I had imagined to read through and get all the papers signed. After all I was here from the past and so the legal ramifications of any future contract were irrelevant. I knew I would only be here a few days at most, so even the payment terms didn't matter. I would be long gone before any money ever changed hands. So, after what I thought was a reasonable time, I flipped to the final page and signed the document.

"No questions Mr. Ryan?"

"Oh no, Marcia, I've signed enough of these before, there all the same. There are only a few clauses I like to read, just to make sure I'm getting the correct rates and such."

"You're not concerned about the confidentiality clause, or the indemnity?"

"Absolutely not. Should I be?" turning it back on her, having a bit of fun.

This shocked her a bit, "Uh, No. It's just standard stuff, as you say." saying this as she quickly collected the documents, displaying perfectly manicured, extremely long fingernails each painted jet black.

After that, Marcia took my photo with a rather strange portable camera and with it proceeded to make me a studio employee photo I.D. that she printed and laminated right there with a rather fancy looking machine set-up next to her desk. This she handed across to me, as well as a somewhat detailed map of the studio.

"You will enter through this gate tomorrow," she said pointing to a gate on the far side of the backlot, "After checking in, you will come straight here. Mr. Evans and his team should have all the troubles sorted out by then. Normal workday is 12 hours, but it could be longer." Marcia was very business-like.

Then after a short pause, something more personal arose, "It's refreshing to see, Mr. Scott, that apparently not all of us need to visit our local slicer."

She said the word slicer, in such a condescending way, it was clear she did not like them one little bit. Then continued her instructions, "Please, don't be late tomorrow, Mr. Ryan. Your natural shape will work out perfectly for this picture, provided you arrive on time."

"Thanks," was my enthusiastic reply, "I'll do my best." then couldn't resist adding, "But if it's not too forward of me, can I ask, if you don't like slicer's, why did you have some work done yourself?"

The inquiry hit home, Marcia outright embarrassed by my question, her olive skin taking on a tinge of red, before replying, "I had this done, not just because it was all the rage, but simply to keep my job. You see when I wanted to get into the movie business, only women with the Barbie doll figures were getting any work. Then, when they eliminated acting altogether, I had no choice but to try something else. I chose to switch to something less obvious, something behind the scenes and so here I am. I just haven't the time, or frankly, the money, to get this changed back." pointing her well-manicured hands at her obscenely thin waist.

"Well, they did a great job on you." I offered, hoping to sound sympathetic.

"No, Mr. Ryan. They did what slicers always do. Made me something I am not," then, after an appropriate hesitation, "and filling their greedy pockets doing so." her harsh tone abruptly ending that part of our conversation for good.

"Can I assume you'll be departing the studio now?" she inquired. Her voice smoother, somehow softer.

"Why, Uh, yeah. If we're all done." no way expecting what was next.

"We are, indeed, all done. But as it happens, I'm leaving now too as well. May I offer you a ride to the gate?" Marcia's suggestion seemed quite contrary to her normally harsh demeanor. It being almost inexplicably unnatural that she would even consider doing someone like me a favour.

"That would be great," I answered, hesitantly, "but I promised to meet at friend up at the museum. Could you drop me off at the AirLift, instead?"

Marcia agreed, and I continued to thank her profusely as we left the building. The tour group had long since vanished and most of the lights were extinguished. I walked ahead of her into the now deathly quiet hall and watched as she turned and locked her office door. The extreme dimensions of her figure were mesmerizing, and I could not help but stare as she sauntered down the hall to the exit, her artificially slim waist protruding above her well-formed hips. She had a sort of classy feminine swagger and combined with the way her high heels revealed the muscles of her calves, easily drew my gaze like moths to a flame.

Outside, she led me towards a very different futuristic looking sedan parked just behind the motion capture building. It was nothing like the Robi-car Christine and I had ridden in on the way to the studio. This car being equipped with a gleaming, mirrored surface finish that sparkled in the dimming sun. The shape of the vehicle was very angular, but also had a genuine smoothness and refined quality indicating it was not only fast, but also very expensive. Its front end was cut and molded in such a way as to make the machine appear almost angry and very aggressive, in complete contrast to several other of its relatively simple looking counterparts, still residing in the parking lot beside it. A very handsome automobile indeed.

The doors opened automatically on command as we walked towards it, but not outward. The rose up at an angle over the roof, to reveal dark, chocolate brown, perforated leather seats, and a fully equipped driver's area with a full-sized, flat bottomed steering wheel. A large open moon roof let in the available filtered lighting, itself enhanced and surrounded by a bright white roof liner in sharp contrast to the jet-black dashboard, carbon fiber finishes and carpeting of the rest of the lavish looking interior. As we entered the luxurious cock-pit accommodations, and the seats adjusted to our differing body shapes, it was evident that the other side of the movies was treating Marcia very well indeed.

And furthermore, as we pulled away, it was interesting to note that the car was completely manual in its operation.

"Is your car not auto-drive like the rest?" I asked, quite interested in the differences evident in what was obviously Marcia's' personal ride.

"Out on the public roads, of course it is." Marcia exclaimed, adding enthusiastically as the wind whipped her short locks, "But within studio boundaries, we are allowed to drive our cars manually, which I thoroughly enjoy."

It was undoubtedly clear that she did, as Marcia obviously knew the studio backlot like the back of her hand, expertly swerving in, out and around the various studios and storage buildings, as if she had been born there. The ride was extremely comfortable, the stiff suspension of the sports car hugging the terrain smoothly and evenly. When Marcia eventually stopped in front of the floating AirLift transport docking bay, we were both having so much fun, I really didn't want to leave.

But, after all, I did have a date waiting for me at the top of the hill. The fancy door opened automatically as we came to a stop and I moved to step out, "Thanks for the ride, Marcia."

"You're very welcome," she responded, then, before I was halfway out the door, Marcia added sharply, in her very distinctive, sultry Asian voice.

"Be sure you're on-time tomorrow, Ryan Scott. Rampant tardiness will not be tolerated, now that you have signed your agreement."

"Absolutely," I replied, "you can count on me." And then, as I stepped toward the AirLift, in a wisp of wind, she was gone, the faint smell of ozone following in the wake of her gleaming car, racing off into the deepening sunset.

Chapter Nine – My Dinner with Christine

The AirLift was even better on the way up, the incredible power and agility of the trackless flying machine, throwing me right back in the seat, as it raced upward towards the top level of the museum. The ascent was almost as fast, if not faster than the decent, the vehicle having enough power to climb at very high speeds. The brisk breeze blowing through my hair, and the late afternoon sun still giving off more than enough heat, provided a very comfortable, yet thrilling ride.

After a very rapid deceleration, my floating vehicle came to a slow stop at the upper concrete offloading platform, bumping gently against the rails. Arriving at the portal, it was immediately obvious at that hour of the day, that most of the patrons had abandoned the museum, just as time had abandoned the buildings within it. The unrelenting heat provided throughout the day now diminished as the sun continued its decent in the western sky, and late afternoon shadows began to form like crouching animals behind every tree and outcropping. Standing up and stepping out of the patiently hovering shell, I walked out through the AirLift attraction's exit and back into the upper part of the museum, humming to myself.

Most of the area was uninhabited, even the museum workers were few and far between. The one or two that were visible only cleaning up spilled debris and refuse. Leaving the sad looking

Simpson's exhibit, I came up quickly to the grey brown archway of the Wizarding World, spying Christine standing there, hands on her hips, one foot tapping as she noticed me approaching.

"What took you so long?" she asked exasperatedly, "After you left, I was stuck on that tram with this weird looking guy who kept eyeing me. He followed me up on the AirLift and I thought he would never leave. I had to ask one of the curators to help before they ushered him out. What a creep!" but she had a quirky smile on her face, indicating it had not been all that bad, "Of course I've had much worse to deal with at the restaurant."

"Well, I'm here now and I have some great news!"

"You got the job!" Christine blurted out.

"I sure did and look," showing her my freshly created, backstage pass, "and I have the keys to the kingdom!"

"Fantastic! Well, I don't know about you, but I'm famished. Let's go get something to eat!"

"Lead on good lady. I'm not sure where is good around here?"

"We can get a car and head into the city or we can find somewhere close by. Any preference?"

"Let's go local, we can eat faster that way."

"You bet!" looking delighted, "We'll still need a Robi-car though."

And off we went, quickly back tracking through all the dilapidated exhibits and then out into the main atrium and gateway. The old City Walk as I had known it, was now a bunch of high cost condos and health clubs. Also detectable amongst these expensive accommodations was what appeared to be a plastic surgeons office, now known to all as the slicers' place.

This future was fantastic; after eating breakfast in your home, one could travel downstairs for a quick trip to the slicer for some body work. All in a day in 2065!

Christine was right then when she said there was nothing within walking distance and so we would have to take a car. We, therefore, headed back to the parking complex in search of transportation. It was surprising to me that with all the residents living in Los Angeles, we were so easily able to acquire a ride for our short trip to a local restaurant retreat.

This time we selected a silver coloured automobile, its interior a tad plusher that our previous vehicle, but not even close to Marcia's luxurious chariot. I had been spoiled. This particular Robi-car also had an odd smell about it, as if the previous user had spilled something and tried to clean it up. They had been wholly unsuccessful. The lingering scent stayed with us the entire trip, and when we alighted at our destination, I was very happy to leave the foul atmosphere for the freshly tinged night air.

We headed into the establishment Christine had chosen, just as the sun completely dipped down below the horizon and the sky lit up with pinks, oranges and reds, coating the few hovering clouds with its final rays and providing us with a spectacular, almost mystic vision. My first day in the Hollywood of 2065 had ended in a truly impressive fashion.

The restaurant Christine selected, from the exterior at least, appeared quite up-scale, certainly a step up from the Denny's where she worked. Immediately, I thought about my present finances and if I would have enough to cover the bill. The inviting interior did not help in any way to reduce this worry.

For once through the large outer doors, we entered a very elaborate greeting area, richly decorated and finished in warm woods and brass fittings. The lighting was very subdued, supplied by high mounted fixtures recessed in the ceiling and several ancient looking wall sconces, but with the recent sunset, it did not take long for our eyes to adjust to the dimmer atmosphere. The walls of this overly lavish reception room were fully encased in cultured timber paneling, the soft ambient lighting reflecting off their dark, glossy surfaces.

Although the immediate entry foyer was graced with an elaborate beige toned Italian marble, the rest of the chamber was floored using black hardwood planks, brightly polished and gleaming in the half-light. The floor was further enhanced by the presence of a thick Persian carpet, in stunning deep reds and yellows, its intricate pattern a distinct and welcome pleasure to the eyes. As our shoes moved across its soft surface, the rugs thick material yielded just enough to demonstrate an over-abundant lushness. Around the perimeter walls were a series of wide couches each covered in sumptuously soft leather, their surfaces worn evenly over time, playing host to the many famous sets of buttocks that had sat reclined in comfort, eagerly awaiting their dinner tables. This gave the brown material upholstery, and brass studded arm rests, a most intricate yet agreeable patina.

A stone fireplace was off to one side, a blazing fire burning in the hearth. Walking by, however, the flames gave off no discernable heat whatsoever and getting closer, I realized it was just a hologram. Not really a fire at all, just another expensive decoration to enhance the lush ambiance of the entry.

A rather short maitre'd occupied the lone podium within the darkened alcove. He wore a very dark suit, with a most interesting cut, but his tie was multi-coloured like the rest of the clothing everyone seemed to wear. Upon noticing me, he made at face as I stepped up towards him in my jeans and leather. Christine quickly moved in, motioning me gently aside and sweetly asking for a table for two.

"Ah, Welcome Christine!" he stated, his voice very nasally, with an obvious put on French accent, "We have not seen you in quite some time. Welcome back to our humble establishment. Can I offer you one of your regular tables?"

"Yes please, but for two, Francois," Christine replied accepting the gentlemen's interesting greeting, "My friend here is new in town and we are out for a quiet meal. It would be good if we could enjoy our meal in peace."

"Absolutely my dear, a pleasure as always. Please follow me." the gentlemen took one further look at me and then back at attractive Christine, swiftly changing his mind, signaling for us to follow him into the swanky eatery.

It was interesting to find out that Christine was known here, and I said so, "So you eat here often then?"

"I used to, in an earlier… before I started work at Denny's," Christine responded avoidantly, "I haven't been here in a while though. I didn't think they would remember me?"

Clearly the maitre'd, Francois was listening, "Of course we would not forget a beautiful face like yours, madame, it is so good to see you back amongst friends." The man's stuck up tone was beginning to grate on my nerves.

The main part of the restaurant was as lavish as its entry, definitely a white tablecloth affair all round. The massive floor to ceiling windows on its north side, letting in the dying sunlight of the ending day, reflecting in off the darkening hills. The carpets were of a plush deep pile and sported bold rich colours, the sterling silver cutlery and crystal glasses all sparkled brightly on the well-appointed tables. Single beeswax candles burned at each location, providing a suitably warm and lightly fragrant dinning atmosphere.

As we wandered through the mostly occupied establishment, I received several looks of interest, some of pure loathing and others of obvious surprise. It was quite unnerving to have all those strangers giving me various unappreciated looks, but I was not to be deterred. The stuffy maitre'd, noticeably amoured with cute Christine, sat us at a remote and intimate table, near the window overlooking the San Gabriel Mountains and Burbank below. He was also extremely quick to assist Christine with her chair, fumbling a bit as he did so. The fact that he knew Christine told me something about her that surprised me.

The good side to this was that he made a point to stay well away from me, so I was able to hastily seat myself opposite Christine, as she continued to smile warmly at the obstinate man. He left the two of us alone, but not before taking one more wanton glance at Christine and then a second, much more fleeting one in my direction, his face twisting up like he had just eaten a lemon, promoting the smile on Christine's face to grow even wider. Finally, unable to resist, she burst out laughing, her pleasant chuckle brightening my difficult encounter with both our host and the rest of the restaurant's patrons.

"Well, that sure was fun," her smile beamed at me across the table.

"Fun for you, maybe," my embarrassment prompting yet another laugh from her petite form. "Clearly, I'm underdressed." I paused, "He obviously likes you though. Were you really a regular here?"

"Perhaps," she again looked uncomfortable with her reply, so I decided not to press the issue. "Hey, the idiot," stating it a bit loudly, twisting around to look at the departing waiter, "he didn't even leave us menus."

"Keep your voice down," Christine hushed at me, "and don't be silly, Ryan, they're right here on the table." And she pointed at the table's clean surface in front of her.

Looking down, I detected an image, not noticed before during the previous awkwardness of settling in. There was what appeared to be a floating hologram of words just sitting there projected above the gleaming, white satin tablecloth. I looked over at Christine and saw her swipe at it, scrolling through the text, accessing even more food selections. As she touched each description, the alphabetized image changed into a picture of the dish itself, providing her a sneak peek at what it might look like. I was fascinated and watched her pace through the various delicious looking offerings with much interest.

"Well, dummy," she looked up, after noticing me staring, her pretty face subtly enhanced by the flickering candlelight, "I thought you were hungry." a sweet smile, creasing her cherry red lips, "Aren't you going to choose?"

"Uh… I guess so. Of course," and briefly flustered, I quickly began to look through my own floating menu.

The selections were all very tempting and looked scrumptious, each floating picture like having a facsimile of your meal sitting right there in front of you on the tabletop. After several minutes, I chose some chicken with pasta that looked especially nice, the best part being its apparently large serving portion. As we had not eaten much since that afternoon, and only the small fried pastry at that, the sheer size of the meal prompted me to select it as my main dish. But it was not only the holographic menu that would be of great interest to me tonight.

A very different person came to take our order and I could tell very easily that once again, one of this future world's famous slicers had been hard at work. The waitress was tall and outfitted in only a skin-tight bodysuit of some unknown shimmery material and a dark pair of calf-high boots. The tint of the clothing was hard to discern, not quite gold, more a bronze, appearing to match the unique skin tone of the woman perfectly but glistening to differentiate its surface from that of her actual body. At a quick glance, it gave the impression the girl was not only painted, but also naked. Clearly, this was not the case.

It was not the clothes, however, nor the skin colour of the server that had me shocked. It was the fact that she had six arms! Indeed, the sparkling girl had two extra pairs of arms extending out below her shoulders, similar to that of a fictional Thai Goddess! Obviously attached for some purpose, perhaps carrying more plates or items, but at present only serving as a tremendous shock to my already thoroughly disturbed mind. Thankfully, at least for the moment, her four additional hands sat unmoving, two pressed gracefully against her lap and two laced behind her back, while her first two readied to take our orders. It was most unnerving.

"What can I get for you this evening?" she said in a very quiet, elegantly smooth tone, which was just enough to pull me out of my stupor, gazing at this strange vision presented beside our table.

Christine looked over and appalled at my shocked expression, at once showed her dismay, now clearly uncomfortable, and not quite understanding my stunned reaction. The multi-armed waitress, however, just calmly stood awaiting our orders, her silvery blond hair, with razor straight cut bangs, hanging gracefully over her perfectly formed, bronze toned forehead.

After I said nothing, she turned away from my slightly dazed look, and asked Christine, "For you madam?" to which Christine immediately read off what she would like from the projected image, still looking at me with a furrowed brow. Trying urgently to save the moment, taking charge of what looked like a rapidly deteriorating situation. Once finished, she prompted me with another mean look that said, 'well get on with it'.

Taking her hint that it was my turn, I had to act quickly as the strange vision turned once more in my direction, "And you, sir?" to which I nervously scrolled through the floating menu, pointing timidly to my choices.

"Very good sir, excellent selections," her tone even, non-intrusive, understanding even. Totally human, except for the four additional arms! "And drinks for you this evening?"

Knowing I was not up on the drinks of the future, I decided to let Christine chose, "Uh, the lady will choose for us," opening my hand in Christine's direction.

She appeared to like that, her expression rapidly improving, no longer overtly hostile and immediately ordered us two drinks. Both of which I did not recognize, let alone know how to pronounce.

As the well-endowed, waitress made to turn away, I added, "Oh, and can I have some ice water as well, please." I knew right away from the odd expressions on the faces of both ladies, I had made another future faux pas.

"Water, sir?" the waitress questioned, first hesitating and then responding with conviction, but no malice at all, "We have not served that here since 2049. I am sorry, we cannot not offer that selection to you at this time." And then she was off, two arms swinging, the other four remaining locked firmly in place around either side of her thinly tapered middle.

"Water?" murmured Christine below her breath, "What were you thinking, Ryan? You know we haven't had fresh water to drink in California since the late 40's. Not since before the industrial poisonings and the massive aqueduct failures." she added with a further distortion to her expression, "Where on earth have you been Ryan, living under a rock?"

"Hah," using my best fake laugh, "Come on... I was obviously just joking. She obviously didn't take my joke very well. Relax, were supposed to be enjoying ourselves."

Christine would not be placated that easily, "And what's with all the staring, anyway? It's like you've never seen an enhanced waitress before."

Then she stopped and considered what she was saying, almost as if it suddenly occurred to her, that she was sitting on the wrong side of the fence. Calming herself, she began again. "You know, that's the only reason I work at Denny's." Christine went on to explain her change in outlook and her motivations, "I don't mind wearing a stupid fancy outfit, and that awful make-up, but I adamantly refuse to add arms to work faster. Denny's is one of only 3 restaurant chains left that don't use augmented servers." finally summing up, "Although I love the food, this place has the reputation of being one of the worst in terms of its waitress adjustment requirements. Their girls not only have to get the additional arms, the poor things have to permanently dye their skin as well."

Christine did not look impressed, now it was the restaurant taking the brunt of her displeasure, "That fancy colour won't come off you know, not without several more visits to the slicer." Then she was silent for a few moments, thinking.

I turned away, taking one last glance at the 6-armed server and then staring out through the floor to ceiling window at the darkening hillside. Absentmindedly watching as slowly, one by one, the overhead lights illuminated, bathing the streets in their diffuse nighttime glow. It was a beautiful evening and the last vestiges of the sunset were just visible staining the dry, wheat coloured grass, of the Hollywood hills, a dark, burnt orange. Here I was, out for dinner with a gorgeous woman, being served by a Thai Goddess, drinking something I did not know existed before today, and knowing water was no longer available. What an evening! What a future!

After the somewhat shaky start, the rest of the dinner passed smoothly, our conversation vibrant and non-stop. The food, as

Christine had suggested, was very edible, however, I very much doubted my personal selection had been real chicken. Eventually, I even got used to our multi-appendaged, attendant, finally getting to see the use for those many arms during clean-up, when she was able to grasp both our plates, our cups and cutlery altogether, cleaning the table in one fell swoop. I could only think how handy those extra arms might come in for automobile maintenance or cooking and cleaning back home. But then every time the waitress came into view, exposing the strange configuration of her body, once again told me that nothing was worth that. I had to agree with Christine. Extreme enhancement was definitely not for everyone, and certainly not me!

Paying the bill was also not as bad as I had originally anticipated. As it turned out it was special night, 2 for 1 on everything, enabling me to scrape enough cash to adequately pay the bill. I remembered my earlier lesson from that morning and did not leave a tip. Still receiving a deep bow and huge smile from our well-endowed server on the way out, told me I had made the right call.

Out in the parking lot, the cool evening wind brushed at our faces while Christine and I found yet another public Robi-car to commandeer, sliding into its comfortable seats and sitting back while the machine drove us smoothly on to our next destination. I was not exactly sure where that might be at the moment, but with my belly full and the fancy futuristic drink paying weird tricks with my head, it was good just to lie back and relax, leaving the driving to the auto-robot.

I must have fallen asleep briefly, for when I awoke, the vehicle had come to a stop outside a fairly upscale looking apartment complex and Christine was looking through her purse to find her keys.

"Have a nice nap, sleepy head?" she teased, smiling at me as she opened the door, "Come on don't dawdle, were here."

"Where's here?" I mumbled, still half asleep.

"Why my place of course!" Christine offered, "I guessed from your situation and your excitement at getting that job today, you probably didn't have a place stay. That combined with the fact you used your last dollar to pay for our meal, made me think you could use a little help."

I looked at her in amazement, "You noticed, that did you?"

"Of course, I noticed that, dummy. Thanks for dinner by the way." Christine was smiling broadly as we stepped out of the car and up onto the path, "So for tonight anyway, you're welcome to stay at my place. On the couch, mind you!"

"Absolutely. That's great Christine, I don't know what to say."

"Thank you might be nice," and she turned and headed into the awaiting complex.

I was pleased just to have a place to rest, because frankly I wasn't sure of where I would have stayed otherwise. And as there was still so much more yet to learn, it was far too early to head back to my machine and I really had nowhere else to go. "Hey, how far are we from the studio? I have an early call tomorrow, you know."

"Oh, don't worry, about that. You'll be okay. We're only about 20 minutes from the side gate by Robi-car." Christine replied, "And I'll come with you to make sure you get there safe tomorrow. Wouldn't want you directing one of our Robi-cars into the Pacific Basin now would we." We both laughed. Then she added, "I have to meet a friend there before my shift, anyway."

"Ah, you know someone who works there, besides me?" I was intrigued.

"Sure," she hesitated before completing her reply, "he works around the studio doing odds and ends. We see each other every now and again."

"Great. Perhaps I might meet him." I offered it as a polite suggestion, not really meaning it.

"Yeah, maybe." Christine appeared a bit unsure, evasive, then continued, "Hey, it's getting cold. Let's get inside. It's late and you have a big day tomorrow."

I did indeed, but little did I know it would be a big day for both of us.

Chapter Ten - Walking the Studio

The rising sun woke me early, the streams of yellow light falling through the unshielded windows. Rubbing the sleep from my eyes, I rose from the crumpled couch, excited to begin my second day here in 2065. First stop was to make my way through to the washroom for a quick shower. I quickly discovered, however, that nothing in this future is quick when you are unaware of how things work.

Just walking into the stall was an experience, as the door was automated, and one could not enter without first finding the access panel. Then once inside, there were a myriad of buttons and selectors for various hygienic devices, most of which I had never seen or heard of before. Then was the choice of soap and shampoo. After getting splattered with all sorts of scented cleansers and gels, as well as a cold spray from below, that was certainly NOT water, I finally figured out the controls of this futuristic "bathing unit". My shower was relatively quick after that but, with all my mistakes, I still left the glazed in cubicle smelling vaguely of some feminine perfume product, which for the life of me, I could not get rid of.

After getting dressed, Christine joked at my ladylike aroma saying it was very endearing, all the while pouring me some of the synthesized café liquid her fully automated galley had prepared for us. We drank it in a rush, before making it out on the street into yet another auto-drive vehicle. My experience in Christine's apartment of the future was short and I was hoping to explore it further when we returned, particularly the functions of the kitchen. That was provided I was invited back, of course.

The traffic was light, as it was still early when we left, the sun peaking over the mountains to the east, the brightening clouds pink and red, dashed with a bit of bright blue sky in-between. The drive time was just as Christine had described the night before, about 20 minutes. We made it to the Universal backlot gate with ample time to spare, just before 7:30 am. Christine had the Robi-car pull up to the curb to let me out, leaning across the seats, taking my hand briefly and wishing me the best of luck. Then she made to leave.

"I thought you were meeting a friend?" I queried.

"Oh, didn't I tell you, they cancelled. So, I'm just going to head into town." Christine replied good naturedly. This was interesting, as from what I remembered, Christine had not been in contact with anyone else that morning.

So, I asked, intrigued, "But your shift doesn't begin until 9, what are you going to do 'till then?" adding, "I hope I didn't put you out?"

"Oh, it's no trouble, I was happy to come up with you." Christine replied, "As far a work goes, I'll just hang around and catch a little breakfast or something. Don't worry about me."

"Alright. I don't mean to be a bother, you know."

"You're no bother, really. Look, don't worry," she stated again, "I'll find something to keep me occupied." Presenting me with another of her big bright smiles.

She appeared in such a good mood I could not argue further, "Okay then. Shall we meet up later?"

"Sure, I can come by and pick you up at 7. We can then find somewhere to get you some real clothes." she suggested, smiling cheekily, "That sound good?"

"Sure does. Sounds like a plan. I'll see you then." then the wide door closed, and she was off.

As I walked towards the gate pulling my pass from my pocket, I noticed in the reflection of the glass on the guard shack that Christine had not U-turned to head back towards town, but instead had headed up and back around the Studios perimeter road. Perhaps there was a café joint somewhere up there for breakfast that she was used to. Of course, Christine's movements were the last thing on my mind. I had something much more important to worry about at that moment, my first day on the job as motion capture actor!

Walking briskly to the entrance gate, I found access through the turnstiles proved fairly elementary. After pressing my identity card against the silver plate, the gates opened up for me with a light beep. The overweight, tired looking security guard in the gate house barely looked up as I went through, paying more attention to his morning café and donut than he did my tall, strangely dressed form. When he did find the energy to raise his eyes glancing my way, I noticed the distinct double take as he spotted my clothes. His actions prompted me to think of how I might explain my evident lack of 2065 apparel to my new boss. That was something, however, to worry about for later. One thing at a time.

The map of the studio Marcia had provided was first rate. I had absolutely no trouble deciphering the graphics that indicated it was just a few minutes casual walk to the entry of the motion capture soundstage. I moved away from the gate house and into the studio proper, making sure to stick on the well indicated, pedestrian footpaths and out of the roadways. At that time of the morning the studio was just coming to life, various delivery trucks whizzing by on their way to offload food, equipment or other consumables. It was a bit disconcerting walking on only a painted path next to the roadway, with no curbs and all of the electrically automated vehicles motoring along beside me. One had to be sure to look carefully over their shoulder every once in a while, because of their completely noiseless approach. Relying on an auto driver in that situation with a vehicle approaching you from behind was a bit nerve-wracking.

Crossing to the other side of the street was a bit easier, as I was at least able to look both ways to ensure my safety.

Passing the studio commissary about halfway through my walk, I mentally noted its central location and distance, as later I would need sustenance having had so little time for breakfast. Passing by the low-slung building, now bustling with early morning patrons, I noticed the figure of a tall, dark haired, elegantly dressed man who I was certain I had seen somewhere before in this new world. Not sure, however, having hardly met any other people except Christine and Marcia, the man still stood out a little from the rest, appearing to be skulking around the pooling shadows at the rear of the structure. He was probably just one of the workers out for a smoke, so I paid it no further mind. There were so many others who were now moving and flowing about the area, everyone dressed differently but blending in, he and I were just two other additions to the melting pot of studio regulars. It was pleasing to be considered one of their colleagues.

Just after rounding the corner on my last leg towards the soundstage, another silent vehicle rolled up behind me. But this one I recognized as it slowed to a stop and the shaded window dropped open to reveal a familiar face.

"Good morning, Ryan," Marcia called in her sultry Asian voice from the driver's seat of her luxury transport, "I am so happy you listened to my recommendation and got here early. I would offer you a lift, but you're almost there anyway. And after all, it's such a nice day. See you shortly." And she zoomed off, a slight flutter of dust rising into my face as the large sleek vehicle spun round the bend. I coughed once, before continuing on my way, smiling at Marcia's bravado. I had really begun to like that lady.

The soundstage was brimming with activity, as I approached, like an ant hill in the summer, and immediately I was drawn into the bustling atmosphere. I passed by Marcia's office, but her door was closed, and so I headed into the studio where I had previously met the director. He was there, busy talking with another man, next to the female camera operator. They both looked up as I entered and just as I raised my hand in greeting, a new face come up behind me, the director motioning for him to take me aside.

"Come this way," his voice was shallow, but energetic, and had a definite squeak to it that got your attention, "Come this way, Mr. Scott, sir, we need to get you suited up."

Following his thin form out of the camera room, he directed me into a well-appointed side chamber filled with benches, mirrors and, off to one side, several items of clothing that hung on a series of rails. The man's name I found out was Angelo, and he had worked at Universal as an assistant costumer and make-up artist for several years. Not that make-up was needed much anymore.

"Here's the change room." Angelo stated energetically, "We have to get you dressed and then back to studio 3. Then we'll see if we can put you to work. But first the size, ah…" and he began to quickly measure me with a tailor's tape, or at least the futures version of one, that appeared from nowhere.

"Where did you get this outfit, it's so… so retro?" Angelo's question was rhetorical as he was not the least bit interested in a reply. In fact, he kept right on talking with himself as he completed his measurements. Done, he turned his back to me and started looking through the suits on the racks, running his hands through them until he had found what he determined to be just the right one.

"Yes, this this should do. Yes, it will do nicely" first holding a dark black, skin-tight ensemble up to my body, then pulling it from the hanger and handing it to me.

"You have exactly…" looking briefly at his watch, "two minutes. Hurry up, we will see you next door," and then he was gone like a sudden wisp of wind on a stagnant summer night.

It did not take long for me to remove my street clothes and pull myself into the silky fabric of the motion capture suit. It was some kind of nylon spandex, equipped with a series of small white reflecting discs arranged over the entire surface of the flexible garment. The suit was furnished with integrated soft soled foot pads and covered my entire body, leaving only my hands and neck exposed. There was also a hood to the costume, similarly, equipped with reflective discs that hung behind my head like a deflated balloon. I assumed it could wait until I was in the studio before putting that on. A form fitting set of gloves completed the outfit, which the aide had left attached separately on the hanger. I deftly removed and tested these, first pulling them on to my hands then getting them to fit by threading my fingers together. Even though I have rather large hands, the gloves fit well and snug, evidently a perfect choice for me.

The form fitting uniform was very breathable and as long as the atmosphere remained air conditioned, I was certain it would be relatively comfortable to work in. Doing a few deep knee bends, I tested the feel of the outfit, getting used to the smooth, pliable texture of the material. My movements felt quite natural, the fabric stretching perfectly with me, so I spent the last few seconds admiring myself in the mirror. The garment was black and rather forgiving but I still detected a slight paunch, which was accentuated by the line of reflecting globes across my stomach. A little less pasta was in my future if I was to make this a more permanent pastime. Now ready, I stepped out of the change room and back into the hall. By coincidence, Marcia had just stepped from her office and was on her way out.

"Ah, I see you are finally dressed for the role." her Asian eyes dropping straight to my belly, "Although it appears a trip to the slicer may be the in the cards for your near future." chuckling as she taunted me, "Remember, I told you the real retro garb was not required. I couldn't help but notice you were still wearing it as you came in this morning. All that of course will be added in post-production. All you need now is the suit." a slight pause, "It does look good on you though." And smiling once again she was off, down the hallway and out into the glistening sun on her way to work behind the scenes.

"Thanks" I said to her quickly disappearing form, "have a great day."

She hesitated, rotating at the door just enough to give me a small wave. The light flickered briefly in her white hair, then her silhouette disappeared, the bright opening closing up as darkness once again sealed the corridor.

"Come on, come on," it was the fussy voice of the assistant, "the directors waiting!"

"I'm here, Angelo, keep your pants on," and then I entered the studio room for my first day of motion capture filming.

It was NOT a pleasant day. Definitely not something I was expecting nor used too. The director was relentless. Do this, do that, spin, drop, run, twist, jump, climb, I did it all. Then later, was told to do it all over again, and again and again. Movie making certainly was not as glamourous as I had hoped and was so repetitive, that it became an outright bore. Thankfully, we broke about four hours later, allowing me some time to run over to the commissary for some food.

When I attempted to head out of the building in the capture suit, Angelo screamed and ran up to me offering some boots to cover the soft pads of the fragile costume. "No going outside in the suit without shoes on, Ryan." he stated bluntly, standing with his hands on his hips, "Now, remember, get back here quick, and don't be late."

Thanking him, I then left quickly, just wanting to get out of there for a break, some fresh air or just a change of scenery, any change at all. Thinking that it might be nice having someone for company, I stopped by Marcia's office on the way out. She was there, with her obscenely thin waist, bent over her desk, reviewing some of the invisible paperwork that seemed to pop up everywhere.

"Hey Marcia, care to join me for some lunch?" I asked, standing at her door like an anxious school kid, a big boyish smile on my face.

She looked up, and her abnormally large, vivid turquoise, Asian eyes stared at me for a moment, a smile creeping across her lips. Almost sure she was about to agree, she gravely disappointed me when she said, "No, sorry Ryan, I just have too much to do today. I'll be at this paperwork all night if I'm not careful. You go on, enjoy your break; you won't get many of them. I'm surprised they've even let you out at all!" and then smiling once more, she looked back down, absorbed in her work.

Definitely disappointed at her refusal, I moved slowly away, moping, but that all changed when the stage door opened to an infinitely blue, cloudless sky, the strong welcoming sunlight hurting my eyes and causing me to squint terribly. For several minutes I had to stand still, pausing enough to let them adjust before I could walk on. It was such an agreeable morning, but like the day before, extremely hot. The sun baked the pavement, the oppressive heat rising and after the cool air-conditioned environment of the studio, only a light wind off the Pacific blowing back against the coastal mountains, provided any comfort. In much better spirits, however, I felt myself getting warmer as my short walk progressed. By the time I entered the cool atmosphere of the cafeteria, my breath was coming in gasps and I had begun to sweat profusely.

The commissary was a large place, and well occupied at this time of the day. It was a single large room, done up in what even I would call retro style, with chrome tables and chairs, brightly coloured linoleum floor tile and a cheerful robin egg blue on its walls. The serving area was all brightly polished stainless steel, and steam rose for the various food service bins, bathing the entire side of the space in an eerie, misty glow. The lighting in the room was provided by huge neon tubes in the ceiling that must have been LED, soaking the area in penetrating, bright white light, allowing no shadows to form anywhere, even under the tables!

I joined the small queue in front of the food preparation area after obtaining a tray from the tall stack located at the end of the counter. The tray was a silver colour and appeared to be fabricated of metal but had no actual weight to it. The material was also faintly glossy and completely scratch resistant, like nothing I had ever seen before. Another miracle of science exposed, then relegated for use in a common cafeteria. Our glorious future at work.

The line moved relatively quickly, in no time placing me in front of several bins of hot edibles, steaming healthily within their warming trays. The vapours wafting up from the display smelled extremely appetizing, making my empty stomach rumble in anticipation, although I could not for the life of me recognize many of the offered selections. Playing it safe, I selected what, for the most part, looked like spaghetti and meat sauce, of which a very generous portion was piled on top of a plate and then handed to me through the steamy cloud hovering above the pleasant-smelling food. Next was on to the beverage counter, upon which sat a single large machine offering beverages of every kind. Not wanting to be surprised, I selected the café, as this was already something I was familiar with.

At the end of the counter was a scanning device of some kind and after watching the patron ahead of me scan and pay for his lunch, I followed suit, scanning my plate and drink in the same way. When it came to payment, however, all it demanded was my security identification card and after scanning that, the display read 'Paid by Universal, thank you, Ryan Scott'. I was so pleased not having to find any money, and would have to thank Marcia for giving me the meal plan with my ID.

Selecting a bench seat in the center of the commissary, was second nature, with the specific intention of people watching while eating. It was not hard to spot the workers behind the scenes and the ones working the cameras. It was a hodgepodge of different folks from all walks of life, including camera men. I spied one of my camera operators sitting with a group of her colleagues, some grounds staff, maintenance crews, front office folks (they were the well-dressed ones) as well as one or two other motion capture actors. It was an enjoyable time seeing the various staff and guessing what each of them did. I made it a game, but soon my very interesting tasting spaghetti bolognaise was done and it was time to return. My camera operator friend had already left and so I knew it was time to go.

Dropping my tray off at the provided alcove, I turned to head out the door, when again the rather distinguished looking gentlemen that I had seen earlier that morning appeared. He was outside, lurking around, watching the commissary as if waiting for someone. I thought that perhaps it might be prudent to call security, but then through better of it. Who was I to make anything about this gentlemen's behavior? He was probably just someone from the head office, watching for lunch hour stragglers. And anyway, I had to get back. It was just the strange recollection that I had seen his face before that morning but couldn't place where that kept tugging at the back of my mind.

The walk back was again extremely hot and entering the soundstage air conditioning was a welcome treat. Angelo was waiting there to fuss over me and commented freely.

"Oh, Ryan! Look! You've made the suit all sweaty. We will have to dry clean it again this evening. Next time go out in your street clothes for goodness sake!" Angelo was not impressed.

The afternoon continued like the rest of the morning, except with a twist. Once scene required me to leave that soundstage and head over to the tank area to be filmed for a swimming scene. This was good in that it cooled me off, but it was very awkward treading water in the form fitting suit. If it was dry clean only, then we were in big trouble. Come to think of it, Angelo was probably just pulling my leg about the whole thing.

When I had dried off, using a very fancy contraption, appropriately called a 'body drier', I removed the still slightly moist motion capture attire and donned my own clothes that Angelo had retrieved from the change room for me. He further assured me that we could find another capture suit back at the soundstage, as we were all headed back there for a few final scenes to complete the day. By this time, however, the entire crew were very tired, the long day of shooting taking its toll, so the walk back across the lot was purposely slow.

We were about halfway there, when a huge and violent explosion shook the motion capture building and the structure bursting into flame. A huge amount of smoke and debris blew out from the damaged facility, one side immediately collapsing into the surrounding roadway.

"Where's Angelo?" I said looking frantically around, as the excessive dust of the failure finally reached us, and the sound of distant sirens started up in the background.

"I'm right here," his shaky voice called, and I turned to seem him come running out of the tank facility, his hands full, dragging who knows what.

"Thank goodness you're here," I stated genuinely concerned, "Was anyone left in the studio building when we left?"

And just as I asked the question, I felt my heart sink as I remembered; Marcia.

Immediately I took off at a run, a bunch of the crew screaming at me from behind, warning me to stay away, but I was not to be deterred. The portion of the building that had collapsed, had effectively sealed off any chance of entry from the south and so I headed across the face of the burning soundstage towards the opposite entrance. The one I had entered only 12 hours previously. The smoke and floating debris was thick, hot and stifling and instantly I found it hard to breathe. Pushing through the metal door, now twisted on its hinges, I fought my way into and along the corridor, the poisonous vapours of the burning plastics and insulation stinging my eyes and nose.

"Marcia!" I yelled, trying valiantly to see through the burning fog, "Marcia, are you in here?"

There was no reply and so, stubbornly, I carried on down the smoke-filled corridor, my body glancing on and off its red-hot surfaces, the faint glow of emergency lights my only guide.

Marcia's office door had blown open and she lay there sprawled at her desk, unmoving. She looked amazingly serene, almost as if asleep, except for the dirt on her face and the small dribble of blood leaking from both her ears. Remaining hopeful, I easily lifted her amazingly light weight, frail, lifeless body up and retreated back the way I had come. Turns out, I left the room just in time, as the inner wall, separating studio 3 and her office, collapsed catastrophically under a barrage of sparkling flames, consuming everything inside. The withdrawal back down the corridor was much faster than entering on my initial search, the two of us soon bursting out into the fading sunlight of the slowly expiring day through the now, nonexistent door. My lungs seared with pain, as I struggled over to a local patch of grass, well clear of the burning structure, and gently placed Monica on to its soft, cool surface.

The firefighters were finally on scene and the first jets of foam retardant were just being released onto the collapsing soundstage. Several emergency workers spotted me and my charge, immediately coming over to assist and beginning life saving measures in a vain attempt to resurrect Marcia's still prone form. They worked attentively for almost half an hour, using all means of life saving equipment and hardware, some of which I recognized, most that I did not. All the while I stood resolutely by, not wanting to go, fearing the worst, hoping for the best.

Several times, seeing me standing there, my outfit a torn mess and my head bleeding, one of the rescue team members tried to take me aside, offering to treat me for my numerous wounds and smoke inhalation, but I would have nothing of it. My place was with Marcia, as the crews painstakingly continued to work on her still inert form.

"Fight Marcia, Fight, damn you." tears welling in my smoke and dirt encrusted eyes.

It was all for naught. Marcia was dead, the poor woman killed instantly by the shear concussion of the initial blast, her brain smashed to a pulp inside her skull, as she diligently sat doing her daily paperwork. It was an absolutely unforgivable tragedy.

What was remarkable, was that I found out later I had sustained several third degree burns on my body that required immediate treatment. But I would only let them see to me after they had finally finished with poor Marcia and had gently placed a white drape over her petite form, shoes still on her feet, now forever still.

Modern medicine being the way it was, I was much better off than my departed friend, as the local ambulance team was easily able to treat me in their mobile hospital unit. First filling my lungs with an aerosol curative and then applying a stem-cell salve to each of my wounds, bandaging them all up, with the great assurances that the treated burns, would be mostly healed by morning.

"Your lungs will be back to full strength in a few days, just don't do any heavy exercise for a while," the young attendant said as he left me, still staring off into space, still in shock.

"Thanks for all your help and concern," I stated mournfully. Gesturing despondently to the shrouded shape on the ground, "I trust it was quick?"

"Indeed, it was sir," the ambulance attendant answered, smoothly, with no hesitation in his voice, "The lady died instantly. There really was really nothing we could have done."

Beginning to pack away his equipment, he left me alone to my sorrows, sitting there on a bench. By this time, the fire had been successfully suppressed, making it no further than the single set of soundstages, but the building was completely gone, the rest of the structure having collapsed in upon itself due to the extreme heat of the blaze. A rising cloud of hazy white smoke drifted lazily up into the darkening sky, as I felt loss for the great lady who had befriended me and given me work, prompting me to cry once again for Marcia's departed soul.

"God speed, Marcia," I mumbled tearfully, mostly to myself.

Sitting there in silence, I watched as the team carefully loaded Marcia's body into the awaiting ambulance. The rescue workers did it slowly, almost reverently, and I appreciated their care and concern. With the lights out, the red and white electric vehicle pulled away, the faint hint of ozone rising to my nose as it disappeared around the corner, the only sound its wide tires humming on the pavement. In its place, stood a plainly dressed woman, clearly waiting for an opening in which to speak to me.

She spoke as she stepped forward, "So, you knew the deceased." It was more of a statement than a question, her voice quiet and serene, no hint of malice or aggressiveness. Straight and to the point.

"Yes, I did," my voice still a little shaky, cracked a bit with my reply.

"My name is Officer Mendez. I'm the investigating detective in charge. I know you've been through a lot today, Mr. Ryan, but I would appreciate it if you might answer a few questions."

She stood there in a dark navy, tailored pant suit wearing very practical flat healed, black shoes. The officer also wore a bright pink blouse under her jacket clearly covering a concealed weapon holstered under her left armpit. The woman's long, dark hair was tied up in a ponytail, reveling a pleasant face, with little make-up. Her manner was friendly, non-confrontational.

"I have nowhere to go," I stated non-committedly, "What can I do for you?"

"The deceased name was Marcia Wong, age, 35. Employed at this studio for most of her adult life. She was occupied, at the time of her death, as a middle manager. Can you tell me a bit more about your relationship?"

"There's not much to tell, Ms. Mendez," stressing every syllable, "I only met her yesterday." I was exhausted, my head still in a fog, my words immerging slowly, as if my voice was walking through molasses. "She offered me a job as a motion capture actor, and then afterwards gave me a lift to the front lot. We talked a bit and then she gave me some advice."

Tired, I just wanted to rest, but after a long pause, continued. "I saw her again this morning and we joked with one another as friends. Then she disappeared into her office to do paperwork while I worked with the crew."

"What happened this afternoon?" Mendez prompted. She needn't have done.

"Well, this afternoon we all went over to the water tank building for more filming. Marcia evidently stayed here," gesturing towards the steaming remains of the soundstage, I was finding more energy the further developed my story became. "We had wrapped up in the pool tank for the day and our crew was heading back here to do a few final scenes before we called it quits for the day. We were about halfway back when the building blew." I stopped, needing a rest.

She prodded me again, "Then what?"

"Well, then I called out to make sure everyone was there and the only missing person I could recall was Marcia. So, I ran in there to get her out. The building was on fire and the doors blown off, but I went anyway…. she had collapsed at her desk."

Stopping for a breath, I concluded my statement, "The paramedic told me she was already dead. I didn't know that at the time, so I pulled her out anyway."

"Paramedic? I've not heard that term used before. Can you explain what you mean," she was very clear cut, non-accusatory, genuinely interested.

"Oh, sorry. The ambulance driver, the rescue guy." This policewoman didn't know what a paramedic was?

"Ah, okay," she appeared satisfied, "Tell me, Ryan. Your name is Ryan isn't it." A rhetorical question.

"Yes."

"Well, Ryan, why on earth would you enter a burning building for someone you've only just met?" she said it almost like I might have something to do with the blast.

Stammering a bit, I said, "Because, Ms. Mendez, I am a human being. And Marcia was my friend, not a good friend mind you, but a friend none the less. I would have done it for anybody."

Deciding at once to put it back on her, I asked, "Wouldn't you?"

She appeared to like that answer and returned, "I suppose I would, come to think of it. Well, you are a brave man, Mr. Scott, I'll give you that. It's not often these days, people show care for others as they do for themselves. I'm impressed."

"Thanks," I replied a bit sheepishly, "I'm no hero, just a guy trying to help. Little good it did."

She was quiet for a moment, then took a different tact, "Did you happen to leave the soundstage at any time during the day?"

"Yeah." I said, "I had an hour around lunch and went to the commissary."

"See anything out of the ordinary, or anyone acting suspicious during that time?"

Ready to respond immediately in the negative I hesitated, for a fleeting moment remembering the finely dressed man lurking in the dining building's rear shadows, but there was no point in mentioning it as he could just have been another studio lackey on a break. "No, I didn't."

"Well," Detective Mendez concluded our interview, "if you do remember anything or see anything suspicious in the future, please give me a call," and she handed me a sliver of clear glass with a barcode on it.

"I'll do that," taking the offered 'card' and placing it in my pocket.

"Have a good day. Nice outfit by the way. Too bad it's ruined" and then she was gone.

I don't remember how I made it back to the gate, but someone must have given me a ride out to the street and, luckily, Christine was there waiting for me. She didn't talk much, just took me under her arm, helping me into her Robi-vehicle and getting me safely seated. The ride back to her apartment was quick, Christine holding my bandaged hand all the way. The last thing I remember finally drifting off into a fitful sleep, after she tucked me in on her couch was her soft voice saying, almost cooing, "I'm glad you made it out, I would have hated to have seen you hurt."

Chapter Eleven – The Grocery Store - 2065

The explosion had taken its toll as, even after a good night's sleep, the previous day's events had left us both scared, shook up and depressed. Myself especially, after the loss of my colleague. As it was the end of the week, I had been told to take a day off and rest. Therefore, after a relatively slow morning at home, with limited conversation, Christine and I decided to do what every other normal North American does when faced with a similar situation; we went shopping.

First on the agenda were some clothes for myself. Especially, when I had to put up with comments like the following the previous morning from my new living companion.

"While I really appreciate your retro look, Ryan," Christine told me, "it would help you to better fit in if we got you some more modern clothes." Of course, Christine didn't say anything that morning, but I still thought it was a good idea.

Who could argue this, as I had already wanted more suitable attire for a while now? And anyway, my only clothes were a complete mess after yesterday's disaster. So, for our next stop, we were off to the clothes store. Clearly, Christine did not shop on the strip, showing no hesitation at all and taking me in a Robi-car to a boutique shopping area a short drive from her residence. It was no Rodeo drive, but as we approached the somewhat grandiose entrance, it certainly reflected a slightly higher standard to that which I was normally accustomed.

The building was of a classic, modern design, a flat roof and lots of glass and steel but with subtle, very expensive looking accoutrements on its frontage, like granite sheets and carved marble. The tall glass doors were highly polished and smoky in shade, reflecting our images as we approached the rather exotic looking store front. We made our way quickly inside, to get out of the hot sun relishing in the relaxing, quiet atmosphere of the boutiques controlled and well-conditioned environment. The cool air that smelled faintly of lavender was welcome, allowing us to swiftly become acclimatized to the lower temperatures, loosening our clothing and readying ourselves for the experience.

At first glance, the obvious thing missing from this shop was the typical, irritatingly attentive salesperson. For there was evidently no service staff in the establishment at all, save for three other customers like ourselves. The stores layout was also unique as there appeared to be absolutely nothing in the place save for a large and empty elevated counter that extended across the entire room. There were also, several low slung but comfortable looking seats along the window and four change rooms, two located at each end of the elongated service table, presumably male and female alternatives. Under the counter were what appeared drawers of some kind and above it a series of floating images, looking like digital picture books shimmering above the marble tops of the service desk. Each catalogue area, was separated from the others with a thin vertical divider rising from the shiny countertop, resulting in about half a dozen available shopping positions.

Glancing over at the other clients, I was immediately immersed in watching the futuristic purchasing process in action with unbridled fascination. Patrons first spent time casually flipping through the various options available on the floating screen. The moment something caught their eye, they selected one or two of these by inputting a command. Once chosen, a few seconds passed after which a green light flashed, and a beep sounded on the drawer in front of them. Stepping back, they pushed a button releasing the drawer. Within it, as if by magic, appeared the garment they had picked, in correct size, colour and style, which they then removed, making their way to the change room to try it on. They made it look so easy.

Another couple had just emerged from one of the other change rooms, obviously with some garments they wished to keep, and others they did not. The ones they wished to keep went through an opening in the top of the counter. The returns went back in the drawer which, when full, or when activated, closed automatically. After another few moments there was another beep, this time the drawer opened to reveal a packed bag, presumably containing the buyers selected items they had placed in the portal above. Naturally, one assumed the rejects disappeared back into the bowels of the store. While this all appeared very quick and convenient, at the same time it felt rather stale and impersonal. But if that was the way of the future, who was I to argue. It certainly avoided one having to deal with any bothersome sale associates.

While I watched these intriguing purchases transpire, Christine had already made her way up to one of the empty kiosks and was flipping through the flickering screen. She too made a few selections, the chosen items appearing promptly in the discharge area below.

"Come on Ryan," she quipped, picking up her items, "let's get moving! We still have a few stops to make! Here, use my screen, my information's still in. My treat!"

"Ah… Thanks," I stated as I walked up the counter, somewhat nervous to begin.

As it turned out, the section process was fairly straight forward. It was like looking through a catalogue, except the display showed what the item looked like on a person and provided size and colour options if available. It was very much like shopping on Amazon back home, but in a very modern, more sophisticated way. I had soon selected a shirt, pants and jacket that appeared to work together. I decided to forgo new undergarments and shoes. As to the former, the selections were just too weird for my taste and the latter, I just preferred what I had, for comfort sake. Admittedly, some of the future footwear choices appeared interesting and comfortable, I just didn't want to risk any possible issues in that regard, considering some of my previous experiences.

Once dispensed, I did make a determined move to try on the garments, just to be sure that men's sizing criteria hadn't changed in my 45 years away. It was unnecessary, as it turned out, all of the clothes fit extremely well, perfectly almost and so left I them on, stuffing my old damaged 20's outfit into the bag provided.

"Much better," Christine quipped, as I vacated the change room. She was patiently waiting for me, seated in one of the comfortable, leather backed chairs, "Doesn't that feel good?"

"I guess so," was my only reply looking down at my new outfit.

"Well, now you look like you belong." then she stopped, "But you've left your old belt on, silly."

"Indeed, I have," I replied, adamant, "I never go anywhere without one. You never know where you might need it."

Christine stared at me for a minute with that look of hers, then shrugged, not really understanding my motivations at all.

Well, I thought to myself, I might look like I belong, but I sure don't feel that way. There were just far too many odd things occurring in this future to make me feel comfortable, and after what happened at the studio, I would have to remain careful, alert and on my toes.

"Come on then," Christine pestered, "I have to pick up my medication, it's this way" and again she was off, back out into the heat, and further down the street to our next stop. I followed sheepishly, trying out my new clothes, feeling how the futuristic materials moved and making every attempt to get comfortable with my fresh, new look.

Turned out our next stop was the future equivalent of the pharmacy. I was a bit worried at what type of drugs Christine might be picking up, hoping she didn't feel I needed any 'pick me up' drugs or some such nonsense. But not knowing what was legal and what was not, might have also been a potential issue. There was no need to worry. As it happened, all she wanted was some vitamins and some newfangled pain medication.

The facility we entered had a much more basic look to its frontage and a colour scheme representing the drug store's type or brand. This one was called, PharmaCon. The interior, however, was much like the clothing store, with just a long main counter and dispensing drawers, with the one exception that each individual purchasing area was in a little kiosk type enclosure, for privacy, and equipped with a small door to seal shut. The counter was also slightly different, in that it was cheaper looking and equipped with what would be considered a small dispensing machine off to the side, at the edge of each booth. The room was all white, with one fancy trim mirroring the exterior branding along its bare walls. The atmosphere smelled faintly of antiseptic, but with a faint hint of strawberry shampoo. Overall, mildly pleasant.

Regular pharmaceutical items like deodorant and vitamins were selected in much the same way as the clothes had been, using the floating selection screen before being delivered in a small automated drawer. But for any medicinal type substances, like Christine's pain killers, she had to insert her prescription in a slot in the stand-up dispenser. This was scanned and accepted with a chime, going through some kind of verification process. Then, several seconds later, one could detect the buzzing, whirling and clicking of machinery as the distributer selected, counted and allotted the drugs. They were then bottled and deposited in a dispensing slot at the bottom of the vending machine style device. All quite neat and convenient! But what if you had a question regarding the drug, how to take it etc.?

When asked, all Christine did was point to a microphone and speaker mounted in the edge of the machine. "Here is where you ask any questions, Ryan," raising her eyes, "But surely, you already knew that!"

Then she added, a little exasperated, "My, it's almost like you've been living in the forest or something?" and she chuckled again, once more laughing at my naiveté of this future time. I took my punches and went with it for what was I going to say? I'm from 45 years in the past?

Once done at the drug store, we caught an available Robi-ride and proceeded to what I was looking forward to most; the future grocery store.

I was extremely excited to see what was instore for me in a supermarket of the future. We parked the car, or rather it parked itself, in the expansive parking lot situated beside a fairly large but also streamlined building. Rather than having expensive exterior finishing's, the structure was very utilitarian in its appearance and offered the external viewer no real information on its offering other than many flat grey surfaces and gaudy but very well-lit signage.

A high curbed sidewalk traversed around its perimeter, equipped with new growth trees, their leaves green with youth, safely nestled within concrete alcoves filled with soil, surrounded by intricate jet black, cast iron grates evenly spaced along the store's frontage. End to end its face offered heavily shaded windows from the top of its concrete foundation to the flat of its roofline. There was a single blue stripe running around the middle, just above eye level, the frontage glass coloured to match, giving the building much more of an industrial look than one of a potential consumer food offering. Through the doors to the right, many patrons could be seen entering, while on the opposite side, an equal number exited, pushing carts heavily laden with brown bagged produce and other consumables.

Clearly, in this time, paper was still used extensively, perhaps because of the fact that plastics had literally overtaken other parts of the planet, and humankind had finally realized that they did not want the glut of non-biodegradable items to infect this still, relatively clean portion of the world.

The supermarket facility we entered was, at first glance, very similar to any grocery shop I had entered, time and again, in the year 2020. We passed through the customary issue automatic swinging glass style entry doors, albeit these new ones were slightly fancier and far better finished than some of the ones I had previously witnessed. They were surrounded by a shiny material that was not aluminum, but not silver or platinum either, something tailored specifically in between. These glossy frames shone strongly in the noontime sun and combined with the glinting rays off the full-height glass, made it difficult to focus as one entered the vast complex.

Just inside the entry was a vestibule of advertisements and posters, as well as the characteristic linoleum floors and basic paint of a typical supermarket, but the area exhibited two distinct differences. There were no actual products present, just their sales ads, and the foyer led directly into the store proper, with a high wall separating incoming and outgoing guests, rather than an open entry/exit, displaying views of the departing customers. The place smelt the same as any food store might, the combined scents of produce, dry goods and bakery items all assaulting the senses together.

One further very distinctive difference was in the construction of the store itself. Rather than having a gloriously high industrialized ceiling, as most similar establishments had in my time, this building, while still relatively high, was completely and spectacularly finished, with only about 12 feet in clearance, providing a far more intimate atmosphere. And instead of being bright and airy, the lighting was muted and low-key, provided only by numerous pot lights recessed into the dark ceiling tiles. Rather strangely, there was nary a shopping cart in site, which was also very mysterious, considering when we had parked, I distinctly remembered the many departing, satisfied patrons equipped with their overloaded wagons.

Not appearing disturbed in a way at all by this fact, Christine continued on her way and so I just followed along, marveling at the many noticeable dissimilarities of this unique establishment.

Christine stopped briefly to 'tag in', she called it, as we entered the main area of the store, flashing what must have been a type of identity card against a silver toned receiving plate. Several lights above it flashed, briefly adding brightness to the dim atmosphere, then, with this sign-in ritual complete, passed on through a turnstile like device into the first area of the store.

This main zone appeared to be set up in rows and aisles as I was accustomed, however, that is where the similarities ended. Because one didn't remove any products from the shelves as was expected. Instead, each time Christine chose a particular product, all she did was walk up to that selection on the shelf, place her card on the plate provided and press a small green button visible next to the price tag and description of the item. At this action, one of the chosen items was dropped on a conveyor mounted behind the shelving and sent off to some central area, as if it were a gigantic vending machine. We continued to walk around the store pressing buttons for our selected products, more than once for multiple items of the same type. The exact same concept applied to the frozen foods, refrigerated items, meat counter and vegetable area; one would select an item and it would be dispensed onto the accompanying discharge conveyor, disappearing somewhere into the bowels of the factory.

Most of these items, like any grocery store, were familiar things like food, consumables and other goods. But that all changed when we passed by the Pharmaceutical area of the giant store. This area strangely enough, was set up like the rest of the store, not like the catalogue shopping of the stand-alone drug store we had just visited. Here all the items were out on display and for the first time, I was exposed to some of the various hygienic offerings of the future.

Unfortunately, none of this was a good thing as I noticed several items illustrating the very scary way our society had evolved. Within the same area where toothpaste and soap were carried, there were also Tylenol and Band-Aids as one might expect. However, there were also items of an extremely unique nature, one of which was so bizarre I could not help but ask about. It was an item entitled not "pregnancy test", but "Impregnating Kit!"

"What on earth is that?" I asked bewildered, pointing at the peculiarly boxed product that sat in a freezer style container with several other boxes similarly labeled, some pink, some blue.

"Oh that!" Christine gasped, "You haven't seen an Impregnating Kit before?" she laughed a little sheepishly before she continued, "Well, I guess not. You're a man after all. And somehow, no matter how sure of yourself you are, you don't strike me as very worldly. Or at least not someone interested in something like that, anyway." How wrong she was.

Then she continued, beginning to enjoy herself at my apparent male discomfort, "That's a kit a girl like me uses when she wants a baby. It's all very quick and straight forward." I listened with detached amazement. "The box contains an applicator and live sperm sample, all safely frozen. Once you request the item for your cart, and it's sent for final packaging, a small on-board cryogenic cylinder is activated to keep the kit refrigerated for up to 48 hours, while you take it home. Once you are ready to apply the solution, you switch off the cryogenic supply, which automatically activates the warming cycle, a green light on the box indicating when it is ready to use. Then you just insert the applicator and inject according to the included instructions."

Christine laughed again at my obvious incomprehension. "Usually, the kits are about 90 to 95 percent effective on the first try, so 9 months later you give birth to a healthy baby. Once in a while, however, they've been known not to take. But," Christine carried on, "If that happens you just bring it back and they give you another one. See, it's all described, just there," and she pointed to an advertising placard for the product located at the end of the row.

Warily, I looked at the poster, not knowing exactly what to expect. The wording of the marketing material hit me like a ton of bricks! What had happened to this future, with words like:

"Pregnancy 100% guaranteed. Just bring it back for another if it doesn't take!"

"Available in both boy and girl selections."

"100% viable sperm included."

"Donor supply 100% guaranteed."

There was also some small print at the bottom which read slightly ominously: "Unfortunately, while Williamson's Laboratory Products Ltd. can guarantee 100% impregnation and the future sex of the user's child, we can take no responsibility for its successful gestation as this can and will be affected by the health and actions of the consumer. Nor can we assure final race, creed or colour. Customers use our products at their own risk."

As I contemplated that most disturbing literature, Christine droned on, both enjoying herself and my embarrassment, making quite a joke about it. "All the benefit, without all the hassle!" she chuckled, "For some women this is their preferred option as it avoids potential partner selection and any of the associated unpleasantness that can entail." only bringing on another chuckle.

"Mind you, I've never considered it myself," Christine indicated, "but have had many friends tell me how convenient it is." she suddenly became contemplative, "Although my dear friend Susan, a tiny little Chinese girl, gave birth to a 10 pound, and very dark, African American boy. Quite a surprise for her strictly devout Asian family." and she giggled, "I'm sure one day the manufacturers will be able to get that figured out. But," Christine shrugged this off nonchalantly, "Who knows, one day my biological clock may start to tick, and maybe I'll try one out regardless." then smiled again as if this was all an extremely normal and natural thing.

Personally, the thought of an "Impregnating Kit" sent chills down my spine, making me cringe at the very image and I wondered just what else might present itself to me as we walked around this store of the future. Luckily, we were near the end of our odd shopping experience and I did not have to see anything even remotely as strange as this one item, although the prepackaged 3 course gourmet meals, made entirely of wafers, and liquid meat were most interesting.

Once we had completed our selections, we headed back to the front of the store. With the afternoon sun now low on the horizon, the variable clouds were beginning to display some very spectacular colours through the high bay windows. I did not realize we had been in there for so long, and it showed as, irrespective of our location, my stomach began to grumble wantonly for lack of food.

As we entered the departure vestibule, the complete absence of cashiers left me feeling unhappy. There were none at all, similar to every other establishment we had entered that day. This prompted the thought of how a cashier was normally one of only a few jobs young people occupied themselves with, at least in my time. It just showed that this future did not appear to have much to offer the early adult, at least in terms of gainful employment, having eliminated all of those types of positions.

"Hey, Christine where are all the cashiers?" I asked a little sullen.

"Cashiers? What's that?" Christine stared at me blankly.

When I didn't have an answer, she stood their looking exasperated, with hands on her hips, chiming, "You know Ryan, sometimes I just don't get you. Cashiers indeed!"

As it was, in their place, each paying customer stood at the end of a discharge chute similar to that at the end of an airport luggage carrousel. As each person leaving the store 'tagged in' at the kiosk, this chute would open up, revealing a shaft through which a fully loaded cart full of groceries, all packed and ready to go, emerged. As we walked up and Christine swiped her identification, a similar wagon was revealed to us, full of all of the items we had selected, all put safely away in crisp brown paper shopping bags, waiting for us to push them back to our waiting vehicle. How convenient!

Christine let me push as we headed out of the supermarket into the late afternoon heat, rising off the continually baking concrete. Our previous Robi-car which we had parked in a choice location near the entry doors had already been taken by another user and so we selected a similar sized transport closer to our exit point. We loaded the numerous bags in the trunk and settled in for the ride home.

"Christine," I asked, and the car pulled out of the stall and approached the roadway, "If all the other stores are set up as catalogue shops…" at the word catalogue she cringed, "Okay then, choice by selector screen," and I moved my hand to imitate swiping through the floating pictures. That appealed to her better, so I continued, "Why was the grocery store set up with items selected off the shelves, rather than at a selections desk? That conveyor system looked awfully expensive and unnecessary." I could not help but be curious as to why that particular way of dispensing items was limited only to grocery style outlets.

"Ah," she replied, "That's an easy one. At one time, some of the grocery stores tried the conventional approach…"

"Conventional approach?" I was a bit afraid to ask.

"Yeah! You know, we were just there, you just described it! Walk up to a display screen, pick what you want and then it's delivered at the discharge funnels. You know that, you dummy!" She looked at me again with a smirk and shook her head.

Then she continued, "Well, it seems grocery consumers didn't like that. They thought it was okay for clothes and shoes and other smaller things, but when it came to food, for some reason, and nobody knows why, they preferred the large displays and aisle style shopping. Turns out no one went to the new conventional supermarkets, everyone still preferring the old 'big store' style. In order to duplicate as close to conventional without scaring away their clients, the Big Box folks decided to use the automated conveyors and self-filling cart system. This was a perfect melding between the two and it stuck. Folks just love it. I do too, when I think about it."

It all seemed so bizarre to me but that was this future, totally and utterly peculiar in every way.

We were both quiet for a few moments, enjoying our journey and the scenery as we continued on our way back to Christine's place. The air was warm and fresh, the almost perfect sound insulation keeping the cabin eerily silent. Just as the cars smooth ride began to lull us to sleep, I asked, absentmindedly, "Hey, I was wondering? Would we be able to go to one of those slicer places tomorrow? I'm really interested to see how they work?"

"Sure," Christine replied, eagerly, "I can take you to one of the places I used once and give you a tour, walk you around a bit." then she added cheekily, "You know, you could use a bit of slicing yourself!"

Not on your life! "Well, we'll see. Let's just get home for some dinner."

"Right you are." Christine mused.

And we enjoyed the rest of the drive back to her apartment in comfortable and peaceful silence.

Chapter Twelve – The Slicer's Office – Special ·Effects 2065

The next day was Saturday and after a short sleep in, unlike the day before, we left the apartment fairly early. During my shower that morning (I had, thankfully, finally learned how to control the darn thing) I saw that my recent wounds had all healed, only a slight discolouration of the skin indicating where they once had been. In addition, my lungs were completely back to normal, and I could breathe regularly again. I was raring to go, being quite excited at the thought of seeing one of those slicer facility's up close.

Christine as always, left home carting her very large handbag. Some things never change, and I always find it fascinating that women carry such big bags. Like most gentlemen, I just carry a wallet and keys when at home. The only time I carry anything more is on one of my adventures, using my compact, but well equipped, waist mounted pack. Even that pales in comparison to Christine's huge leather purse, stuffed with who knows what. Remembering back to the day of the riot, however, and the welcome refreshment the drink bottle had provided when she pulled it from her bag, I felt it best not to complain too much. After all, I didn't have to carry it.

As she had promised, Christine assured me we would be visiting her favorite slicer, so we headed out into downtown, using an available Robi-vehicle as usual. The day was sunny as it always seems to be in southern California and the inherent lack of smog provided for glorious views all the way out into the Pacific. For a treat on the way, Christine requested the car to drive us along Mulholland drive, so we were able to look out at the magnificent vistas of the city, mountains and ocean, the vehicles auto drive allowing us to pay attention to all of the wondrous views flowing around and below us. The special suspension on the car and exacting climate control even prevented the typical land sickness that some folks experience when travelling on a very windy stretch of road as that one. With the sea to the west and the city skyline stretched out beneath us, it was a most worthwhile detour.

Soon though, within no time, we were back in Beverly Hills, travelling past numerous tall glass and steel structures that were obvious new additions to this previously expensive housing area. Some of the huge residential estates remained, but many more had evidently been demolished to make way for this new, thoroughly industrial looking development. The car soon drew up to the curb, and at first, I thought we had just pulled aside mistakenly for some reason, until Christine began alighting from the vehicle. Following suit, I found myself on the sidewalk at the entry to our supposed slicer treatment facility.

Quite contrary to what you might expect a hospital like setting to be, a three-story sprawling campus surrounded by parking, this medical facility was a towering glass and steel monster stretching up into the cloudless blue sky. Rather different than what I had pictured.

Looking back and turning to gesture at Christine as she moved around the hood of our car, I did not notice a tall, well dressed individual bounding away from the main entrance of the building. He was looking constantly behind him, as if chased. In a very big hurry, and not looking where he was going, he bumped right into me on the forward approach stairs. As I was part way up at the time, I was knocked off balance and would have fallen, if not for the large man grabbing hold of my toppling body in panic.

"I am extremely sorry," he said, speaking in a deep, attention drawing tone, all the while balancing me rightly on the stair. He held me gently at arm's length and looked up, intending to say something further, before I cut him off. Now able to look directly at him, I was sure that his was a familiar face.

"Hey, I know you," I said, regaining my balance, as the man suddenly and very abruptly let go of my shoulders, "I saw you at the studio the other day, hanging around the backlot."

The tall man jumped back, as if burned, first embarrassed and unsure, then aggressively stating, "I am afraid you are mistaken sir," after which he immediately swept past me, speaking very smoothly to Christine as he did so. "Are you finished with this vehicle, ma'am?"

"Why yes," she stammered, also showing some recognition at the gentleman's face, "it's all yours."

"Thank you. Thanks very much," and before we could say any more, he had jumped in our freshly vacated automobile and zoomed off, directing the vehicle to move even before he had closed the door and settled in the seat.

"Well, that was strange." I commented, reflecting on the man's odd behavior, before adding. "I'm sure I've seen him someplace before."

"Of course, you've seen him before, that's Gordon Flichette, the fellow from the rally the other day. He was the one on the podium giving the speech." Christine chastised me, "don't you remember?"

"Ah," I admitted. "You're right. That was him. Riot man. Of course."

Christine gave me a somewhat glowering look, mumbling something that sounded like 'riot man indeed' before turning and walking off, approaching the fancy medical buildings entry doors. But instead of following, I stood there for a minute contemplating what had just occurred as more than just a chance meeting. Certain that the rally wasn't the last time I had seen that particular well-dressed individual. No, I mused, I had definitely seen him on the studio lot as well, the day of the explosion.

"Well, are you coming or not?" Christine shouted from the top of the stairs. She had stopped and turned, and was looking down waiting for me to follow, her hand motioning, eager to get going.

"Sure, I'm coming," and began jogging up the pavement steps, the image of the tall elegant looking man still on my mind.

Those thoughts were fleeting, however, as I wandered up the rest of the stairs to the front door of the complex. A large crowd had assembled there to greet us, positioned against the side of the glass wall, lining up in front of the vast doors. There was a doorman/orderly carefully holding back the group, who were noisily moving about in anxious expectation. It looked as if they were waiting for tickets to a rock concert or something.

"What's up with them?" I asked Christine stepping up behind her, a little out of breath.

Christine's face wrinkled as she viewed the lineup that consisted entirely of both males and females between the ages of 18 and 30. "That's what I would like to know as well," she huffed, almost as if she was angry at the noisy throng of gathered, bubbling youths. She couldn't possibly know any of them, so I though her reaction very peculiar.

We walked directly up to the fellow holding back the crowds and asked what was going on. He was of medium height and build, not even 6 feet tall, but clearly in very good shape. The tendons on his exposed neck bulging out above the scrub style shirt he was wearing. Which appeared at least one size too small, the way it clung smartly to his muscular frame. He wore dark pants and soft soled running shoes and did not appear to be enjoying his present task of holding back the waiting queue of eager young adults. I did not quite understand his initial reply, but he mentioned something about a sale, until Christine cut him off.

"Are we able to go in?" Christine inquired, "We're just here to visit Dr. Johansen's office. I'm a past patient of his, here to show my friend around a bit."

"Oh, so you're not here for the special, then?" The orderly inquired.

"What special?" I asked. Christine was silent, still looking a bit upset with the crowd.

"The one-day event to look like Donny Dunn or Suzie Shine, you dope," he commented. Then considering us further, taunted, "But hey, on second thought, you two look way too old for that. Although, it looks like you," pointing a thick sausage finger in my direction, "certainly could use a bit of slicing yourself."

Why did everyone seem to think I needed slicing? It was beginning to make me feel rather self-conscious.

Then I heard, "Go on up," The man continued gruffly, "if you're not here for the special, you can go right in."

Christine and I walked quickly past him, and the line of excited youths, glad to get away from the clearly unhappy, almost hostile attendant, passing through the high glass swinging doors and into the vast lobby of the medical complex.

As the door closed, behind us, I heard, "Hey, how come they get to go first?" shouted by a young girl at the front of the line.

"Calm down," stated the bad-tempered orderly, "you'll get your chance. You've all got your place. There're just here for a tour, not slicing." That seemed to be the end of it.

The atrium we moved into was huge and airy, the bright sunlight passing easily through the glass sheathing, illuminating the grey and silver coloured entry hall. The atmosphere was quiet, and the air conditioning was working overtime, so I immediately felt a slight chill as we came in out of the rising heat of the day. The floor of the vestibule was a dark grey limestone, the walls etched in silver accents, and with all the surrounding glass, the overall effect very bright and sparkly, each ray of light gleaming off the polished accents and reflecting throughout the vast area.

Without hesitation, already knowing exactly where she was going, Christine took us right up to the first set of elevators. It happened that one was sitting, doors open, awaiting us as if it knew we were coming. The small rooms' walls were constructed of fully reflective material and it had polished metal floors as well as a brightly lit ceiling. And as the doors closed, exposing yet another mirrored surface, with all of our multiple reflected images visible around us, I imagined we had entered some kind of fun house attraction, with no way of escape. It was most disconcerting.

Displayed in the infinite multiple images surrounding us, Christine still looked troubled, her earlier pleasant demeanor appearing to have been melted away by the morning sun, revealing a slightly hardened edge. I opened my mouth to say something but did not have a chance as the lift was so fast it seemed the doors, having just closed, were almost instantly opening again. I was reminded for a minute of the magnetic bars spinning on my time machine, and sighed. As the elevator panels glided silently aside, they exposed a wide, very inviting hallway leading to a massive reception area and check in desk.

Advancing out of the lift and forward, I was able to catch a better look at the person sitting behind the counter and recognized a look that was vaguely familiar. I say familiar, because although I did not know her, the face was identical to that of our tour guide and the two girls in the Denny's I had seen on my first day. It was obviously not either one of those girls, however, because while her face was identical in looks to the diner twins, she was very petite and sported vibrant, bright green hair.

"Can I help you?" she asked pleasantly, as any respectable attendant would, before adding "I can see you two are obviously not here for the special!" smiling at me warmly, "You sir, somehow, don't strike me as the Donny Dunn type."

I was about to respond with a friendly quip, when Christine rudely cut me off, "No, we are not here for any special. We are here to see Dr. Johansen," she stated, rather abruptly, "I am a previous patient of his and I have brought my friend in for a tour."

"Oh, Yes, well…" the pleasant young receptionist was taken aback at Christine's rather violent retort, almost as surprised by her rudeness as I was. This recent aggressive behavior was very unusual and did not really make any sense. Christine was normally so very nice to everyone. Evidently either the meeting with the man downstairs, or the crowd of young folks waiting eagerly at the door, had put her off in some way.

"As it turns out, Dr. Johansen, while in surgery at the moment, is due for a break in about 10 minutes." rebounding quickly, the vibrant girl was quickly back to her jovial, overly helpful self, "If you would care to take a seat, I will call him when he is done with his latest patient."

Having no more to do with the 'copied' girl, Christine turned quickly away, and walking briskly, selected a comfortable bench in the waiting area, as far away as possible from the sleek reception desk and the young girl behind it. I followed directly, but not before mouthing a silent apology at the emerald crowned attendant. She took it all in stride, however, evidently used to all sorts of characters in her line of work. Shrugging her shoulders, smiling brightly again once more, she returned to her work, staring at a holographic image of some text displayed in front of her, similar to the menus we had at our tables during dinner several nights ago.

"Hey, what's up? What on earth got into you back there?" I gently probed Christine, making my way across the waiting area and sitting down, "You weren't very nice to that girl, and that's not like you. You're clearly upset about something. Was it anything I did?"

"No, it's nothing you did," Christine returned. She was quiet for a moment and then, "Not you or her, although she's one of them too.

"One of them?"

"Yeah, another one of those slicer copies, but it's not that, it's those screaming kids downstairs."

Then she finally opened up, clearly upset with herself, "You see, I'm a bit choked up at this whole 'Special' thing. Dr. Johansen never used to be a screen slicer. It's the main reason I came to him. Instead of going to just any another slicer joint."

"Screen slicer?" I had done it again.

"Yeah, screen slicer." Christine continued her explanation, "They're the ones who specialize in recreating screen characters on young folks who want to literally," and she said it while making air quotes with her hands, "be their favorite screen icon. Danny Dunn. Suzie Shine. You know! The artificially created screen actors from the movies. Like that one over there!" Pointing to the green haired attendant.

She sat heavily back in her chair, "Well, in the past Dr. Johansen never used to work on young folks like that. He used to only specialize in making people better looking as they were, using the technology to improve on their own personal image, not changing them into some... some cartoon. I guess he succumbed to the pressure and his pocketbook. He's no better than the rest. Slicing teens into screen icons like everyone else!" Christine exhaled dramatically, "I'm really disappointed. I really thought he was different." Then she sat there silent, her eyes searching the ceiling, quietly contemplating, completely distracted.

Not wanting to interrupt her very understandable brooding, my eyes wandered, looking out at the vast seating area. It was a well-appointed, very richly designed space, with over 30 chairs. Apparently, this Dr. Johansen was doing quite a business!

As I continued to admire the room, the young receptionist turned and smiled at me once again. But I realized soon enough, it was not me at whom she had beamed, instead it was at the excited girl who had just stepped out of the elevator. This was the exact same young lady who had occupied the front of the waiting line downstairs, and was now eagerly rushing towards the counter, waving what appeared to be a ticket in her hand.

Not more than 18, she was already quite pretty, in a girl next door sort of way. She had flaming red hair, high cheekbones and a cute button nose, apparently all of which was soon to be changed into something completely different. Just another misdirected youth of this society in need of a new, seemingly more common identity. A bit of a shame, considering her already very agreeable appearance.

"I want to be Suzie Shine, Suzie Shine," she squealed.

"Yes, yes alright, that's fine, just fine" the receptionist spoke in a calm, even tone, in no way condescending, like one speaking to a child. This was suitable as the young person she addressed really was a child, in a way. "Please just relax. We have you all taken care of …." looking briefly down at her list, "Sondra Clements isn't it?"

"Yes, yes, that's me," the young girl stated, the gentle tone not phasing her in anyway, as she excitedly brandished her identity card, "but soon I'm going to be Suzie Shine!"

"Yes, indeed you will be," smiled the attendant, "indeed you will. Now, quietly if you can, just head on down here with James and he'll get you all set up and ready for treatment."

A tall orderly had emerged from a passageway behind the desk, dressed in slightly wrinkled set of light green scrubs and clearly showing signs of extreme fatigue. I was not sure how many operations this place could perform in a single day, but evidently, he had been at it for quite some time.

His weary voice called to the red headed girl, looking down at the chart provided by the receptionist, "Come on then. Let's get you ready, ah, Sondra."

"It's Suzie, dummy!" Sondra quipped as James' eyes looked to the ceiling in despair and he headed back into the clinic, the exuberant the young lady following in his footsteps, skipping and dancing as she went.

Fascinated, I glanced over at Christine, evidently not impressed, ruminating over the obscene display. She was fully put out at the blatant commercialism of Dr. Johansen's new screen slicing business and she was not afraid to show it. All of this, however, was interrupted when an extremely tall, almost basketball player, height of a man, in a long white coat, approached us.

Dr. Johansen was a very attractive African American gentleman, clearly having taken full advantage of his own slicing technology, sporting a very Romanesque nose. He was clearly older, with an ample sprinkling of grey at his temples, but his ebony skin was flawless and smooth, like that of an 18-year-old. His voice was light and jovial as he spoke to Christine, opening his arms for a welcoming hug.

"Christine, my dear, so good to see you again," Christine stood and embraced the doctor. "It really is good to see you. Let me look at you."

Holding her at arm's length, he motioned for her to spin around, Christine reluctantly obeying. "You are looking very well. The treatments appear to be working marvellously."

"Hey, Doc," Christine replied rather sheepishly, completing her turn, "it's nice to see you too. But I see you've changed things around here a bit since the last time I was here."

"Indeed, we have. Just the nature of the game I'm afraid. Business just wasn't the same after the change. We had to begin screen slicing just to stay afloat. And as you can see, we even have to have sales days just to keep up."

The doctor motioned towards the departing Sondra, just disappearing around the bend, exhausting a big sigh, "Suzie Shine, Donny Dunn. That's all we do these days!" the Doctor looked down dejected, "but here you are. What can I do for you today?"

"Well I'm here with a friend of mine, Ryan Scott," and she turned to me, "Ryan, this is Dr. Johansen."

"Nice to meet you, Ryan, the doctor held out his hand and I shook it. His grip was warm and firm, "Any friend of Christine's is welcome here."

"Thanks." I said quietly.

Then Christine looked back at the doctor, "Ryan was hoping for a quick tour, see what the artistry of slicing is all about."

"Well that's fantastic, welcome Ryan," the doctor's smile widely. "As you know its special day today so I will have to get back to my patients soon enough, but I'm sure I can spare a few moments for you," he leaned in jokingly, "and it will be moment before young Sondra's ready for me anyway." he motioned for us to follow, "Please come with me and I'll show you the basics."

Christine hung back and then stopped, "Hey listen, Ryan. I've seen this all before, so tell you what. I'll just head back downstairs to the café house in the lobby," she was already on her way to the elevator, "I'll meet you down there when you're all finished. Okay?"

"Ah, alright, I guess," was all I could offer, looking forward to having her company in this uniquely strange place.

"Don't worry, we'll take good care of you," the doctor drew me towards the back corridor, "Great girl that Christine, you've found a good catch there. By the way, have you ever considered a slicing treatment for yourself?" Oh boy, not again!

As I looked back for support, Christine smiled cheekily at me, walking away towards what appeared to be the ladies' room. Obviously, her mood had improved, and the positive change bode well for what remained of the day. Not to be discouraged, and still very much looking forward to the tour, I obediently followed the doctor past the reception area and behind the scenes into the real world of slicing.

Beyond was literally a blindingly bright, virtual snowstorm. First was the look; the main hallway walls and ceilings were white, the floors were white, and the doorframes were white, there was no colour in the place at all, save for the view beyond the many windows which lined the access corridor. Second was the noise; there were staff of all sizes and shapes, running to and fro, getting new patients ready, taking patients to recovery, escorting healthy, but significantly changed, patients out, and bringing equipment and materials into each of the many rooms. It was a literal mad house.

The hallway we were in was generally equipped for regularly dressed staff, or street clothes for want of a better term. But beyond the main corridor, in each of the adjoining chambers, the environments were set up like cleanrooms in a computer chip production facility, fortified with airlocks, and staff adorned in coverall suits, booties and masks. Demonstrating a hygienic set up even more stringent and controlled than any hospital operating theater in 2020 might have been.

The first room we observed, through the myriad of viewing windows, was the client recovery area. An exhausted young lady, her shoulder length, brunette hair matted with perspiration, rested on a comfortable lounger, still dressed in the light wrap a patient might wear, laying haphazardly across the bench, her pasty white legs clearly visible. A scrub nurse attended to her, monitoring an IV connected to her arm, adjusting her position, placing a blanket on her more delicate areas, all the while speaking words of comfort to the patient, I could not hope to hear through the thick glass. The girl's new visage, obviously freshly applied to her face, was still wrapped behind bright white bandages, just waiting to be revealed.

Within the room were several other additional loungers, all available save one, occupied by a young male, resting comfortably, clearly anxious to go. His straight blond hair combed over the exposed face of a very fine-looking gentlemen. High cheekbones, a stylish roman nose and pouty lips, all falling to a deep cleft in his chin, clearly the image of this Danny Dunn that I had heard so much about. It was now apparent why there was such a long line up downstairs.

"As you may have already guessed, this is our recovery area," said the doctor. "As you can see the young lad there is almost ready to go, his new Donny Dunn look ready to display and show off. The young lady, on the other hand, has just come out of surgery and will remain covered for another, ah…" and he looked down at his fancy chronometer, "about two more hours. At that time the anesthetic will have worn off and the synthy flesh will have completely fused, so she too may go home to show off her new Suzie Shine persona."

"Excuse me, doc. Did you say synthy flesh?"

"Yes, I did. You see, Ryan, there's no way human flesh can possibly heal in the short time we have to slice our patients, even with our stem cell healing accelerants. So, in order for things to work faster, we complete the modifications and repair using synthesized human flesh, essentially a micro-plastine derivative, that looks and acts like skin covering the new face. This material can be exposed to sunlight within only a few hours of treatment, revealing completely new healed skin outside, while behind the scenes as it were, the actual patients remaining flesh, bone and muscle repair themselves beneath. Quite handy on these 'Special' days." And he smiled brightly.

He continued his narration, "I like sales days because I can program in the chosen silhouettes in the computer long in advance and just call up the details directly, one for the male patients, and one for the female. Although sometimes I can be surprised." he paused for effect, "It's quite interesting how a few of the young gentlemen that come in want to look like Suzie Shine."

Then he laughed heartily, "But to each his own. Of course, for more custom work, like your friend Christine for instance, I have to set up unique programs for each individual, researching the exact details of their facial structure, musculature and bone make-up." he hesitated before going on, "That's why I decided to get into this screen slicing business. Over time, the studios have cut back on new computer-generated main characters, re-using them as much as possible. This has considerably reduced the numbers of different actors over the years, making the likes of Donny Dunn and Suzie Shine quite popular. And feeling their own personal identity is just not enough, that's all the young kids want these days, anyway."

He held his hand up vertically against the side of his mouth and lowered his voice before adding, "And I happen to have a friend in the animation department at several of the studios who can supply the data base for the face constructions to me direct. I don't even have to make up the program for some of them!" Then he chuckled loudly, his laugh filling the hallway, feeling very proud of himself. What a business!

Next, moving on down the hall, was the slicing room itself. This was what I had come for! Through the large crystal-clear windows, one could see the entire area consisted of a stainless-steel lined environment, equipped with a single, centrally positioned, floor mounted table surrounded by numerous robotic arms, tubes, hoses and other embellishments of which their origin or function remained a mystery. These all hung from a series of concentric discs mounted circumferentially around the central light fixture right above the main operating surface, allowing 360-degree rotation and unlimited access.

Beside this primary table were a series of smaller, secondary surfaces, each equipped with various devices and accompaniments, some manual, some tied into the robotic arm control system. Two rotating, low backed chairs orbited on either side of the main slab, having access to both the patient and its own control console immediately attached. Mounted in the ceiling at the middle of the room were a series of cameras and other mechanical items and accompanying them, on either side wall in clear view of the dual seats, was a large flat screen, installed for what I assumed to be viewing during the actual procedure. At present, the immaculately clean operating theater was unoccupied, apparently now patiently awaiting the arrival of young Sondra, after her pre-op preparation was complete. It was wondrous to behold, and I only hoped that the doctor might let me observe him slice his next patient.

"This of course is the main procedure room," the doc touted. "Housing the state-of-the-art slicing technology, touchless, automated sanitization, and a fully equipped synthy flesh distribution network." he actually puffed out his chest proudly, "my pride and joy."

"So, this is where it all happens then, is it?"

"Yes, my friend indeed it is, and soon," the doctor was excited to be showing off his equipment, "I will have to scrub up yet again and proceed with little Sondra's Suzie conversion" And he laughed again.

"Would I be able to watch you perform your magic." I asked tentatively, extremely keen about the prospect of watching all that gear in operation.

"Normally, for confidentiality purposes this is not permitted, the viewing areas are really only for immediate family members. But provided you're willing to stick around, we'll see what we can do. The actual procedure does not really take that long, it's the preparation that's the hard part, but first, let's move on, I have more to show you." And we headed on to the next window.

"This," the doctor stated as we arrived at the next window, "is the very brains of our facility," and he smiled, proudly presenting the room in front of us with a grand sweeping gesture of his hand.

The brains, as Dr. Johansen called it, was another technologically advanced, contamination protected chamber, but instead of stainless steel, this room was ceramic tile lined, from top to bottom, wide expansive beige tiles on the floor, smaller rectangular ones on the walls, similar in size and shape to white subway tile, and finishing off with a strange cement covered ceiling. At the very center of the room was a sort of donut shaped scanning machine, similar to a modern MRI machine, set up around a horizontal stone table upon which lay our excited Sondra, her street clothes now removed and wearing only a light hospital shift. From what I could see there was not one item of metal visible in the entire room.

"Now you see what makes this magic possible; our dTBM scanner, or as we like to call it the DOTBAM machine!" adding with a flourish, "our deep tissue, bone and muscle scanning unit." Then he excitedly pointed into the ceramic room, "Now just watch, as the machine is put in motion for our next client."

Young Sondra, I could see, was lying excitedly on the table, gently strapped in place, while a laser scanning screen generated from the donut was projected downward onto her face. The donut slowly moved from the top of her head to the base of her neck, registering all of Sondra's specific dTBM data. This the doctor stated was stored in a computer to be used for later.

"The next part in most interesting," he stated further.

Soon after word, the attending nurse, James, standing at the side of the machine and viewing a local monitor, selected a face on the screen. It was completely different from Sondra's cute high school looks, with sharp cheekbones, aquiline nose, rounded chin and a set of lips that were so pouty they almost appeared to be crawling off the visible facade. This image looking exactly like the receptionist up front, the two girls at the Denny's and our tour guide at the museum. The Suzie Shine I had heard so much about.

With a touch of a button, this image was projected from the laser streams and layered over top of Sondra's own, the differences highlighted in a deep blue, all of which the computer registered in its data base. Then almost as soon as it had begun the procedure was complete.

"Of course," droned on the Doctor, "our rather special DOTBAM machine can not only do the face, but the entire body as well. We need only program the exact requirements and the scanner can register the patient's complete body image into its memory banks. If I remember correctly this is the style of treatment your friend Christine requested when she came in for her slicing." then he added, "But today, with our special, it's only the face that need concern us, which is good, as it makes things go that much more quickly for each client."

By now Sondra was already on her feet. And was being escorted through the airlock into the operating theater.

Not quite resisting the urge, I asked a question nagging at me, "Doctor, I notice this room is tile lined, not stainless steel like the operating room. I would have thought that stainless would have been better for sanitary reasons, why the difference?"

"Ah, very good! So, you are paying attention," he replied, always ready to provide more information, "Stainless steel is of course better from a hygienic point of view but our DOTBAM requires a completely metal free environment. It seems that elemental iron impedes with its scanning and transmission abilities. Thus, this room contains not one ounce of steel, and we have to be very diligent to ensure no metal of any kind finds its way in there. The results for the patient could be disastrous." adding thoughtfully, "Even the rebar used in the concrete construction of the building was coated with an inhibitor and the walls adjoining the stainless lined operating room are specially treated to shield the unit in order to insure no inference makes its way through the adjacent cavity."

Then he stopped for a breath before continuing, anticipating more questions. When none were forthcoming, he continued, "Well Ryan, we don't have that much time left. Come, we have just a few more minutes to visit my office before I have to return to my doctoring duties." And he led me all the way to the end of the hallway, through a tall door.

This door in contrast to the rest of the corridor, did not have an airlock and was constructed of incredibly thick and heavy, hard wood, stained a deep burgundy brown. The room we entered was a masterpiece of modern interior design, hailing from various centuries in look, feel and accompaniment. The floor was ultra-modern, with its checker-plate stainless steel finish, which differentiated sharply from the dark brown hard wood wall paneling around its perimeter. The ceiling was painted black and retained a series of bright recessed pot lights to illuminate the space. The walls were covered with fine art, all in elaborate and very expensive frames, that enhanced the works without taking away from their beauty. Each piece of artwork was provided with its own individual illumination from above, heightening the viewer's experience. Finally, there was an extremely wide and ornate Victorian desk in the center of the chamber, under which the edges of a fine Persian rug extended to provide a notion of warmth to the otherwise most utilitarian floor surface. All in all, a great space, demonstrating that truly Dr. Johansen was doing very well for himself.

"Please sit," he motioned to a very comfortable, wing back chair opposite the desk, into which I sat, enjoying the elaborate and luxurious feel of its soft leather. "I hope you enjoyed your tour of my facility, or as I affectionately refer to it, my special effects department."

"Most certainly, doctor. You have shown me some truly fascinating stuff," realizing I had truly been impressed.

"Well, we only have a few moments as I must see to our young Sondra." for the first time the doctor spoke in a rather melancholy tone, "Such a pretty girl. It seems almost tragic to covert her over. But I'm only a humble slicer, not a psychiatrist."

"You must have a choice, surely," I inquired.

"Indeed, and contrary to what you might believe, I do try my best, especially with the younger ones, to talk them out of the procedure." he sighed, "But unfortunately, Ryan, it's all the rage and all of their friends are doing it and, to be quite frank, despite what you might see, it is not all that expensive to accomplish in this very competitive marketplace. So, they demand, and I see to their needs, for if I don't, someone else surely will."

The communicator on his desk beeped and I caught the detached voice of the emerald haired receptionist, "Doctor, sorry to disturb you but your next patient is ready in the procedure room, please go on in."

"Well, that's me." he said, standing up, "Sorry to have to leave you, but here's the thing. As you are not a family member I cannot legally allow you to watch the procedure, but," and he chuckled as he said it, "if you just stay in the office here after I leave, then follow me out a few minutes later, you will reach the procedure room just as I am about to alter our patient. You should have a clear view of the entire process on your way to the elevators. See you, Ryan," and he extended his arm to shake my hand, "It was very nice to have met you. Take care of Christine for me." before adding as an afterthought, "And if you are ever in the market for an upgrade, please feel free to call." Then he was off, the very solid door closing tightly behind him.

Shocked at the casualness of it all, I sat there stunned for a moment. Modifying your face, in just a few hours for the right price, just to be like everyone else? It was amazing. This future world was definitely an interesting and thought-provoking place. As I sat brooding, I stared out over downtown L.A. The day was still very bright, and the rising towers of the downtown core glistened and shimmered, rising up to meet the sky, their edges slightly out of focus in the rising thermals.

Allowing what I thought had been enough time, I rose from the chair only to be suddenly knocked down flat, my head knocking firmly against the leg of the desk, as the chair toppled, and a loud explosion ripped through the building. I literally saw the heavy office door bend inward with the pressure, until the strain was too much, and it blasted its way into the room in pieces, devastating the interior, portions of it continuing out through the huge picture window, reducing it to dust. If I hadn't been thrown to the floor with the initial blast, I imagine I would have been impaled like a vampire, then followed the shards of oak out of the opening, falling swiftly to the hard ground. As it was, the wing back chair that was heavily forced against me, bruising my ribs and upper thigh, had acted as shield, protecting me from the worst.

A wave of heat and dust entered the office, through the now open doorway, as the last surge of the initial blast dissipated. The pain in my leg made it difficult but after finally standing, I was able to survey my present situation. I could see several small fires had broken out throughout the room, none of them yet quite large enough to set off the sprinkler suppression system. I pulled down one of the heavy curtains from around the nonexistent window and expertly put out the small budding flames, hopefully saving the few of the Master works that had not already been torn from the walls with the flying doorway. Then I made my way out into the corridor in search of an exit.

Looking both left and right I spotted the closest stairwell, but upon entering could see my options were very limited as the staircase appeared in extremely rough shape. The landing had disappeared and the metal treads and handrail, normally used to descend to the next level, had also torn free from their supports. Together with the landing, everything had fallen down, and were now several stories below. As I did not have a repelling rope set-up handy, I retraced my steps back into the main corridor, heading along it towards what was hopefully the central core and an alternate escape route.

The building behaved as if deserted. There did not appear to be anyone else alive, or none that would be able to assist in anyway. I continued down the debris strewn, strangely silent corridor, the emergency lighting my only guide, smoke and steam hissing from all sides, water dribbling from bent and broken piping. Small fires continued to burn in several corners, but with not much fuel left to consume, were slowly extinguishing themselves. The dry wall was torn and ragged, its plaster surfaces falling everywhere, making the footing very uneven, the concrete flooring evidently having heaved upward or downward in numerous places.

It was not too long, however, before I heard an urgent scream, which first began as a whimper but ascended in volume on closer approach. The DOTBAM room was a complete shamble, the machine having been forced right off of its concrete foundation, the expensive, ceramic donut laser scanner shattered. The walls and floors displayed large cracks and numerous smashed tiles and various fittings lay haphazardly on the floor. The viewing window had been blown in, the particles of clear green safety glass strewn to all corners of the room and the door of the airlock hung twisted and bent on its single remaining hinge. I carried on past this devastation, the sounds of desperation unmistakably emanating for the next chamber along.

It was the operating theater that had taken the brunt of the explosion. The entire outside wall of the tower had been blown away, steel and glass tumbling unchecked to the street below. The gaping opening allowed the morning wind to blow inward, swirling the dust and debris evenly around the destroyed room. The hallway viewing panel for this room was also gone, revealing that the airlock had completely disappeared, evidently now also lying 30 stories below. There was a massive chasm in the middle of the floor, the concrete having sheared and cracked and was currently hanging from only a few exposed, iron reinforcing bars. The sheets of stainless flooring had separated at the gash, and was bent up like a soup can, twisted and torn.

I stood on one side of this open crevasse, and on the other, screaming for assistance, was young Sondra, still safely strapped to the operating table, hanging at an angle in space, still mounted to the precarious, ever tilting floor slab.

The ceiling appeared in good shape and the apparatus and arms hanging from above the table remained securely in place, so I entered the remains of the room slowly, taking a quick glance behind, surveying the full extent of the damage. The good doctor lay sprawled against the inside wall, a cut on his head but breathing. James was there as well, the orderlies leg a bloody mess, but with it already beginning to clot, his femoral artery obviously still intact. They both looked okay as they were and I even detected a slight groan from one of them, so they could wait. With everyone else apparently out of action, I knew my first job was to help Sondra.

Young Sondra hung there in space, perilously poised above a 30-story drop, in desperate need of a death-defying rescue. The dangerously tilting concrete floor slab was clearly showing extreme stress and about to let go at any moment. She continued to squeal, all the while strapped on the bench and I could see that, with each subsequent movement, her actions were putting additional unwanted strain on the shifting slab. Moving without thought, stretching one foot over the gap, I tentatively placed some weight on the other side, knowing immediately as I did so that it was no use. My foolish actions caused the slab to shift yet again, instantly forcing me to step back off. It looked like there was no way I was going to climb across, in any normal way, to help the frightened girl.

Struggling to see another option, another solution, anything to save the poor girl, I surveyed the room once again, looking every which way, including back and up. There seamed nothing I could do, nothing within reach. Panicking, I began to perspire, the beads of sweat forming on my brow, dribbling down my dirt encrusted face. Wiping the irritating flow away before it got into my stinging eyes that had begun to lose focus. A feeling of utter helplessness tore at my mind. I was absolutely frantic for a solution. But there was nothing I could do. The tilting floor shifted again, drawing yet another horrific shriek from the petrified youngster.

The room began to fill with haze as a small fire had erupted behind me in one of the wall cabinets. A jet of water spurted drunkenly from a broken sink. A piece of the floor broke loose and plummeted to the ground, taking a large chunk of stainless-steel sheeting with it. A sticky fluid dripped on my shoulder from above, possibly some of the synthy flesh from the overhead pipe and hose work.

That was it! I swiftly removed the belt from around my waist and then reached up to one of the rotating mechanical arms surrounding the table just within reach. It took an extreme effort, and almost made me topple into the widening chasm in the floor while doing it, but ultimately, I managed to loop my belt around, pulling the end through the buckle to firmly attach it to the metal arm. The dangling leather now served me as a firm hand hold, and I wrapped the strip of pliable leather around my wrist and then palm, testing the strength. It appeared to hold my weight with minimal deflection.

I did not have much time for just as I prepared to jump, the floor slope altered once again, Sondra suddenly yelling with a renewed sense of urgency, her wailing screams a desperate plea for help, cutting like a knife through the thick, smoky air.

As soon as I had made the first lunge, I knew it was too hard, providing far too much momentum and without any choice, lifted my legs as I sailed over the table in a wide circle, dropping back to the floor where I started. After that aborted effort, my next effort would have to be an extremely careful one to get it just right. The second time, however, too nervous and too anxious, I once more overshot the table. But on the third try, with just a light push off this time, I slowed to a halt just above the surface where Sondra lay, lightly placing my feet on either side of her trapped body on the very edges of the operating surface. I felt the floor shift again with my added weight and so, pulling against my left hand and wrist, I took all the burden on to my arm and hanging belt, reaching down to untie the frightened girl.

"You're going to be alright, Sondra," I said in a relaxed tone taking a deep breath, trying to calm the girl. "I'm here to help. Just please, you must calm down and try to stop moving. Here let me get you unbuckled and then you grab on to me." I didn't need that last part, as already with one arm free, Sondra had taken a firm hold of my extended arm, putting even more load on my suspended wrist. I felt my left shoulder crack, and could almost sense the joint stretching, as the added weight attempted to pull the arm straight from its socket.

Painfully, one by one, I released the rest of the buckles restraining the girl. After each came lose, the slab would move closer to falling, Sondra would yell and hang on harder, pulling with greater force at my body. The blood began to drain from my upper hand, and by now I could no longer feel my left arm.

The last buckle, however, just wouldn't budge. No matter what I did it wasn't going to come lose. Sondra's shifting weight had drawn it taught and it was immovable. Reaching down, still perilously suspended above the slab, I reached across my chest and into my holster, withdrawing my knife. I rapidly began sawing it across the fabric, felling it slowly fray as I worked. Within moments though, I had her free at which point she shifted entirely, lifting herself up, putting her arms around my neck, holding on for dear life. I dropped the knife, wrapping my available arm around the girl's shivering torso.

With her free, all that was left was to push off and away from the table to spin us back to the stable side of the floor. As I did this, the outside portion of the steel deck finally give way, and as the two of us swung back around to safety, the tilted section of the room, containing the recently occupied operating table, plunged away, falling speedily down to the ground. For one precious instant, we were suspended over an abyss before being safely secured on the far side of the procedure room floor. I immediately dropped the hold on my belt, and the pair of us toppled to the cold steel surface, myself spinning in the air to hit first, protecting Sondra's frail body with my own as we fell.

My left arm began to throb, then tingle, the blood slowly returning to my hand as we lay their sprawled on the debris strewn floor. Certain I had dislocated something during the fall, I had also suffered a cut on my leg from the sharp edge of the torn stainless floor, only now feeling the itchy flow of blood dribble down my ankle onto the cold surface. But it didn't matter, because we were safe. We were both safe.

I breathed a deep sigh of relief, remembering with utmost horror, the brief vision of the floor giving way under us and my momentary view, 30 long stories straight down to the ground. I said a prayer in thanks and then rolled away to see if Sondra was alright. The girl was cut and bruised as well as covered in what appeared to be several small burns, but all in all appeared in reasonably good condition.

She lay there whimpering, muttering over and over, "I will never visit a slicer again, I will never visit a slicer again."

The light shift, she had on, however, was a complete mess, torn right through and with the exception of a light pair of panties, the young woman was wholly unprotected. I pulled off my fancy coloured jacket, now grit encrusted, and slung it round her shivering torso. Yanking off my boots as well, I placed the oversize footwear on her soiled and very chilly, bare feet.

After a few more moments rest, and a good set of strong breaths, I stood, helping her gently up. Then holding her tightly by the shoulders, the two of us, hobbled out of the room, passing the unconscious doctor and his aide, and down the hall towards the exit stairway.

"What's your name?" I asked, just to ensure the girl remained awake.

"Ah, my name's Suzie... no, Sondra," then she said it with more conviction, "yes, my name is Sondra."

By this time, the rescue crews had arrived en masse, and we were met at the stairwell entrance by a young firefighter who, dropping his axe, gently lifted Sondra bodily into his arms and carted her immediately away, down the stairs. A second rescue worker, similarly, abandoning his fire gear, took hold of me and escorted me down the stairs, helping me all the way.

"There are two more injured and unconscious folks up there," I coughed, already breathless.

"Okay, thanks," stated the fireman, "we've already got out the receptionist and several others and have more crews on the way up who'll take care of them. You just save your strength; you've had a busy day." And for the remainder of the decent, the two of us continued down in silence.

With the slowing of my adrenaline and slight relaxation of my muscles, I began to feel the various pains begin to wrack my body, as previously forgotten they had now slowly come back into focus. It was lucky the firefighter was supporting my right arm as the pain in my left shoulder, elbow and wrist was almost unbearable. Also, just realizing that sometime during my ordeal, my face had been burnt, the feeling of excessive warmth like a halo around my head. Various cuts and abrasions adorned my arms and legs, and my muscles felt soft, lose and jellylike.

The surface of the concrete stairs felt cold and gritty on my stocking feet, and our progress was slow, the dank and musty smell of the stairwell enhanced by the smoky, sooty residue of the previous explosion. Eventually, we emerged at the lobby level, just in time to see Sondra carted away in an awaiting ambulance, the lights flashing furiously, its tires squealing as it sped away. With no other units readily available, and myself not in such bad shape, my savior propped me up on an available stretcher and pushed me across the road, heading over to a triage center that had been erected for the various hurt and wounded.

As we left, another firefighter ran up and briefly stopped us midway across the blocked road.

"Hey, are you the guy who rescued the young girl?" he asked.

"I am," my voice was scratchy, my throat dry, so I could offer little else.

"Well, I have something here that I think belongs to you. She said she was very appreciative of all you did." as he said this, he dropped my boots and torn jacket at the bottom of my stretcher. Before finishing with, "Man that was a real good thing you did. It's what we're trained for, but for someone like you to put his neck out like that for someone else, well, I got to hand it to you, Bud. You're a real hero in my book."

His kind words sank in, making me feel warm inside, so I replied as best I could, my voice still rough, "Thanks. It was what anyone else would have done."

"Well, maybe not anyone," he observed, "Hey, thanks again."

Then he was gone to help another in distress, and we were again on our way across the plaza, the wheels of the stretcher hissing on the pavement.

Relaxing on the slightly firm but more than tolerable temporary bed, was a delightful repose after all my recent activity. As we approached the medical tent city, I spied Christine as she ran over, looking frightened. She had evidently been crying, and bent down to hug me, placing a big wet kiss on my dust encrusted lips. Unfortunately, unable to remember much else from the moment, I finally passed out, worn down from the shocking events of what was supposed to have been a simple morning trip to the local 'special effects department.'

Chapter Thirteen –
Aftermath

.

Much later in the day, in the aftermath of the slicer disaster, once I had awoken and been successfully treated and supplied with glorious, futuristic painkillers, Christine and I huddled together. We were still seated on a gurney in the temporary emergency shelter erected by the rescue teams across the street. The facility had been located in the extensive, open-air mall between several of the towers directly across from Dr. Johansen's slicer building. A myriad of ambulances, fire trucks and police cruisers remained haphazardly parked around the immediate area. It was a large contingent, the paramedics attending to the wounded, the firemen cleaning up the foam distribution hoses and equipment and the police officers, who were still busy holding back the gawking crowds and lining the area with yellow crime scene tape in preparation for their upcoming investigation.

Holding my attention, in the center of the vast concrete plaza was an extremely large and attractive, ornamental fountain, constantly spraying copious jets of crystal-clear fluid into the air from its many nozzles. Shortly after release, the liquid persistently fell back in on itself, the droplets toppling, mixing, and coalescing back together in an endless circle of renewal. The continually rising flow and returning showers glowed brightly as diamonds under a spotlight, generating small rippling waves in the tiled receiving pool, sparking brilliantly in the late morning sun.

My ears still rang from the blast, but the soothing sound of the recycled liquid travelling in its perpetual circle, was just loud enough to remain quite relaxing and therapeutic, easing my troubled mind. In addition, with an intermittent light wind blowing, a delicate spray occasionally made its way across the square, cooling my slightly burned face. The only unfortunate thing was an odd medicinal smell surrounding us, most likely emanating from the main triage tent nearby. Christine cuddled next to me crying, while I sat staring out at the fountain, the devastation and all the activity around me.

"Christine," I asked unhurriedly, my voice still rough, "Is that really water coming up from the fountain over there?"

She raised her head up slightly at my question, before dropping it back down, her voice also scratchy and irregular, "Of course not, you dope." giving me a light punch in the shoulder on which she was resting, "Jeez Ryan, I would have thought you had got it by now. There is no water. That's an alcohol fountain. They use specially treated grain alcohol which they recycle through the fountain over and over again. Keeps itself clean as no bugs can develop in the solution. It's replenished every day after sunset. Don't you smell it?

"Yeah, yeah, I was just making sure," I replied distractedly, deflecting my ignorance yet again. So that was the unusual aroma in the air. An alcohol fountain! What will they think of next? Then I remembered my morning showers. If there was no truly water, what was used for that? I couldn't, no, did not even want to ask, so I looked up and away from the flowery liquor display.

The front face of Dr. Johansen building had been torn open like a ripe melon, the wide opening in the surface of the glass and steel structure, like an evil eye glaring down from its blackened facade. Dejectedly, not being able to stare at the opening anymore, I looked away from the gaping wound, down to the ground near the entry stairs of the now abandoned tower.

There lay the shattered remains of the large slab of dark grey concrete and stainless steel, now destroyed, broken into component parts after its long fall. This rubble of course had been a part of the infamous slicer room floor that, unbelievably, less than a few hours ago, had given way beneath me. Thankfully, just after I had been lucky enough to retrieve the young girl Sondra before she fell with it. By now she would be safely in bed at a local hospital, and I could just imagine the fuss she would be giving the nurses in that facility, relating the details of her hair-raising story.

Sitting in complete disbelief, I still could not entirely fathom what had happened. How twice, in the short span of three days, I had been forcefully engaged into an all-out rescue following a massive, devastating explosion. In this instance, however, unlike the previous situation with Marcia, I had been successful in the attempt. Somehow, I was convinced there was absolutely no way all of this trouble could be just a coincidence, but what it all meant was still a complete mystery.

While deeply contemplating my strange twist of fate, with the smells of the smoky aftermath of the explosion still wafting over from the battered and blistered tower now obliterating the slight alcoholic tinge to the air, the familiar silhouette of Officer Mendez, stepped in to block the view of the carnage, placing the two of us in shadow. She was wearing a very similar outfit to the one she had on the last time I saw her and was obviously still packing the same concealed weapon. Today her hair was loose, falling lightly on her darkly clad shoulders.

"So," with no preamble, she started in, "fancy finding you here. Mr. Hero. I understand there's a young girl in LA County Hospital that can't say enough about her miraculous rescuer." she began taunting me, counting on her fingers, "Not a fireman, nor a policeman, not even an ambulance attendant, mind you. No, just a regular guy, who apparently likes entering burning buildings as a hobby."

"Hello, Ms. Mendez," I offered sheepishly, "I know what you're thinking, but it's really just a coincidence that I was here today." She glared at me, with her dark eyes, "Really, I was just here for a tour."

"A tour? Don't make me laugh." The detective was full of bluster but frustrated as the cool air blew her long hair into her face. She wiped it away swiftly, then put her hands on her slim hips, "Okay, hotshot, who brought you here then?"

"Officer Mendez, I would like to introduce you to my good friend, Christine," and I gestured to Christine who had sat up at the approach of the policewoman and was now rubbing her eyes. "Christine happens to be a previous patient of Dr. Johansen's."

"He is going to be alright, isn't he?" Christine asked, tentatively shaking the Detective's outstretched hand.

"He'll be fine," she said, returning the offered hand swiftly to her side, "He was only knocked out by the blast. He should be back to slicing before the weeks out. Provided," as she said this, she turned towards the mauling gap in the tower behind her, a slight grin apparent, "he can get that fixed first."

Ignoring her dark sense of humor, I inquired about the young orderly, James, "Oh, it looks like he'll be okay too, he'll be in the hospital a few days with that leg of his, and will have to have a slicer tidy it up a bit, but he should be back on his feet in no time."

"That's great, he looked to me to be a good kid," I stated to no one in particular.

"So, Mr. Scott, as I mentioned it is very interesting to find you here," she continued, "Is there anything at all you can tell me about this particular incident that might shed a bit of light on the situation."

"As I already told the fire chief, who stopped by earlier, I had just finished my tour and sat talking with the doctor in his office. He was called into his next operation and I was on my way out, when, boom, the building erupted and I was knocked over. When I got up, I headed directly towards the nearest exit, but it was blocked. I ran down the hall to find an alternate one, but on my way could not help but notice young Sondra's predicament..."

The detective cut me off abruptly, "How did you know the victim's name was Sondra?" she asked, accusingly.

"Well, Ms. Mendez, two reasons. The first is that the doctor told me her name and second, the young girl happened to introduce herself directly to me after I rescued her," visibly, I was now upset at this woman, "so I would appreciate it if you would lose your accusatory tone and stop treating me as a criminal."

"By all means, Mr. Scott, forgive me." As she apologized, her tone adjusted, now more even and reserved, "I am only trying to get to the bottom of these attacks. You see our preliminary investigations have shown that the type and strength of explosive used here, appears to be similar to that which was used the other day at the studio." With her next words, she then confirmed my own assessment, "So it looks like we have a crazy on the loose who likes to blow up studios and slicers."

She continued, "Frankly, we are a bit worried at this latest development. Several years ago, we had a similar situation with various bomb attacks when the studios made their first move to eliminate actors with the computer-generated ones. We had all kinds of incidents back then, and many fatalities. Trouble was, we never did find the culprit or culprits. It appears we have the same thing brewing all over again, and under very comparable circumstances, with the latest announcement regarding voice actors." she hesitated before finishing, "And you, sir, just happened to be in both places when each explosion occurred." another pause, "Also, I decided to take a closer look at the surveillance video from the recent theater riots. And low an behold, I noticed that you were also there as well. You must understand how this looks."

"What I understand is that you should be out looking for your crazy, as you put it, not harassing a Good Samaritan who just happened to have been in the wrong place at the wrong time…. twice. Then added, "and with regards to the riot, that was just another coincidence. I had no plans on being there at all. It just…. happened."

Silence reigned for a moment and while thinking, I suddenly realized the officer's very valid concerns. "I assure you I had nothing to do with either of these attacks. But, while being an unwilling participant, I did my best to help the victims where I could. One shouldn't be penalized for that, surely?"

"No, you're absolutely right. And we appreciate your help. I know the young lady sure does." Mendez looked at Christine, "And you miss, what do you do?"

"I work at Denny's on the boulevard," Christine responded evenly, "I've been showing Ryan around." adding unnecessarily, "It was really my idea to go to the rally. He decided to tag along as he was new in town."

"New in town, eh?" she started again.

"Don't get any ideas officer, just because I'm new to town doesn't mean I'm a mad bomber," again my voice rose in response to her inquiries. "You knew it was my first day on the job at the studio the other day. I already told you that the last time we met."

"Indeed, you did, Mr. Scott, just not the new to town part." and she made a small notation in her notebook, before continuing. "Well if I can ask, since we are all friends here, did you see anything out of the ordinary or strange occur before the explosion?"

"The whole subject of slicing is strange to me," I quipped, "but no, nothing that stands out."

"How about any people, seemingly out of place, or odd behaviours?"

"You mean besides the line-up of crazy kids who want to look like movie stars?"

The detective gave me a look.

"No…" then I hesitated, "No, wait a minute, I mean Yes, Yes I did see one guy," and I turned to Christine, "You remember, that tall, good-looking chap with the cleft chin, who bumped into me when we got out of the car." Christine nodded in agreement.

"So, what about this 'chap'?" Mendez asked, emphasising the word chap.

155

"Well, just after we arrived this morning, when we got out of the Robi-car at the curb in front of the slicer building, just over there," and I pointed to the pile of rubble and steel lying in the road, "This guy comes flying down the stairs, clearly in a rush, not looking where he was going, and bumps right into me. Then he ran straight into the car we had just vacated and shot off. I remember it clearly as he was not even seated before he instructed the thing to go. He must have been in a real big hurry!"

"Can you describe him?"

"I can do you one better," I looked at Christine, "When he bumped me, we looked at each other and I thought I recognized him. Apparently, he was the key speaker at that riot... I mean rally you mentioned, a few days ago outside Grauman's.... I mean the Chinese theater." Now I was really flustered, "Oh, just tell her, Christine, you knew his name."

"Ah yes," Christine offered, "it did look a lot like him. His name is Gordon Flichette. He used to be...."

"An actor, yes," Mendez cut her off, "I remember. Quite some time ago, in fact. Also, quite famous as I recall, just before the change." again, she wrote on her notepad. "Anything else?"

"No, not that I can think of, Christine?"

"Ah, so you were there too?" Mendez inquired.

"No, not during the blast. I was downstairs getting a café. I had left Ryan upstairs for his tour." Christine appeared slightly reserved as she replied, but she was tired, as were we all, "I had been there so many times before, but I knew Ryan was looking forward to the tour so, not wanting to spoil it for him, I left him with the doctor. I was rushed outside with the rest when the building was evacuated. We only met back up here, in the triage center, after." her voice trembled, "I was so worried, I did not know what to think?" and she hugged me once more.

"Fine, Fine, well thanks for the enlightening information. I'll leave the two of you for now. If I need you, I assume you're staying in town?"

"Yes, we're staying at my place, The Waterford Towers." Christine offered. Officer Mendez's eyebrow raised at the mention of Christine's residence. For what reason I couldn't possibly fathom.

Before heading away, she took one last look at me, "You still have my card, right?"

"Sure do, Ms. Mendez," and I pulled the bar-coded, sliver of glass from my dirty pocket to prove it.

"Fine, feel free to use it, and by the way, my name's Anne."

Then she was gone, leaving Christine and I to convalesce in relative peace.

Later that day, with the excitement having finally died down and the rescue crews almost done packing up, we were released on our own. The two of us supporting each other as we made our way across the plaza to find a vehicle, just wanting to get home. It did not take us long and we were soon safely encapsulated in a comfortable Robi-car and on the road back to Christine's apartment. The day had changed as we waited, the sky filling with fluffy white clouds, blocking the rays of the sun for the first time since I had arrived in this bizarre future of 2065. The lessening of the harsh daylight was welcome, almost soothing and put me in a better mood as we arrived at the apartment's door.

As we wandered up the entry path, I took a better look around, noticing the pristine landscaping, the elegant fountains (alcohol ones, presumably) and the elaborate treatments and materials used in the construction of the building. Come to think of it, quite a fancy place for a Denny's waitress. Perhaps this was what had promoted Anne's rather strange expression when Christine had revealed her address. But we had both been through a lot today and as we passed by the front doors, waiting patiently for the elevator to get us up to Christine's floor, I decided not to press the issue that evening. That could wait for later, a discussion for some other time.

Once we were in, the two of us retreated into the living room and sat on the couch. Instead, I asked Christine, "Hey, this sliver of glass Officer Mendez gave me. How does it work?" and I pulled out the barcoded chip.

"Oh, that's a call chip," she stated, matter of fact. "You just insert it into any com panel, and you are connected with the person listed on the chip."

"Com panel?"

"Yes, just like the one over here." and she got up to point to a small box on the wall. It was a tiny silver device with a light-up panel, and a slot upfront, so small it had not even registered to me before. "I don't have any use for it much without any call chips of my own, but these are standard issue in any apartment these days. Hey, I can go rustle us up some café, are you thirsty?"

I was a bit, "Sure thanks. If you don't mind though, I'll just sit here."

"Sure, make yourself comfortable, I'll be back in a few minutes."

Being very tired, I chose to lie down and rest my aching head and muscles. Thinking I would close my eyes, just for a minute. I could smell the café brewing in the kitchen and Christine humming some kind of unfamiliar tune. But then, come to think of it, everything in this time was unfamiliar. Within a few moments the adrenaline that had previously coursed so rapidly through my body had completely worn off and fatigue began to take its toll. Finally, fighting a losing battle, and my body worn out, I fell into deep, restful sleep. I never did get my café.

The following day was a whirlwind of errands and other activities Christine had planned, that ended up totally wearing me out. The clothes shopping was easy as I had done it before, all I needed to do was replace my outfit, that had become damaged during the rescue, with a similar style and cut. In between the stores and a nice walk in the local park, we lunched at a small café where I was able to sample more of the interesting food from this future. The menu system was now old hat and so our experience did not result in much embarrassment for my companion. It certainly helped that our waiter was unenhanced, possessing just two arms and legs just like ourselves. But we were on the go so much, by mid-afternoon I was tired and asked to return to her place for a rest. We were also so busy, I never got a chance to ask Christine about her fancy apartment, so was determined to do so that evening.

After a short rest and relatively peaceful afternoon at home, later that day, Christine and I sat around the kitchen table. A fine dinner, courtesy of the automated cooking system, socked away in our bellies, a fine wine in our glasses and a fine mood resounding through the dimly lit room. There were several candles burning, giving off a warm flickering of orange light, and the slight fragrance of the recently consumed, very tasty meal, remained in the air. The two of us sat opposite one another, ready to chat about anything and everything. Now was my chance.

Slowly, I sipped at my glass, the fine aroma touching my nose, the light taste of fermented grapes basking on my tongue, while the subdued lighting created wispy shadows on Christine's beautiful face. It was a great moment, a relaxing moment, after the terrifying events of the past few days.

I decided to begin our conversation with a question on something else that had been bothering me, "So, tell me, if I'm not prying. I very interested to know why on earth such a beautiful woman, as yourself, would ever even think of going to Dr. Johansen's in the first place. It doesn't seem to fit you, being so self-confident and all."

This appeared to jolt her a little, making her slightly uncomfortable, "Ah…"

Realizing my mistake, I quickly cut in, before she continued, "Sorry, I didn't mean to be to so personal. Or to pry. That was stupid of me. Look, don't worry about it. Forget I asked. Let's talk about something else."

"No, no, it's okay. It's just that... it's a little hard for me to say..." and she trailed off.

"Take your time." I encouraged, "We have all the time in the world."

Christine took a gulp of wine and then slowly continued telling her story, "Well...there was..." she hesitated again. Clearly bringing up her past was not a pleasant experience, "Well, you see I had...an accident when I first started at work and it was...quite bad. It required some reconstructive surgery."

"Was this an accident at the restaurant?" I asked, probing.

She hesitated, thinking back, remembering, "Yes... yes, I was burned. Badly burned on my arms neck...and my face. So, I had to see a slicer to get things properly repaired. The only unfortunate thing was, as I had never been to a slicer before, they did not have a record or scan of my facial structure, and so Dr. Johansen could only recreate my visage from photographs. It was a long, pain staking process." she took another long sip of her wine, her hand shaking.

"I'm sorry." was all I came up with, "It must have been hard for you?"

"Yeah, it was. But I got over it. And now that it's all over, I am back to normal and working again. And all is right in the world." she still sounded distant, melancholy, not her usual self.

It was time to get away from this awkward discussion. It was obviously upsetting her, and I did not want to spoil the evening. Changing the subject, I ventured, "Hey, strange about that tall guy wasn't it?"

"Sure was." Christine answered, still a bit distant.

"What was his name again?"

"You mean, Gordon Flichette?" she had brightened suddenly.

"Yeah that's him." glad the new direction of conversation was improving things, "You knew him, didn't you?"

"Only by name. He was a big-name actor several years ago. Before the change."

"There's that phrase again 'before the change'. Officer Mendez used the same phrase, earlier. What exactly does that mean?"

"Oh, it's just the term everyone uses for the time before the actors were put out of work. When every studio switched over to all digital characters, almost overnight. For us here in Hollywood, it was a big change, hence the term."

Tentatively contemplating this, I was silent for a moment, considering the drastic change the people associated with the movie and television business would have gone through.

Then, I decided to return to the tall man, "Do you really think Officer Mendez will chase that guy, what's his name Flichette, down? Talk with him?"

"I really don't know?" Christine mused, "All I know is that the police got quite upset the last time the bombings occurred, just after the change, and so I guess they are more prone to action this time. So, yes, probably she'll track him down."

"It's interesting because I recall also seeing him a few days ago at the studio. The day of the bombing. Do you think he still works at the studio?"

Unexpectedly and without apparent provocation, Christine suddenly got all flustered at what she must have viewed as continuous questioning, "How am I supposed to know, I don't work there!"

"Well," sheepishly responding, "I just thought, since you said you had friends there, you might know?" not anticipating her outburst at all, trying my best to deflect away her rising agitation.

This reply seemed to calm her down a bit, "Well, yeah, you're right, I do," then she apologized, "Sorry, I snapped. It's been a long few days." thankfully resulting in a softer look.

We both sat in silence for a few moments, and I took the time to finish the last of my wine. Then, even though I really wanted to ask her about the apartment, I chose not to risk any further upset and instead, decided to call it a night. "You're right it has been a long day. And I am still rather sore. On top of that your wonderful wine is putting me to sleep. If you don't mind, I think I'll call it a night."

Just then the com panel on the wall blipped and Christine got up, sauntering over to unit muttering, "Who on earth would be calling me by com?"

"Hello," she stated tentatively, her voice back to normal, "this is Christine."

"Christine, good evening. This is Officer Mendez, is Ryan Scott available?" The policewoman's voice was perfectly replicated, with absolutely no distortion. It was an extremely realistic, almost stereo effect, like she was standing there next to us in the room.

"Just a moment," then calling over to me, "Ryan, it's Officer Mendez. She apparently wants a word." then more to herself, as she walked back to the kitchen "That explains why she's calling by com."

Walking slower than before, the pain in my joints still on the mend, I wandered over to the panel on the wall.

"Yes, Detective. What can I do for you?"

"We chased down that lead you gave us. Apparently, this Mr. Gordon Flichette has disappeared. He's not at his home, or any of his normal hangouts. We'll keep a watch out for him, but please, do me a favour. If you see him again, can you let me know?"

"Will do, Officer... sorry, I mean, Anne."

"Goodnight then, Ryan"

"Goodnight," I said, and the panel went dead. All was quiet again, but just for a moment.

I had just turned away, when suddenly, the panel burst back to life, bleeping loudly once again. I had not seen Christine do anything in particular, so I just spun around and said "Hello?"

"Ryan, this is Angelo." with no preamble, "Director Evans wants to start filming again tomorrow. We've managed to set up an alternative motion capture studio temporarily on another part of the lot. Security will tell you where to go. Tomorrow morning, 8 am sharp. Please don't be late."

I opened my mouth to offer a reply, but again the panel's illumination disappeared. Angelo was gone.

"Well, that's a surprise." I stated loudly, towards the kitchen.

"What?" Christine asked.

"Looks like they want to start filming again already. They haven't even buried Monica yet!"

"Well, Ryan that's the movie business." stated Christine rather harshly, "It's all about the money with those guys. I suggest, however, if you want to keep your job, you get some sleep and head down there early. As a matter of fact, I'll come with you as I have an early shift at the restaurant too. Looks like this has been our day to rest. Come on, I'll tuck you in."

And a short while later, I was once again safely reclined on my comfortable couch bed, my heavy eyelids closing, for what was certain to be another somewhat agitated slumber.

Chapter Fourteen – Unlucky Day

The next day, was like any other in Southern California, the sun rising reverently over the coastal mountains, revealing a bright pink and orange glow, bathing the new day in a glorious symphony of light. The grey and decrepit Hollywood sign, just visible high up on Mt. Lee, still looking like a torn blister over the rest of the warm light brown surface of over baked grasses on the hillside.

After a rushed shower (I still did not know what had replaced the water) and breakfast, Christine and I left the apartment early, easily finding a Robi ride close by, making our way directly to the studio gate. Being still tired, all of my muscles remaining stiff from my previous ordeal, made getting in and out of the car a bit of a chore. But soon after, with a good stretch and deep breath of the fresh morning air, I felt rejuvenated, reinvigorated and ready for the day.

Christine said goodbye from the driver's seat and so, after rounding the far side, I gave her a light kiss on her cheek through the open window. She smelled faintly of roses and talc; her excessive work make-up not yet applied. It was a nice look. Seeming to appreciate my affectionate gesture, she first smiled and then reached a hand up to caress the area. But it was all very fleeting, for soon she had closed the window and was off again, taking the same road she had done before, the light scent of ozone following in the Robi-car's wake.

On my way to the guard house, to both show my credentials and obtain a map showing the temporary motion capture studio's new location, in behind me walked Angelo, very chipper and perky for such an early time in the morning.

"Hello, Ryan, so nice to see you here. And on time! Hey, Frank!" he shouted, as he turned to the guard, "I'll show this guy the way, don't worry."

"Sounds good," growled Frank uncaringly from the booth, his back still facing the newcomers, attention not once waning from his projection screen. Today it was some kind of underwater sporting event, involving both divers and swimmers, engaged in a collage of complex activities, one would clearly have to understand the rules, just to decipher. Frank, bless him, obviously knew what was going on, for he seemed to be thoroughly enjoying the spectacle.

"Hey, Angelo," patting my new colleague on the back as he scanned in, "Glad to see you've had your coffee... I mean your café, today." foolishly, laughing at my own joke. "It is good to see you though, how are you holding up?"

He just nodded, "I'm fine, still a little shaken, and I miss Marcia, dearly."

Prompted by his words, I decided to inquire on a slightly more serious matter, "Have they made any arrangements for her service yet?"

"Nope, we're still working on the funeral arrangements. In fact, yours truly is doing all the arranging." and he placed both sets of extended fingers against his chest, "But I should have it all wrapped up bit later in the week." he smiled, weakly, "I'm to let everyone know when it's all set."

"Okay, thanks. Just don't forget. Even though I only knew her a short time, she was still a good friend to me."

"She was good friend to us all," after which Angelo's went quiet for a minute.

The walk across the lot was a fair distance further than my previous hike, as we had to work our way much further into the expansive backlot to locate the new studio. As we passed the commissary, I could not help but glance over in the hope I might see the tall man there, but all I saw at the rear of the complex were the morning shadows blooming around the refuse containers.

After his slight pause, Angelo remained extremely talkative as we walked, filling me in on all that was to occur during the upcoming shooting day. When finished with his hourly play by play, he began, rather enthusiastically, gesturing here and there to various points of the backlot revealing historical, mysterious, sometimes even intimate information regarding the assorted places, almost like a tour guide. I teased him about this.

"Hey Angelo, it looks like you missed your calling. You would make a wonderful tour guide!"

"Oh, don't be foolish, Ryan," he quipped, swiping his hand through the air as if swatting a fly, "That's a job for computer sims, not actual people."

Touché. After that, I decided to save my jokes for another time.

We came upon our new, but temporary facility soon after, Angelo leading me straight in and over to the change room.

"You know the drill, get into the suit and then meet me in the hall." Angelo directed, staring at his display pad as he left me to my devices.

As the dressing affair was now old hat, I quickly selected one of the motion capture garments from the available rack and slipped into its slick material. The strange material gliding perfectly onto my body, almost as if lubricated. This was helpful as I did not have to bend and twist as much as I had when putting on my regular outfit earlier that morning. Once dressed, I stored my street clothes in the nearby locker and headed back out to meet Angelo.

Certainly, the word temporary fit the new film soundstage well. Or perhaps a better description was; fresh. As the containment walls encircling the room had evidently just been erected and being constructed of fresh lumber, they still emitted a faint scent of pine. Their surfaces where plain plywood, that had been hastily covered with green screen and the floor was freshly painted, feeling a tad sticky with each foot fall. The camera crew, however, was raring to go and even though director Evans was deeply engaged in talking with one of the camera ladies as I entered, he turned away immediately upon my entrance.

"Great, you're here!" Evans stated, impatiently, pulling himself away, "let's get started."

And so, it began, another day of motion capture bliss. As we worked through each scene, I got a bizarre sense of déjà vu as I was certain that the blocking and movements the director had me perform were identical to those completed on the first day we worked, with one exception; I was doing everything from a different perspective. This time when I should have been right, I was left, where previously I had sat on the west end of the table, I now sat east and so on. This was a mystery to me, but I was certain to eventually find out what it all meant. Barring that, if no explanation was forthcoming, I could always ask Angelo.

With thanks, I was permitted a small break at lunch, this time remembering to remove the suit and change, prior to vacating the soundstage. As before, the walk back to the commissary was a pleasant one and I felt myself remembering the most interesting time I had had so far. But as I sat eating my meal, my mind drifted to the two very nasty instances that had occurred in my travels to this future Hollywood and I began contemplating what it all meant. Officer Mendezs' ongoing concerns, the mysterious whereabouts of the tall man that I had seen just before each explosion and Christine with some of her recent reactions and behaviors. Finally, what our current relationship might be turning into. It was an extremely, thought-provoking lunch hour.

I must have dozed off because I was roughly awakened by Angelo who, in my absence had obviously been sent to track me down.

"Ryan what are you doing?" he asked, exasperated, "I've been looking all over for you. We thought something had happened! And yet here you are. And to find you sleeping no less! Get moving! We need you at the pool tank!"

As before, the time in the tank was similar to my previous exploits, only, like the morning had been, opposite in every motion in relation to each side of the pool. The cool liquid, which I knew was not actually water, was nonetheless very refreshing, particularly after running to get here through the afternoon heat, beaming down on the backlot paths. The motion capture suit felt and acted like a neoprene scuba suit, allowing the *water* to enter, creating a thin wedge of fluid between my body and the garment, that eventually warmed up to near body temperature, creating an insulating blanket between my skin and the cold liquid of the tank.

The afternoon flew by, and soon I was out of the tank and drying off. Angelo let me know that I was welcome to put on my own clothes and did so, thanking him for all of his help.

"Thanks Angelo. You've been a great help, these last few days" as I toweled the last of the *water* out of my hair, "What's next? Are we heading back to the soundstage for more shooting?"

"Nah, Director Evans has what he wants for the different parts of the whole shot and so it's time to look at the dailies."

"The dailies," I asked, mildly interested.

"Yes, dummy. That's where we take the film we've shot during the day and head over to the screening room to view the final images. They'll use your shots from before, together with the ones we made today, combine them together, then add in the computer characters, creating the completed shot. Then Director Evans can see if we need to make any adjustments for tomorrow."

"Is there any way I can come see these… dailies?"

"Well," the assistant hesitated, "normally, the director likes to complete these himself. But since you're genuinely interested, and I like you, I'll go ask him." then he flew out of the room as if burned.

With what Angelo had said I began to piece together the puzzle, figuring out my role. He mentioned the shots made earlier and those made today were to be merged. So, the only thing I could think of was that I had stood in for two characters in the same scene. One day I had been the first character, the next day I had been the other. Quite interesting.

If I did get a chance to look at these dailies, I would be able to prove my hypothesis. Satisfied, I completed getting dressed, and was combing out my hair when Angelo returned, slightly out of breath.

"He said yes! Can you believe it? He actually said yes!" Angelo was beaming, very proud of himself, "I think he likes you too. But of course, I did put in a good word for you. When you're ready, I'll take you right on up! Director Evans is already on his way!"

We headed out of the *water* tank building together and into the late afternoon air. It had cooled slightly and there was a soft Pacific breeze making its way across the studio lot, bringing in a calm sea wind that smelled slightly of saltwater. The screening room was a smaller, two-story affair, nearer to the front lot and so our required stroll took several minutes. Angelo, like an automaton, fell into his guide mode as we made our way towards the viewing area, forever spouting some distant historic fact, or scrumptious detail about an actor and his hateful wife, or a rendezvous between star crossed lovers, married to other people. These very enjoyable stories, thankfully, kept me occupied, preventing me from dwindling back to thoughts about other, much darker memories.

The front entrance of the building was hidden in an alcove at the front of the structure, the sign above it stating simply, Screening Room One, in gold lettering. As we walked through the very solid entry doors, in my peripheral vision, I caught a glimpse of a tall individual moving off to one side, nearer the lane between our building and the accompanying sound stage. At first, he reminded me of the tall man, but it was such a momentary glimpse and the individual was wearing worker's overalls and not a suit, so I didn't think any more of it. We continued into the darkened interior and made our way up two, short flights of stairs.

The reason we had to enter from the upper floor was that the screening room was essentially a small theater, with a sloping seating area and a rear projection booth. At the lower level, beyond the limited rows of seats, was a small, flat stage and behind it a screen, not a full movie size screen, but still significantly bigger than any home theater screen I had ever seen. Above the display was a series of suspended, blackened steel, lighting ladders, holding up large studio lights oriented in numerous directions to illuminate the screen and area around it.

At the top of the stairs was a set of washrooms, the entrance to the projection room and a luxurious seating area, presumably in which to sit and discuss the dailies after viewing. The couches were of very plush material, equipped with large fluffy pillows and between each was a side table with drink holders. Beside these lavish recliners was a small bar, well stocked and ready for use. Most assuredly for those important post review conversations, where the director wished to elicit actual responses from the attendees and not restrained reviews held in check by unlubricated consciousness.

Angelo and I wandered in the darkened theater to see that Director Evans was already comfortably seated several aisles down, in the middle of the row, putting, himself immediately front and center of the screen. Until Angelo gestured, I was headed in that direction, but instead, at Angelo's insistence, we sat down several rows behind the director and slightly off to one side.

"Director Evans doesn't want anybody sitting next to him during the dailies viewing." Angelo whispered to me. "That's why we have to sit here. So, we do not disturb his musings."

"Sounds good to me," I replied, "I can see perfectly from here anyway."

And it was true. It was almost as if the room had been configured in such a way, that any of the chosen seats was a prime viewing position for the massive center screen.

"What's taking that moron so long to reel it up," we heard the director mumble from his seat. Almost as if on cue, the lights dimmed even further, and an image splashed onto the screen.

It was Danny Dunn! The fellow I had seen the other day at the slicers, sitting in the recovery room anxious to leave. Except of course it wasn't, not the same person anyway, but a computer-generated character there for all to see. He was moving across a room, in a very much similar way to that as I had done, moving across the soundstage. I was amazed at the combined efforts displayed above and how they perfectly duplicated reality. Shortly thereafter, another character joined him, this time it could only have been Suzie Shine. Remembering her image from all my previous encounters, but most recently from the projection made on Sondra's face I had viewed emitting from the dTBM machine in Dr. Johansen's preparation room. This striking female character was moving from the opposite side of the room towards Danny, duplicating the movements I had just made that morning.

It was amazing! And the two human characters were just so incredibly lifelike! I sat there flabbergasted and utterly engrossed in the action, knowing I had been a part of this marvel of modern film making.

This continued for several minutes, all of my movements displayed, the two characters duplicating them in exact detail, the images of the two computer actors effortlessly moving as if real, showing that real life and computer-generated fantasy could be blended into one seamless reproduction of the real world. Then all at once the screen went blank.

"Okay. That was great." Evans shouted from his seat, his head rotating on his skinny neck, "Spool up the pool footage."

"Two minutes, sir!" came a soft female voice through the speakers.

"Humph!" Was all we heard from the director as we saw him slide back a little in his seat.

Angelo and I sat still, not wanting to disturb the director, anxiously awaiting the next reel of footage. I was eager to see how the images filmed in the *water* tank turned out, prompting a very strange, almost surreal thought. If they used my movements for a female character, would I look good in a bikini?

Five minutes went by and nothing happened, the director began to shift impatiently in his seat. When the delay reached 10 minutes, he suddenly jumped up and maneuvering out of his row, tromped up the stairs towards the projection booth. The rear door briefly opened, bathing us in a bright blinding light, before we were again trapped in darkness, the automatic closure on the door doing its duty.

"What's going on?" I tentatively asked Angelo.

"I don't know, but the chief is going to be pissed!" Angelo had never sworn before, so this must be something new.

"Hey, do you mind, if I took a quick walk to stretch my legs? Since it appears we have a bit of time, I would like to take a better look at the screen."

I inquired this of Angelo as a courtesy, because even though I was interested to have a look at the front of the room, he had been the one to invite me in and I didn't want to step on anybody's toes.

"Shouldn't be a problem." he replied, "But if the lights dim, get yourself back up here and into your seat pronto. The chief doesn't like anyone in front of him when he looks at the dailies!"

"I promise! I won't be long," quickly popping up and heading down the stairs towards the front of the theater.

I didn't get very far. For, upon reaching the last step just prior to the stage, the lights dimmed once again, prompting me to turn frantically around as an image appeared on the screen. But there was no soundtrack, as at that very moment, the building rocked with a great explosion, the entire upper section of seats disappearing in a blinding flash of brilliant fire and smoke.

I was knocked down flat on the floor, my feet still on the last step the rest of me sprawled on the stage. There was a secondary explosion, and with it the first lighting ladder trapeze hanging from the ceiling, the one closest to the seating area, broke loose and plummeted to the ground. With extreme speed, it smashed heavily against the first row of seats, one of the recently extinguished lights nearly decapitating me in the process. Not fully escaping its wrath, I felt multiple shards of shattered glass hit my face, cutting me in several places but also burning me in others, as the material was hot, superheated by the high wattage bulbs contained within.

The developing smoke was thick in my eyes and I began to choke, poisonous fumes filling and burning my lungs. Making to immediately escape the swelling inferno, I attempted to lift myself up for a quick sprint to the nearest exit. However, while I could move my body, my legs had been pinned by the collapsed lighting support. Twisting in place to discern the extent of my peril, I noticed that, gratefully, my legs, feet and ankles while trapped solid, appeared unhurt and were still able to move under the twisted structure. For the life of me though, regardless how hard I struggled, I could not withdrawal them from under the heavy aluminum rack that had befallen them.

In desperation, I looked up, noticing that the cable support at one end of the second spotlight ladder had also been damaged. It had slowly begun to unravel, the individual wires whirling around, getting thinner and thinner, as the combined weight of the lamps and ladder support pulled at the torn restraint. Yelling to expend my frustration, yet not having anywhere to go and with another threat just waiting to happen.

Futilely, I struggled once more against the broken aluminum and wiring trapping my feet, pulling furiously, tearing my skin and drawing blood now screaming out in pain. But the battles were all for naught, my wasted exertions doing nothing to loosen the horrific grip imposed, only serving to intensify my existing injuries.

Gazing up once again I realized with some hope that the far end of the ladder support was still intact, so theorized there might still be a possible chance of reprieve. Straining against my bonds, I moved my body at an angle, moving as close to the edge of the stage as possible, bringing my hands up to cover my face.

Just in time, the near end cable support parted, and the ladder plummeted down. It fell like a huge gigantic axe being swung by some evil, demented titan. It swung directly down, right at me. Then at the last second, while completing its arc, it just missed my head. The wind caused by its travel briefly whipped at my hair before ultimately smashing apart as it crashed into the stage floor surface barely 2 meters from my face. I was saved any further pain from more white-hot flying glass shards, as only two of the lights ended up colliding with the ground on the supports far side, thankfully sparing me from their fragmented wrath.

Safe from one more close call, my body shivered with energy and pent up anguish. Even with my adrenaline flowing profusely through my body, I could still feel myself passing out from the fumes. Foolishly and without thinking, I attempted to hold my breath, only to cause spots to arise in front of my eyes as I neared suffocation.

Virtually at the stage of passing out, I detected vague movement, after which a large figure came into view. He was out of focus but had entered from the lower entrance door and was wearing a studio worker's maintenance coverall. A large cloth had been wrapped around his face to fight the smoke, but I could see he was a tall, dark-haired man. Without hesitation, he ran to my aide, grabbing a large steel pole from the side of the stage. That combined with the lower stair, he was able to erect a fulcrum, getting the strong metal end under the edge of the first fallen lighting rack trapping my legs. With a massive grunt, his muscles straining and the veins on his large neck bulging, he managed to lever it up, just enough so that I could pull myself free. He waited until my feet were clear before grunting again, dropping the heavy support back to the floor, the metal twisted and bent.

As he helped me up, I was able to briefly glimpse the image still miraculously projected on the towering screen despite the expanding holocaust. The bright image that knifed its way through the intensifying black smoke, rising like a ghostly portrait, was of a beautiful mermaid swimming towards the camera. Her face was plain, but extremely pretty and sparkled in the shimmering water lit from above. She had big eyes and generous lips, a well-formed upper figure, tapering out into the luxurious mermaid's tail. I had never before seen a mermaid of mixed ethnicity, but this one clearly was, nonetheless appearing very exotic, sensual. Her long curly black hair floated in the water gently framing her face just as the image melted away, disappearing as the projection screen burst into a crimson sheet of red flame.

"Come on, we must get out of here, there's no time!" my rescuer yelled at me, as he pulled at my slow-moving body. Forcing me to shift and supporting me aloft by my shoulder so that together, we stumbled as quickly as possible towards the lower exit doors, fiery remnants falling all around us. Behind us, the last roof support gave way, releasing the third and final lighting rack. It plunged from the rapidly disintegrating ceiling, each individual spotlight smashing itself into an infinite number of sharp fragments in our wake. With a last surge, we were out of the opening and into the gently developing twilight and most welcome, fresh evening air.

The sounds of sirens filled the sky as the two of us headed away from the burning building. Crossing a service road illuminated in the flickering orange flames, we dropped heavily onto a bench, near the outside wall of a soundstage across the street. Coughing violently, my lungs attempting valiantly to clear themselves, I looked back, hacking incessantly. My eyes could still not properly focus, but the screening room was now fully aflame, most of the roof having collapsed, fire flowing out of the sides of the building, its walls beginning to give way. The concrete skeleton of the structures upper section, housing the projection booth and reception area was now visible, the combustible contents completely consumed in the inferno, nothing remaining except blackened concrete. Of the viewing area itself, there was nothing left, the end housing the screen having collapsed into the seating space, everything else consumed in the hellishly unrelenting, fiery blaze.

"Goodbye, Angelo," I said remorsefully, and I bowed my head in prayer. A tear rose from my right eye, dribbling down my cheek, wiping a clear, flesh toned track in the black soot and grime engrained there, before at last dropping off my bleeding chin, as I finally passed out.

Chapter Fifteen – Second Aftermath – Astounding Revelation

What could only have been moments later, I awoke, sitting there with my unknown rescuer, more than just stunned, but completely shocked and dismayed. It had happened again, not twice, but three times. Violent explosions, like a jilted lover, kept chasing me wherever I appeared in this outlandish future with no explanation, and no understanding of why. How on earth had I managed to get myself into so much trouble and yet still be alive.

Twofold, I had been the rescuer, but this time, if not for the man beside me, I would have been the latest victim, burning alongside my poor friend Angelo. I looked away from the remains of the inferno and over towards the man who had saved my life.

He sat there beside me, still out of breath, the soiled white cloth around his face not yet removed. His hands were burnt in several places and the coverall he was wearing showed holes in the material where the fire had found refuge, blazing its way right through to the skin. He groaned and looked up, pulling the wad of stained fabric away from his face, leaving a dark line of soot above his nose, at once revealing a very large cleft in his prominent chin. He turned to me, anxious to see if I was alright, care and concern expressed in his large, dark eyes, the face of someone I knew, or at least recognized. The face of the tall, well-dressed man; Gordon Flichette!

The so-called crazed bomber had rescued me. But how was that possible? Would an insane fellow, who indiscriminately planted and set off bombs in anger, really risk everything to save a complete stranger? And then I remembered what had been said of me the other day, and my reply hoping that others might someday do the same for me. Detective Mendez didn't believe it, but here was another man willing to risk his life to save another. This was no bomber. This man was a hero!

"Thank you. I really appreciate what you did." I coughed once again, "You saved my life. I owe you one."

"All in the line of duty, my friend." his voice was as deep and penetrating as it had been the day of the rally. "It's not every day you get to rescue someone from a burning building is it?" and he laughed at his own joke, intending to break the mood, ultimately make us both feel better. All it did was encourage another fit of coughing from us both.

"I was close by when I heard the explosion," Gordon began his story, "avoiding some shrapnel, I ducked down, meaning to move away, and call for help. It was only then that I spotted your predicament through a newly created hole in the wall of the building. Wrapping one of my work cloths around my face, I came in to get you, and of course you know the rest. The only thing is, what on earth was it that made you hesitate on our way out? You had started moving and we were almost at the exit, then for some reason you just froze. You realize we were almost hit by that last lighting array as we left. We were very lucky. I do hope she was worth it." and he smiled.

He must have been referring to my glance at the beautiful mermaid on the screen as we left. I laughed a little, the action prompting a fresh fit of coughing and hacking. Again, I marveled at how stupid it had been to have stopped, but there was something about the image of the pretty mermaid that stuck in my mind, something I just couldn't put my finger on. So, together, we sat on the bench against the wall, getting back our collective breath, waiting patiently for the rescue crews to arrive.

Several minutes later we were still both sitting, but this time in the back of a portable medical unit, sucking on oxygen, getting our lungs in order, and our various burns, cuts and bruises seen to. The stem cell salve had been applied to my new burns and my largest cut had been safely sutured shut with dissolvable stitch work and a prepared dressing placed on top. My lacerated ankles had also been smothered in the miraculous healing lotion and wrapped in gauze. Gordon's burns had also been similarly treated and the two of us remained in place, waiting for the inevitable visit of Officer Mendez.

We did not have to wait long, as within moments of our successful treatment, she appeared at the triage area, anxious to see me and my companion.

"So, Mr. Scott, fancy seeing you here?" Her voice full of vinegar. "How is it possible or even conceivable that you could be in the wrong place at the wrong time, three times? And who is this beside you, another victim, you've saved?"

"You have it all wrong once again, Ms. Mendez…Anne. Please let me introduce Mr. Gordon Flichette," and her face burst wide in surprise. "Mr. Flichette was the one who decided to go out of his way to rescue me this time. I was trapped with nowhere to go, and Gordon here risked his own life to help me. This time, it is I who has someone to thank for my life."

She stood still for a moment, her mouth slowly closing, and then without further ceremony, reached back to retrieve the handcuffs off her belt, as she bent down to arrest the man.

"Hold on a there a minute, Detective…" I held up my hand, palm out. "Just before you do anything rash. I know what I had stated before, informing you all about Gordon's strange behavior. But you can ignore all of that as he has a simple explanation for it all." adding quickly, "And no, he is not your bomber, I know that now."

She stood there flabbergasted and stopped mid-motion, correcting her movements at the last minute, changing her mind about withdrawing the handcuffs based upon what I had just said. But it was obvious she needed some reassurance of her own.

"So, Mr. Flichette…?"

He cut her off, "Please call me Gordon."

"So, Gordon," Officer Mendez continued, "You have a lot of explaining to do. You don't mind if I ask you some questions, do you?"

"Absolutely not. Most of it is out now anyway, so no harm at all." he actually smiled at the still shocked detective.

"Okay, let's start with an easy one. Can you enlighten us on the reason for your presence here at the commissary the other day? Apparently, you were hanging about, skulking behind the building."

"Of course, I was just having a break before work" and he pointed to himself. "As you can see, I am now part of the maintenance team for the studio." The detective squinted her eyes. "Yes, I know it's quite a step down from my previous employ within these gates. And so, needless to say I find it somewhat embarrassing to have it widely known. Ever since before the change, there has been very little work and now, with the elimination of voice acting, the only solution was to join the maintenance team just to keep food on the table." he finished with a flourish, still a very proud man, "It's not a glamorous job, but it sure pays the bills."

"Well then, how do you explain your behavior the other day at the slicer's office?" The detective was relentless. Gordon put up with it, patiently, keeping a very positive face.

"That madam officer, is even more embarrassing than my new career." this time he turned red as he spoke, "It just so happens, regardless of my new occupation, I still wish to maintain my persona as a beautiful actor. This requires a visit to

Dr. Johansen's facility now and again. You see this cleft in my chin?" and he pointed to his wonderful identifying feature. "This is a construct of my friend, Dr. Johansen. Every so often my face starts to reject the wonderful artistic work he creates, and begins to revert back to my previous, plain old chin. It is quite annoying!"

Ms. Mendez and I smiled as he continued his long story, "Well this awkward situation requires me to return to him every so often to correct the problem. And just so that I'm not seen, I make certain my appointments are scheduled very early in the day, as I hope to get in and out, without being noticed."

Gordon was on a role, "It is not good for my image as a past great actor for the public to see me sliced as frequently as I am. I had specifically chosen Dr. Johansen's facility because he did not do the popular work," and he gestured, "you know, slicing the young kids into their movie favorites." he took a deep breath, while Mendez nodded in understanding.

"But alas, at my last visit, the one just the other day, I happened to foolishly choose an appointment not only after Dr. Johansen had started his new screen slicing business, but one on a sales day no less. I was appalled and had to get out as soon as I could. It was all quite humiliating." You could see Gordon was beginning to blush again, "Not only did I not get out unseen, I nearly knocked over poor Mr. Scott here. A very unfortunate situation all round." he was now finally out of breath and ready to stop, "When I heard of what happened later, I was absolutely horrified."

Detective Mendez silently considered this for a while, more to give Gordon time for rest than to mull over what he had said. I could tell from her expression that she already believed every word and I was glad. Like me, it looked like Gordon had just been in the wrong place at the wrong time.

Finally, Anne asked her final question, just to complete the puzzle. "Alright, provided that's all true, the fact remains, Mr. Flichette, we've been trying to find you for several days with no success. You were not at home and not at any of your regular hangouts in town. How can you explain your sudden disappearance?"

"Oh, my dear, that's very simple," and he chuckled, smiling broadly, "I was up the coast at my sisters for a few days to relax. Because you see, I do not allow the doctor to use any of the synthy flesh on me, which is part of the reoccurring problem I have with my cleft growing back in. But I am adamant and unmoving in this regard. Usually I go to my sisters to recuperate so as to hide the bandages. She has grown so accustomed to my visits so, even though I did not get sliced that morning, I still went up to visit anyway." he ended his defense, "So feel free to call her and you can verify my whereabouts for the last few days, no problem." and he proceeded to recite his sister's name and contact information that the officer dutifully wrote down into her small notebook.

"Well, that appears to explain your activities, but it does not explain anything for you, Mr. Scott," Ms. Mendez was now looking directly at me, "So, what happened here today?"

"Just another coincidence, Anne," using her first name in the hope of some deeper understanding. When this appeared to have no effect, I continued.

"Angelo and I had accompanied the chief…" smiling at my use of Angelo's term, "sorry, I meant the director. Well, we were in the screening room viewing the dailies when apparently there was a problem with the projector. Mr. Evans got up and went to see what the hold-up was about. After he didn't come back, I got up for a walk, and just after that, the entire back of the building exploded. I was thrown to the floor and one of the overhead lighting supports fell and trapped my legs. The fire was getting closer to me when Mr. Flichette…"

"Gordon, please!"

I smiled at my new friend, "When Gordon, here came to my rescue, using a bar to lift the fallen material and release me. After that we rushed to the exit, just as the rest of the ceiling came down. We stayed for a few moments across the road until the emergency crews showed up and they brought us here. They were just getting finished patching us up when you arrived."

Just then, Christine came pushing through the crowd, crying and blubbering. Running over, the light wind blew tendrils of loose dark hair in her face. "Ryan are you okay?" she was weepy and clearly upset.

I was looking at Detective Mendez and did not actually notice Christine until she was right up close. The falling sun was just behind her, illuminating her gently from behind, the light wind continuing to blow the hair around her face. I looked over to her, knowing she was anxious, wanting to tell her I was alright only wanting to reassure her.

One look in that lighting, however, and my mouth dropped open in recognition, total realization finally dawning on me. Christine was the mermaid! Christine was the image I had seen in the dailies! She was an actress! What on earth was going on?

"Christine?" I croaked, sound barely escaping from my throat.

"Oh, Ryan. Whatever has happened to you now?"

It was interesting that she had shown up so suddenly, and after my revelation, my mind was muddled, so I spoke slowly, "I'm okay. There's been another explosion. But how did you know?"

"I was coming home and heard it on the news, it's over all of the networks! The big explosion at the screening room! So, I came right on over."

At this comment Officer Mendez gave me a strange look but stood aside, waiting until the two of us had said our hellos. Christine dropped down beside me, wrapping her hands around me, holding on tight. Still confused and unsure, I reached up and gently wiped the tears from her eyes, while Christine reached into her purse for a Kleenex.

"Young Lady, if you don't mind, I have a question," the detective started, "can you..."

But she never finished her inquiry, for off in the distance, another explosion rocked the studio, the four of us looking immediately in the direction of the disturbance. Each and every one of us shocked, and totally and utterly speechless.

Chapter Sixteen – The Reveal and the Chase

If you'll excuse me." Officer Mendez stated as she ran towards the blast, "Don't you three go anywhere!"

Then, after motioning to several other officers and emergency workers, the group of them took off quickly on foot in the direction of the explosion. We could see a pillar of thick black smoke rising over several of the buildings and knew just where she was headed.

"Don't worry," I called after her fleeting figure, "were not going anywhere!"

"Are we?" I said gently to Christine, who had jumped up at the sound of the loud discharge.

"Absolutely not." she replied sitting right back down and putting her arms around me once more, "My place is here, I have to take care of you." and she hugged me again putting her head under my chin, "What on earth were you doing in the screening room anyway?"

"Well, the day of shooting was over, and I asked if I could view the dailies."

"I'm just glad you got out of there safe and sound. I was so worried. How did you escape?"

"That's the big news. You'll never guess who helped me out of there. Saved my life really."

"Who?"

I beamed, pointing at the tall man sitting beside us, "It was Gordon Flichette! Gordon here was the one who came to my rescue!"

"Not the man there're chasing as the bomber?" and she looked over at Gordon with a funny look, shifting in her seat, as if only noticing him there for the first time.

"One and the same. But Gordon here's no bomber. You see he's a friend, not this crazed bomber, Officer Mendez and I proved that. He's just an unfortunate man of circumstance, like myself, who just happened to be in the wrong place at the wrong time. Except this time," I added with a flourish, "he was there at the right time. The right time to save me anyway!"

"Oh, Ryan! I'm so pleased!" it was stated sincerely, but her voice held an edge, almost as if something was not quite right. It was even more pronounced when she thanked Gordon.

"Thank you, Mr. Flichette," she stated plainly, "Thank you for saving, Ryan."

"You're welcome, my dear. And it's Gordon, young lady. Of course, it was really the only thing to do," Gordon clearly did not hear the same change in tone I had.

Then I thought to ask the big question, "but I have a question for you."

"Yes, Ryan anything?"

"Well, this may sound a bit bizarre, but when I was watching the dailies, there was a sequence with a computer-generated mermaid. Now, I only saw it briefly, just after the explosion, but the face of the girl reminded me of you."

She sat back suddenly, as if burned, "Oh…, don't be silly, Ryan. You must be mistaken."

"No, no, I'm sure it was you. Mind, I only got a glimpse, but it sure looked exactly like you."

"Nah, you're imagining things, you dope. Why on earth would my face be on a movie screen? I'm just a local girl who works at Denny's." she continued, "Come on, you admitted it yourself, it was at the end, after the explosion. You were probably delusional, suffering smoke inhalation, and you would have seen the image through the smoke. There's no way you can be sure."

I did not reply, immediately thinking her argument was quite valid. Maybe I had imagined it all, in the heat of the moment, wanting so desperately see Christine again. "Yeah, maybe you're right. Yeah, come to think of it, I probably did imagine it."

"That's better. You were scaring me for a minute. Why on earth would my face be on a movie screen?"

I don't know what did it. Maybe it was because she had said the exact same thing twice, maybe it was that she specifically mentioned her face, maybe it was the mention of the smoke, maybe it was the way she denied it so vehemently, or maybe it was just the way she said it. But now, I was absolutely sure it had been Christine's image up there that had swum out of the screen at me. But why would she lie to me. What could it possibly mean?

Then Gordon spoke up, his deep voice reverberating beside us, "Ryan was not mistaken, young lady. It was you, because I saw your image as well." That did it.

Christine was silent, not having any response to that. She slowly stood up, cautiously, nervously, "Uh, Ryan, Mr. Flichette, I mean Gordon," and she nodded, "I hope you don't mind. My mascara's a complete mess. Can you give me a sec while I go freshen up?"

"Oh, I don't know, I think you look kind of cute," my mind was racing, what could I do?

"Don't be silly, you dope. I'll be back in a minute." she was not to be deterred.

"Hey wait!" I called after her, "Officer Mendez told us to wait here."

"Don't worry, I'm not going far. I just have to use the little girl's room." Giving me that wide, cheeky smile of hers, "Really, don't worry, I'll be back in a jiffy." and then she left, walking off towards the side door of one of the soundstages on the other side of the road.

"Okay, I'll be here," I said mostly to myself. And then it struck me, how would Christine know where the closest washrooms were, if she had never worked here? On second thought, how did she get by security without a pass? Something was up, and I did not like it, not one bit.

Just as Christine disappeared from view, Detective Mendez rounded the opposite corner running rapidly in our direction. She was yelling something and appeared very agitated, her jacket was open, and her shoulder holster and loaded weapon were visible as the wind tore at her coat. Her hair was flying lose and the last vestiges of the late afternoon sun caught it, releasing its deep auburn colour as she ran. Anne was completely breathless when she finally reached us.

"Where's Christine?" she immediately asked, chest surging, bending down, her hands on the front of her thighs.

"She just went to use the washroom; I was going to say…" but she cut me off right away.

"Which direction did she go?" Mendez was frantic.

"Uh, that way." and I pointed, "Just opposite to where you just came from." I was confused.

"Well, get yourself up, let's go! We must get after her!" Gordon also rose, but she motioned him down with her hand. "You stay here with Officer Peacham, there's still some more information we need."

I was still uneasy, looking toward the soundstage, "Why? What's going on? What's wrong?" but deep down, I already knew.

"What's wrong? What's wrong is that last blast was just a decoy, a small incendiary charge in some garbage bins on the other side of the commissary." my heart dropped in my chest as the detective continued, "It's your friend Christine, Ryan. She's the bomber."

"No, that can't be…" my voice trailed off as I said it, but again, I had already felt it in my bones.

"I know you don't want to believe it. But it's her, alright!"

Then, looking at my shocked expression, Anne told me of her conclusions, "Yes, the newswires were indeed carrying the story about this afternoon's blast. But we kept it quiet as to which part of the studio was attacked. How then, did Christine know it was the screening room? And how did she get here so soon after? How did she get on site for that matter" then adding for good measure, "And just as I was going to confront her about it, she reached into her purse, and must have activated the dummy charge as a distraction, by some kind of remote?"

Then I too remembered Christine reaching into her abnormally large purse for the Kleenex just as the bomb went off.

It was now all coming into focus, the image on the screen, the convenient rides to the studio, the non-existent friends, the sudden disappearance at the slicer's office and the unexplained knowledge of events of this afternoon, all gelled into only one firm conclusion. Christine was the bomber!

"Come on!" Anne yelled again now running, in the direction Christine had gone, "We have to catch up with her."

Jumping to my feet and doing it much too quickly, I felt the blood rush away from my head feeling faint, but the adrenaline that was now surging in my body because of the horrific discovery, got me vertical again. Gordon stood, holding my shoulder, helping me with my balance.

"Are you good?" he asked.

"Yeah, I'm good," still a bit woozy.

"Well then, what are you waiting for? Go get the bitch!" and stumbling on only my first two steps, I immediately followed in Detective Mendez's wake.

The two of us ran straight to the door Christine had just entered and were instantly plunged into darkness. Only a single emergency fixture was operating, blanketing the doorway with its meager light. We stopped just inside, trying to see further into the pitch-black room, patiently waiting for our eyes to adjust. Then we heard an unnerving voice taunting us from the shadows, echoing off the barren walls.

"Hey, Ms. Mendez!" Christine cackled, the sound of her words now a haunting duplicate of her once sweet, provocative voice. "I see you've finally figured out the truth. My silly mistake for slipping up! It was the screening room thing wasn't it? I knew from the look on your face." she continued to taunt us, "But you won't catch me. I've worked in this studio for so many years, I know it's every nook and cranny!"

"Well, Christine, you may know this studio, but I know your type, and you will never get out of this studio or escape me, except in handcuffs! Why don't you just come quietly and save us all a lot of trouble?" Officer Mendez said this knowing perfectly well the answer would be negative, but saying it, nonetheless.

"No can do, Detective! I'm afraid you're just going to have to come get me!" and then we saw a dazzlingly bright light appear on the opposite side of the soundstage, as evidently Christine had opened up another outside exit, and we briefly spied her lithe silhouette as the far door closed again leaving us back in darkness.

"Let's see if we can cut her off!" Anne yelled, and we turned around and headed back out the way we entered, running quickly around the outside of the building, the only sound our heavy breathing and our shoes, scratching against the hard pavement. The chase was on and from the look in Anne's' eyes, I knew this would end only one way, Christine in custody. Or dead.

Just as we rounded the building's corner we spotted, our prey, Christine, jump in one of the available director golf-carts and speed away, up the service road.

"Well, if that's the way you want it," mumbled Anne, running over to a second golf-cart, jumping aboard and activating the starter. I was barely on board, and nearly fell out on the ground, when she began speedily moving up the hill, giving chase.

"Hurry up! Come on!" as I slumped back on the slippery seat, the vehicles small tires squealing on the asphalt. "She's getting away!"

And sure enough, Christine had already crested the rise and was well out of site, before we were at full speed. "Damn can't this thing go any faster?" Anne yelled at the cart, as we continued up the hill after my would-be girlfriend, turned insane bomber, the whirling sound of the little vehicles electric motors whining furiously.

Reaching the peak, our speed was now so great, the little transports tires raised right up off the road, but not for long. Soon after we came crashing back to earth, almost dislodging both Anne and I out of our seats and onto the asphalt. We held on for dear life, rewarded for our diligence noticing Christine just ahead, as she continued on her way, heading toward the front lot. I didn't know what she had in mind but guessed it could be nothing good. Winding out way past the computer graphics building we had seen on the studio tour, our golf-cart began to approach the lower level of the museum, the towering building housing the old Transformers ride visible in the distance.

Christine was already there, threading her cart between it and the old Mummy ride and turning at the bottom of the hill. We lost track of her briefly as we approached the two ancient theme ride buildings, and as we turned left between them, spotted the rotting archway of the abandoned Jurassic World attraction. Beyond that we were presented with an interesting development in our ongoing chase. Christine had abandoned her golf-cart and was busily mounting one of the light blue AirLift cars!

Thinking she was going to quickly ride it all the way to the upper level, it appeared we would just do the same, continuing our pursuit on foot through the abandoned upper atrium. Aware I was in no position to run very far, I still had full confidence in Anne eventually winning that part of the pursuit. Everything looked to be coming together, and Christine would soon be in custody.

It was a great shock, one that left me dumbfounded and my mouth dropping open in shear surprise, when Christine's floating machine did not head rapidly up the hill, but instead broke free of the ride constraints and flew away from the docking platform heading east, over the surface of the backlot. Was this even possible?

Then thinking back to our first ride, the only way this quasi-miracle could have been achieved, was that some way, she must have accessed the manual override controls!

Whatever the reason, Christine was now racing away from us at three times our speed in a rocketing hovercraft! We need to get one, and fast!

"Did you see that? I asked worriedly.

"I sure did," Officer Mendez's returned, "We need to get one of those little beauty's ourselves. We'll never keep up with her in this dinosaur!"

"I agree. I only hope we can get those manual override controls to work!"

"Oh, don't worry about that, Ryan. I have a few tricks up my sleeve. It's standard procedure for the police staff that operate in the district around the studio to be trained on how to use the emergency overrides on the AirLifts!" she laughed, "We shouldn't have any problem!"

Without hesitation we whizzed right up to the ride entrance, and abandoning our trusty golf-cart, we leapt out, jumping quickly into the first available AirLift.

"Now, if I remember this right," Officer Mendez was talking to herself, while she fiddled with the control panel on the front of the car, "Yep, got it." and the small front panel, which I had noticed on my first ride down the hill, popped open to revel a short control stick and throttle control.

"The only problem is," Anne stated a simple limitation of our new ride, "these things don't have any brakes." then she chuckled, her smile addictive, "If you want to stop, you just release the throttle and the air friction halts the craft. So, get ready for one hell of a bumpy ride!"

With a light push on the throttle and quick shift of the control yoke, we were off!

As we pulled away, or at least attempted to depart, it was quite obvious that Christine retained the upper hand with respect to control of the AirLift vehicles manual operation. While Detective Mendez had thankfully recalled how to access the physical controls of the unit, she clearly did not share the same experience in regard to operating the sleek craft, and it showed. Christine was already moving smoothly away from the launch area into the backlot and we were still trying to get the thing to behave.

Stupidly, in the heat of the moment, I stated the obvious, "Uh, I hate to remind you at this delicate moment, but she's getting away!"

"I know, I know. I'm working on it," Anne yelled in frustration, glaring at me. "While they taught us how to access the controls, it's not like I've had many hours training on how to drive this thing!"

We joltingly moved away for the platform, in the vague direction after the departing Christine, and hopped and bobbed roughly along for a few more moments, until Anne got a feel for the strange craft. As we began to accelerate, the AirLift became easier to control, finally beginning to obey her commands. Moving swiftly away from the ride entrance, the AirLift soon passed beautifully between the abandoned Jurassic and Mummy facilities, less than a meter above the roadway!

The AirLift vehicle, however, turned out to be strictly a hovercraft style of device and not an airplane style flyer. Because, while fast as a cheetah, there was still a permanent requirement to have some kind of solid surface beneath the craft in order to maintain its forward motion. For when we got too high, the craft slowed and reduced height until the lower engines could once again bite into the grounds familiar surface. Almost as if the vehicle required something of which to 'push off' to stabilize it and ensure its rapid movement. The faster we flew, however, the higher we could go, enabling us to easily clear low bushes and other smaller hurdles. Which was a good thing because we clipped many of these landscaping impediments during our shaky start. But, no matter how fast we travelled, we could not completely fly over the taller obstacles, such as buildings, only make our way around them. Discovering this the hard way with a near disastrous collision with the first soundstage we encountered.

Mind you, I was sure we would have been able to fly *through* the structure provided the large truck doors had been opened at either side, but that was no help to us now, with most of the soundstages closed down for the day.

Pushing the throttle to its limits, the speed began to increase exponentially, our craft rising much higher away from the ground. Anne continued to race us through the various soundstage buildings, where all the computer programmers were busily keeping their heads down, creating new and interesting characters, completely oblivious to the pursuit going on around them. Feeling a little like rats in a maze, dodging in an out of the various rectangular, three-story structures, all the while trying to keep Christine in view up ahead.

After many more frightening twists and turns, both of us now very dizzy, we turned the final corner past the last, full size sound stage. We had finally reached the end of the studio's front lot and the landscape began to flatten out, our AirLift now racing over the picture car storage area. With no more asphalt or concrete surfaces, I felt the dust whip up as we passed, covering the age-old vehicles with yet another layer of dirt and grime.

"Can you still see her?" I asked, the windstorm of the push drives, blowing grit into my eyes.

"Yep, she's still there," Anne pointed with her spare hand, "about 500 meters ahead and to our right."

And sure enough, I could just spot the light blue shape of Christine's AirLift, speeding in advance of our bouncing machine. She was dashing towards the abandoned backlot, which we had recently ridden through together as passengers on the ancient tram, our AirLifts moving ever so much faster than the old tour vehicles, now idle at the end of the day.

We skipped over a slight rise and I immediately recognized that we were now belting down the dry cobblestone road of the familiar old village, next to the yellow adobe buildings with the red tile roofs, following the exact trail that the flash flood used to run in the old days. Our craft ran up against some of the branches of the trees lining the way as we swerved back and forth, Anne still getting the hang of the turns.

By now we had nearly caught up with Christine and as she turned left at the crossing bridge, she looked back nervously to review our progress. We soon saw that glancing behind at us was a mistake, as she turned too quickly, clipping one of the ancient road signs, putting her craft into a light spin. Holding on tightly, she managed to fight her way out of it as the pair of us continued on now entering the old western village, both our vehicles at maximum throttle.

Through the dusty streets, we flew, each trying to best the other. Then I noticed Christine fiddle with something beside her and drop it over the side. It hit the ground, just as we passed, both of us realizing at the last second that it was a small explosive device.

"That damn girl's playing hardball now! Hold on!" Anne yelled.

In a desperate effort to avoid the *mine* that Christine had just dropped, Anne dipped our craft down, swinging us wildly to the right, right off the center of the western street and tight up against the gray wood siding of the closest building. We unexpectedly found ourselves trapped, sandwiched between the porch canopies and the clapboard sidewalk, as if in an ancient, grey wooden tunnel. The only open side, off to our left, revealing the gravel street beyond.

The charge detonated, the explosion behind us rocking our AirLift, raising a huge amount of dust and dirt up in our wake. Then there was another huge thump and a jolt as we hit one of the pillars holding the suspended roof and the entire structure began to shake violently around us. The remaining support posts flashed by on our left, the wind whooshing in our ears with each successive one we passed. It was definitely time to leave.

With one more frantic tilt of the control yoke, Anne had us back out in the open, but because of our excessive speed, she had not judged the timing correctly, snapping off yet another fragile column in our way. As we finally left the shadow of the cantilevered awning, the entire suspended roof came down around us, crashing to the ground, small bits of wood raining down on the rear end of our vehicle, barely missing us. The disturbance sent our car twirling sideways into the forecourt and Anne had to cut back the throttle to bring us to a slow, uneven stop.

"That was too close," I said anxiously.

"Yeah. Let's not do that again," Anne replied, but turned to me smiling, obviously enjoying herself, once again accelerating to full throttle, shooting out past the last vestiges of the old western street, determinedly following in the other AirLift's wake.

Next, it was down another dip and into good old New York Street, two futuristic AirLifts chasing through the chasms between the glass buildings, pawn shops, museums and fancy brownstones. All just frontages of course, but still solid, forcefully directing us through the only one clear path. Christine jogged left through an opening so suddenly, we missed the turn. Forcing us on to the next intersection before altering our own course north in pursuit.

This brought us out into courthouse square, the famous old backlot set that I had now witnessed time and again on the tour, the old concrete pillared courthouse still there standing majestically at the east end of the plaza. We had obviously surprised Christine, because where she had kept on the same path, we were now at right angles to her as she sprinted towards the old law building facade, effective cutting her off. She could not turn, and unable to travel over the tall frontage, had absolutely nowhere to go. I made a small yelp of victory seeing as she was set to collide with the face of the abandoned structure, holding my breath.

At the last minute, Christine did something to her car, making a strange movement with the control stick, pushing the throttle to the maximum, prompting the nose of her AirLift to rise. I don't know how she did it, but she was suddenly using one of the columns as the push drives surface and climbing the face of the clock tower! She flew over the top just as we swiped across in front of the building powerless to stop her. Her momentum carried her over the short roof and then she plummeted down behind, bouncing perilously up and down, before once more regaining the ground as her propulsive medium. We careened around the side of the building to resume the chase, the two of us retracing our route through another part of the backlot.

"What on earth was that?" I shouted, flabbergasted at the move.

"I don't know, but she sure knows how to fly these things!" Anne yelled, "I thought for sure we had her that time."

Up through the asphalt streets, past all the roads that had in the past been used for any city in America; Chicago, LA or Akron, Ohio. The pursuit was back on and it appeared our adversary had us outmatched. We might be finally losing the battle.

We sped up another rise, suddenly surrounded by what used to be, at one time (as I was losing track) beautiful trees, flowery shrubs and manicured lawns as we entered the backlot's residential street. The derelict craftsman homes, barn houses and New England estates, rising around us. But it looked like Christine had made an error. I remembered from the tour that this was a short street, one of every kind of home, but all installed on a tight cul-de-sac! No way out! Again, we had thought luck had gone our way and we had her cornered as she raced down the street between the opposing sets of faded whitewashed picket fences.

"We've got her now," was all I could offer.

But I was wrong, because Christine did know the studio. While each of the homes may have looked opulent from the exterior, all they were was a bunch of light wooden frontages, with no rears or interiors. Only exteriors were ever filmed on the residential street, all of the interior work being done on sets in a soundstage. So, there was nothing behind any of the homes!

Christine knew this better than anyone and dropping down in her cockpit she approached the last house in the row, heading right for the large bay window that beckoned to her.

Her AirLift easily penetrated the fragile faux glass work cutting through it like a hot knife through butter, emerging completely unscathed on the opposite side of the house, and high tailing it further into the surrounding woods.

"It looks like she has all the luck." I quipped, foolish to have thought we had her cornered.

We passed through the gaping opening, the last vestiges of the light frame and glass sprinkling our AirLift as we passed, and once clear, again rocketing after our fleeing culprit.

"Boy, she's good!" Anne offered, "Where to now I wonder?"

Where to indeed. We continued our faithful chase down another lane, over yet another copse of trees further west. As we rounded the line of timber, we began riding over the 747 jumbo jet crash scene, silent that evening, the grass and weeds still clasping on to the bits of wreckage strewn about the hilltop. Anne brought the car to a gradual halt as we had finally lost sight of Christine and her AirLift. Her sudden and complete disappearance baffling.

"Where did she go? Did you see where she went? Have we lost her?" I yelled hysterically.

"Ryan, get a grip. Stop it with the questions!" Anne reprimanded me. "I can see, she's disappeared! Well, she can't have gone far, let's have a look. Systematically, instead of getting all worked up!

I chastised myself for my foolishness, "I'm sorry, Anne. I can get a bit excited you know." I felt terrible.

"I know, this is getting on everyone's nerves. I thought for sure we would have caught her by now!"

Slowly we trolled around the false crash site, looking at the burnt-out house frontages, the grass verges, everywhere.

Suddenly Anne figured it out, "She's hiding in one of the fuselage sections!" we accelerated again, flying past the largest pieces of airplane's wreckage.

Christine had indeed pulled a fast one, flying right through the largest of the sections and lay hidden in the aisle way between the destroyed rows of seats. As soon as we attempted to enter, almost coming to a complete stop, she accelerated away, shooting out of the tube like a bullet from a gun, heading east down the hill.

"Damn, I knew it!" was all Anne could offer, and we applied the throttle and moved on after her.

The flight took us past the Psycho House and the Bates Motel then a reverse turn behind us towards another road and into the rotting Whoville set, one that had not even been included on our recent tour. I only remembered it from my experiences in 2020, and it looked bad then. Now the set was a complete mess! All of the foam, mesh, plaster and steel structures completely collapsed, and falling apart, no longer representing a fictional Christmas village, but a pile of moldy, wasted junk, completely overrun by the mini jungle that surrounded it, destroyed forever. We just viewed Christine's AirLift as it moved past this sorry looking sight and turned through yet another tree lined road. The numerous twists and turns of our flight were making me dizzy, and I was completely lost, only hoping Anne knew where she was going. I just held on, not knowing when this rapid, very different circle tour of the backlot was going to end!

The flight continued, along another dirt road leading down the hill into the drained and dried out Jaws attraction. The little hamlet of Cabot Cove sat next to this set, quiet and undisturbed for a generation. Flying over the collapsing docks, we passed right by the battered body of old Bruce the shark, his toothless grin once again smiling up at us as we passed. As we cleared more of the surrounding trees, we saw Christine try another fancy move to fly over the tattered and damaged blue-sky backdrop of the now dry exterior water pool, attempting to shave off some time rather than go around.

This time, however, she had made an error. As she attempted to lift the nose of her AirLift, the push dive of the craft, because of the number of torn openings in the backdrop screen, lost hold of a sufficient surface, causing it to falter in midair, forcing its nose back down, taking her not over but right through the rotten plywood sheets of the façade, but still beautiful Southern California sky!

It first appeared that her craft had made it through successfully, the pointy nose of the AirLift cutting the ancient plywood as if paper, but as it continued on its path, some of the larger metal frame work pieces, caught the vehicle, twisting it as it passed, the light windshield of the craft braking off as the AirLift tilted and then tumbled heavily to the ground, spaying dirt and debris into the air, cutting a trench in the soft soil. It's push drive having completely failed, the small craft was smashed apart in the wake of the crash.

We were so busy watching the calamity, we swept right on past the accident at high speed, just able to spot Christine's AirLift crumple disastrously into the ground, before we were long past, almost back at the residential street.

"Turn around, turn around, she's down this time for sure!" I chanted excitedly.

"I'm trying to, you numbskull! Give me a minute." Anne was angry as she wrestled with the controls, our craft not as nimble as it once was, the engine apparently beginning to overheat from the long-extended chase.

After a few false loops, we finally managed to turn around, first completing a brief flyover the crash site, before landing near-by Christine's battered AirLift. As we bobbled to a bouncing halt, we could see that her bright blue craft had been torn to shreds, the steel siding all opened up like a tin can, the paint scratched and the engine scorched. We noticed a small fire in the yellow grass, but it was slowly burning itself out, for luckily most of the area behind the backdrop was in shade and the ground was dry and barren. As we got closer, we were unsure of what we would find, but not taking any chances, Anne had her gun out and was approaching cautiously.

We popped our heads over the side of the tattered remains of the open cabin, expecting the worst. The small AirLifts windshield had sheared right off, its remnants lying on the front of the bent and dented nose. The leather seat was torn, white stuffing bulging out and the control yoke had snapped clean off. The rest of the insides were a mess. There was fluid of some kind draining onto the surrounding soil and the wreckage smelled of burnt oil and charred plastic. But no Christine! Not even an inclining that she had been there, except for the stained safety harness that lay opened on the seatback!

"Where is she?" I asked, unsure of what I was seeing, "Do you think she made it out?"

"Hold on." Anne replied and then slowly made her way to the other side of the craft, gingerly avoiding the strewn debris, noticing for the first time another fluid, dribbling down the opposite side of the cockpit. This time it was red; blood!

"She must have survived the crash." Anne's statement resonated, "The only way would have been that she ducked down at the last minute before colliding with the backdrop. But Christine can't have gone far, she's injured" and she pointed to the small dribbles of blood on the cowl of the broken AirLift.

"But which way?" I questioned anxiously.

"Give me a minute," and she went about on a search to see where Christine had made off to.

Eventually, we discovered a small trail of blood leading around behind the remains of the mural and then off, back through the trees, toward the Jaws pier.

"She must have headed down the hill as we were turning, and we missed her." Anne reasoned, "Let's go find her!"

And we began to jog down the incline, back towards Cabot Cove.

At first the trail of blood was relatively easy to follow, and we were able to trace it back through the outdoor Cabot Cove set, around the shark tank where it disappeared. We frantically searched for another clue and then finally found one back on the entry road.

"Looks like she's got us chasing her like a wild goose again." Anne fumed, pointing "Look! The trail now heads back up the hill along the other road."

And sure enough, there were small droplets of blood providing us a trail back up the road and away from Bruce the shark.

"But why come all the way down here only to go back again? I asked.

"Who knows? Maybe, she's delirious, got her directions mixed up or maybe she thought we would continue down back to the New York Street." Anne was already on the move, "Doesn't matter. Come on she's up this way."

We followed the road for part way until noticing the trail cut across its grey surface, and down into the ditch on its far side, passing into the row of shrubs lining the road. We stopped a minute for breath. The air was a lot cooler now with the sun beginning to fall and the westerly wind picking up. Working our way first through the bushes then a thin width of woods, we broke out on the other side. Standing in full view across a gravel lane was none other than the Bates Motel. A small line of blood still directing us, now visible crossing the roadway and the dusty parking lot out front.

The Bates Motel set had now existed at this studio for over a hundred years, but unlike the Colonial street, was completely furnished and built out; a real motel on the Universal backlot. Back in the day, before the tram tour, full sets were sometimes used, as the area could be cordoned off, saving the need to duplicate the room set on the soundstage. This would also have inevitably been done anyway for Hitchcock's famous shower scene, considering actress Janet Leigh would have been almost naked and no doubt a closed set imposed. However, to make the several shots where both the exterior and interior were in view together, the small building had been completed to make filming of the motel scenes easier.

"She must be hiding in one of the rooms," Anne had a determined look on her face, "We'll search them systematically, one by one, starting there." pointing to the closest room, "You watch the exit, and hold the door open, while I do the searching."

She took a hold of my arm, as we crossed the expanse between us and the motel, "Remember she's injured and not going anywhere. But we don't want to spook her, she may be armed, or worse, may still have some explosives left over. So, be careful!"

Stepping up the two short steps onto the full-length porch, we began our search. We searched one, two and then three rooms, and more, nothing. It was going much slower than I expected, Anne was very systematic and thorough in her investigations, leaving no stone unturned, looking in the bathrooms, in the closets and under the beds. Each of the rooms were identical and open, the door locks having seized many years ago. One of the entries we encountered was jammed shut and we had to break it down, with a firm kick of my boot, but the room was as empty as the rest, only cobwebs and mildew to welcome us. Most of the bathrooms had been either gutted or never built out and, in the few rooms that actually had them, the mattresses were moth eaten, homes to various rodents living within.

The last room, closest to the manager's desk, showed promise, as there was a small spotting of blood visible on the clapboard sidewalk outside the door. But, unfortunately, like the rest the units, it too was deserted. Both Anne and I were now getting frustrated, the last vestiges of the late afternoon sun, dissolving into heavy twilight, and the area throwing shadows everywhere. It was getting harder and harder to search each chamber. Luckily, there was still just enough residual daylight spanning through the age encrusted windows enabling us to continue our search. I chastised myself for not having my pack and trusty Zenon flashlight with me, now resolving, that no matter where I was in any other future, I would never be without it again.

The last place to look was the manager's suite, the largest of the rooms behind the reception area. As we entered the check in vestibule, I noticed the old décor, reminiscent of the age and the old keys still hanging on the peg board behind the reception desk. As Anne looked around the space, the last residue of dwindling light, drifting through the main picture window above the desk, uncovered the door to the owner's suite behind and a small bloody handprint that had starkly displaced the years of accumulated dust.

"This is it!" Anne instructed, removing her gun, "You go outside and wait for me there. I'll bring her out."

"You're sure?" I asked, "Wouldn't it be better if I stay with you?"

"No, as a civilian it's best you're elsewhere, but if you want, wait for me by the door, I'll be right back." and she pushed open the entry leading to the back room with her back, revolver held at chest height in a two-handed grip.

"You be careful," I cautioned.

"You bet," Anne returned, stepping slowly into the room, the creaking of the door cutting into the harsh silence of the coming night.

I moved forward to the other side of the desk, closer to the open door and waited.

It had been several minutes, and I was getting worried. In the intervening time, the night had fully closed in, so it was almost dark, the moon not yet fully risen, providing just the gentlest of blue light, spanning through the exterior windows. The bright lunar surface was welcome sight, but it also created all kinds of shadows in its wake. Long, dark and ugly shadows. An owl hooted in the distance and the wind blew, rattling the branches on the skeletal trees outside. All about was still, the air cool, the night stagnant, unmoving. Then I heard a scream!

Anne came running out of the back room, slamming into the frame of the open door and yelling at me to move!

"Move! Move! Move! Outside quick!" she barked, vaulting the counter, myself following, running around it, the two of us flying through the outer door, across the wooden porch, and finally spilling out onto the weed infested, gravel drive.

"Get down!" was the next thing she said and before I knew it, she had knocked me flat on the rough surface, grazing my bad knee in the fall, the two of us rolling clear.

That's when the night turned into day again and the Bates Motel shockingly exploded in an amazingly bright, very catastrophic, conflagration. In its wake, burning wood planks began flying directly over our heads, raining down across the gravel frontage. The concussion of the tremendous blast hurt our ears while pushing us flat against the ground, the heat of the raging flames burning our backs.

Being constructed of old, dry wood, the Bates Motel was a venerable tinderbox, so within moments, the entire set was ablaze. Igniting almost immediately following the initial blast, the flames now eagerly consumed the building in its entirety, a vast plume of black smoke rising into the night.

We crawled away on our hands and knees, further afield from the scorching fires, only turning to look once we had reached the edge of the roadside, putting plenty of space between us and the massive inferno.

"That bitch!" Anne yelled, literally exploding herself, breathing heavily, attempting to sit up, "She set a trap! An explosive trap! The cow obviously did have a few tricks left up her sleeve. Well, this may go on longer than I thought. Looks like she still has a bit of fight left in her."

Then she recited her last movements, "I went in and was doing my careful search, closets, bathroom, bed, when I noticed more blood on the rear window ledge. That's when I first realized the window was open, or had been opened, which was very strange. Looking out I saw a silhouette on the stairs, heading up the house on the rise. Wanting to follow her directly, I quickly turned around to tell you where I was going, and at the last second, spied the charged explosives set behind the door!" Anne took a short breath, "She must have set a delayed timer, hoping we would be in the room when it detonated. Oh, boy! We were lucky to have gotten out."

Then she continued, with renewed determination, ready at once to resume the chase, "Well, if you're ready, we have a someone waiting for us up at the house on the hill," and together we looked up at the Psycho House, its foreboding upper window staring down on us from its lofty perch above.

"I'm in! Let's go!"

And we stood as one, brushing ourselves off and headed around the still burning motel, toward the distant stairs, to what was sure to be, one way or another, our final confrontation with Christine.

Chapter Seventeen – The Final Confrontation

Deep night had descended. Now having completely risen, the moon was full, a bright grey-blue orb gleaming in the sky. Its misty light enabling us to make our way towards and up the cliff side stone staircase. The raging fires behind us, while still burning and hot, had almost consumed the bulk of their fuel. Despite the fact they were beginning to subside, they still provided an additional eerie glow that spilled across the rock steps and surrounding hill, as we made our slow but determined climb to the top. We decided to take it in measured, easy steps, both of us still suffering, partially from shock, as well as overall soreness from the fall after our close brush with death. No doubt Anne was taking her time to help me out, considering all the pressure I had placed on my injured leg, with all of our walking over the past hour.

At the peak of the stairs, Anne and I stood still together for a moment, slightly out of breath from the ascent. Both of us, taking the fresh evening air into our lungs, and just listening to the sound of the night, trying to calm our weary minds. It was difficult, glancing up at the antique, rapidly deteriorating, wooden structure and its hauntingly familiar façade visible before us. The eerie looking place was starkly illuminated by both the glowing moonlight, and the remnants of the cherry red afterglow rising up from the still burning hulk of the Bates

Motel. This faint crimson aura provided the house with a devilishly, evil look. A very peaceful moment marred by its ever-fateful, troubling presence.

The ancient building was a mess. Many of its wood shingles had fallen off or were lose, spilling to the ground like discarded shavings from an overworked woodchipper. The old porch, its rusted iron railings twisted and bent, tilted sideways on the front of the house, looking as if built by a drunken carpenter. The wooden steps rising up to the faded door, were half rotted and sagging, with most of the old windows smashed, shards of glass hanging loosely in their partially broken frames. The worst injury was the massive damage to the left side roof of the house, which had occurred on account of the collapsed tree branch. But beyond the age, damage and neglect, the most disturbing part, was the still intact, high mounted oval window of the central tower staring down at us out of its face, like a repugnant eye. Likely hiding all means of fiendish secrets behind its incessant darkness. A portrait of pure, unadulterated evil.

"Interesting looking place," Anne commented, still staring up at the old mansion, "looks kind of... I don't know. Scary looking?"

"You have no idea." I replied evenly; my voice strangely calm despite my building trepidation.

Gingerly crossing the thin road and overgrown grass to the bottom of the abandoned house's wooden steps, we noticed some of the tall, sun-bleached weeds had been trampled. That and several visible dark spots, indicated Christine had indeed passed that way. We approached carefully; Anne had her gun out once again, slowly mounting the creaking entry steps, stair by stair. Upon reaching the porch, several more of the dark spots became noticeable on its greying surface and crossing the entry threshold of the now, wide-open door.

I experienced a frigid chill just being there on the brink of entering one of the most famous movie houses of all time but was somewhat sure that Anne did not share my apprehension in the least. Obviously, from her apparent unfamiliarity, she had not seen nor witnessed Alfred Hitchcock's famed thriller classic, and so the house did not resonate as much with her. But for me, it represented ultimate malevolence, and I suppose, marked a particularly appropriate location for the conclusion of this rather disturbing adventure.

Unhurriedly, we moved inside, each footfall, creating weird and extraordinary sounds on the loose and weakening floorboards. As we did, the lighting dimmed slightly, but thankfully we did not lose either the bright moonlight or the last remnants of the burning motel fire. Their combined illumination being more than enough to make our way deeper into the deserted house. The main entry opening and the wide front picture windows, permitted the residue of the deep red glow to be reflected off the straight and narrow staircase heading up to the second floor, while the tall side windows bathed parts the vast entry hall in a startlingly blue-white, lunar light.

The house smelled old, rotten and stale, mold and mildew everywhere. Immediately evident once we made it inside were the small pools of blood on the floor, and a few more drops of red blood on the main stairs. On closer inspection, however, this macabre splatter extended only up the first three or four steps before puzzlingly disappearing. Based on the amount of blood in the main hall, the presence of these rather limited spills had to be a ruse, Christine wanting us to think she had gone up, when I already knew, deep down, exactly where she would go. To the only place a sick and twisted, criminal mind would go. To where the insane character of Mr. Norman Bates had kept the rotting, dried out corpse of his *Mother*. The basement cellar!

"She's down this way." I whispered earnestly, pointing, already heading towards the basement door under the stairs.

"Why that way?" Anne whispered in return, "From what I can see, it looks like she's gone up?"

"No, she hasn't," I was adamant, "That's just for show. Look closely." gesturing to the blood spotted lightly on the stairs, "The stains only go up a few steps."

Hesitating, looking into Anne eyes directly, I presented my conclusion, "She's downstairs. I know it."

"How do you know? What makes you so certain?" Anne asked worriedly, a bit confused and, for the first time, looking a little frightened.

Whether it was the scary location, the thought of going into the building's dark basement, or my bizarre precognitive abilities, I did not know which.

"I just know." firm, resolute, "It's a long story. I'll tell you about it sometime."

"Okay, I'll take your word for it." then shrugging her shoulders, attempting to shake away her mounting fear, she followed obediently.

This time I took the lead, walking in the dim light of the moon still shining down the hall, before gently opening the old creaking door at the top of the cellar stairway. The eerie sound echoed in the quiet house, interrupting a sleeping rodent that scurried away along the baseboard. As I had suspected, the top step was slippery with blood. The door handle also showed spotting, leaving a sticky residue on my palm. My supposition had been correct, only a vicious criminal with nowhere to go, would head into a basement with no possible means of escape. We proceeded with caution, carefully mounting each step, descending slowly into the dark recesses of the Psycho House.

It was extremely quiet, there being no noise save for the creaking of each wooden riser the deeper we went. The walls were old stone, a remnant of the ancient foundation, the thin grey mortar, lose and crumpling. There was a musty, moldy smell in the air and the walls were moist, in some areas moss covered, clearly unmaintained for decades. A light drip of water could be heard from somewhere below, the sound resonating in the tight space. Seemingly to fall in time with our footsteps. It was very dark, but as we got about halfway down, the dull red glow from the surviving motel fire at last became visible through the long broken, high mounted window hanging like a mist. The blue moon glow was even more effective, shining down in rays upon a tiny portion of the cellar floor, creating a distorted white rectangle in the dusty soil.

The natural illumination allowed us to complete the remainder of our downward movements unimpeded. The expansive room below us looked to be deserted, the dirt floor rough and barren, but with most of the area still cast in shadow, we remained vigilant, slowly and guardedly descending to the bottom of the rickety staircase.

Upon reaching the lower stone landing, our point of view had shifted enough to reveal an old craftsman wooden rocking chair as it arose from the shadows, appearing like a wicked specter, unexpectedly exposed by the unceasing, filtered azure moonlight. It was gently rocking in place and, with each movement back and forth, it creaked hauntingly. Out of place in this deserted cellar, no motive means for its unsettling action yet evident, it continued like a pendulum on a clock. Expecting at once to see a ghostly rendition of Mrs. Bates anxiously waiting to expose her shriveled skull, gaping mouth and dark, hollow eye-sockets. A shiver went up my spine and I began to perspire. For the first time in my life I was scared. Deathly scared.

"Who's there?" Anne called, gun drawn, pinned to the moist wall, evidently as frightened as I was.

Silence, no noise except the incessant rocking of the phantom chair. We looked at one another, unsure.

"Hello?" Anne called out once again, "Is anyone there?"

Still it remained quiet, the relentless creaking now getting on my nerves. I took a long step forward.

Then suddenly, making us jump out of our skins and scaring us both to death, a shrill voice cut through the silence. Not that of a dead mother, but of an unbalanced criminal mind. Injured, tired and worn-out, fed up with the chase, content to surrender. Almost ready to admit defeat.

"It's only me, Ms. Mendez," Christine said, turning the chair around, with an extended, shoeless foot, exposing herself to the falling moon rays, sitting, slouched down in the rocker. Her hair was matted to her skull and there were two large cuts on her face, one eye bruised and almost closed. Her left shoulder was badly shredded, the arm broken or at least dislocated with the rest of her clothes torn in numerous places. A long, ugly looking gash gaped open on the front of her bare leg, bleeding profusely. And, lastly, a mostly empty, very dirty handbag hung limply from the damaged arm.

"Christine?" was all I said.

"You win. You bested me. I'm done." her voice was flat, no emotion evident. Her breathing began again, gurgling roughly in her chest, for she had been previously holding her breath, in a vain attempt to escape detection.

Then, very subtly, her good arm dropped limply towards the floor, resulting in a dull thump as her palm opened and something impacted the dirt beside her chair. I looked down to see a small explosive device, which had been hidden in her hand, now lay on the ground, glowing red numerals on its detonator timer counting backward.

"We'll all go to hell together," she said it almost as an invitation, a vindictive solicitation.

The activated bomb lay there on the floor. Initially, neither Anne nor I made a move, both frozen in shock. Then my brain began to work again, and, without further hesitation, I leaped forward, unconsciously noting the timer read 9 seconds. It was at 6 before I reached it, and 4 before I had it grasped firmly. With all the strength I could muster, at 2, I threw it up, up and out the broken basement window towards the shimmering moon.

I pushed Anne flat to the floor just as the device exploded, filling the night anew with blinding yellow light, the concussion of the blast slamming back through the open window, sprinkling the remaining glass, as well as exhaustive amounts of dirt and organic debris, down upon us both. The catastrophic noise echoed harshly in the chamber, stinging our already damaged ears.

And ultimately, illuminating the entire dank basement, revealing Christine's demented snarling face, sitting in the chair as she cackled insanely, like the horrifying monster she was, covered with blood, and ready to kill, the sound of her hideous, screaming laugh filling the gradually returning night.

Chapter Eighteen – Aftermath Redux and Retribution

Even with Christine as badly wounded as she was, she struggled like a trapped lioness, requiring Detective Mendez to handcuff her floundering injured hands securely behind her back. Rather cruelly, I would suspect. This would have only made the pain of her damaged shoulder unbearable, but she took it all in stride, crying, shrieking and grumbling as the policewoman pushed her all the way up the stairs and back out of the old building. I think Anne took a guilty pride in strapping Christine up like that. I and did not really blame her, considering the circumstances.

Christine's final gift to us, the bomb, had detonated just clear of the front of the house, near the edge of the ridge road, blowing in the remaining windows, and collapsing what was left of the porch. It had taken with it the lane, the stone steps and the tree that had done so much damage to the house over the years with its fallen limbs. The trunk itself had become completely uprooted, toppling and sliding down the hill inverted, towards the burnt-out motel, its exposed roots now reaching towards the sky in mock surrender. The pathway in front of the house was an irreparable mess, but after braving the thoroughly destroyed front staircase, we were able to make our way gingerly over the loose chunks of dirt and gravel making up the still crumbling hillside, towards the remaining section of roadway rising up from the lower levels. Several small fires were amassing in the tall grasses near the side of the house, and I was uncertain, if left unchecked, they would proceed any closer. Not even mentioning the potential threat, we hurriedly continued away from the ancient structure.

Finally, after detecting both the explosions and the fires, emergency services had begun to arrive, ambulances and fire trucks as well as a few police cruisers. They had already established a perimeter and had just begun setting up a triage facility well west of the house. We headed in that direction.

Christine by now had lost most of her previous fight, the massive loss of blood obviously diminishing her once powerful resistance. Her violent struggles now concluded, she hung between Anne and I like a wet noddle. Despite her small size, she was very heavy as a dead weight, so it was a difficult walk around the far side of the house towards the amassing rescue workers.

We were both glad, several minutes later when two paramedics, spotting us and our injured charge, came to assist and we could finally let go of Christine's broken form, passing it on to someone else. They soon dropped her down on one of the available stretchers laid out for the injured. Two more attendants came to assist Anne and I, providing our own places to sit, under the cover of the hastily erected hospital tent.

"She's a suspect! Don't let her go anywhere!" Anne stated sharply to the two men, as they strapped Christine into the stretcher, immediately connecting an IV and swabbing her leg wound. "I want an officer, no two officers, with her at all times."

"Yes Ma'am, well get on it right away, but we first have to get her to hospital for treatment. Can you take off these cuffs?"

"Not on your life, and I don't care about the hospital, you will wait until I release you." Detective Mendez was adamant. Screaming over at two local police, milling about the edge of the blast zone, she motioned them over, "You two. Come here!"

After pairing up the officers with the two attendants, the combined team loaded the still cuffed Christine into the nearest ambulance, Anne busy making sure everything was secure and that the prisoner remained safely neutralized. Once all was arranged to Anne's satisfaction, the ambulance then took off, its sirens blasting, heading through the crashed 747 diorama on its way to LA County General. Then and only then, would she settle down to be looked at herself.

The two of us sat still on our stretchers while we were examined. Luckily having only suffered superficial burns, scrapes and bruises, nothing even close to Christine's massive crash wounds. They patched us up as we sat there, very quiet in our contemplations, staring off into space.

"You're all set," said one of the attendants, "looks like you'll survive."

I nodded in thanks as the man moved off, looking for work else ware.

Then we both heard a loud yell, followed by more frantic hollering, this time that of several men, jarring us both from our rest, the two of us jumping off our comfortable seats and walking out of the shelter to see what was going on.

My supposition had been correct, fully expecting the sight next witnessed, as bold orange flames began to consume the lower floor of the Psycho House. Without remorse, the devilish tendrils passed on quickly through to the second floor, annihilating everything in their path, and before anything could be done to quench the raging flames, the entire structure was soon fully ablaze. The bright reds and yellows filled the night with a spectacularly eerie light and I just stared as the horrid house met its final destiny.

Regrettably, it turned out that, the fire trucks had accumulated at the lower portion of the road, beside the still smoldering motel and were busily dowsing the embers in white foam when the fire in the house first started. Apparently, none of the rescue workers had noticed the brush fires intensifying next to the structure, being so busy with taking care of us. These flames had continued to build in strength unhindered, finally working their way to the porch of the house and, shortly afterwards, the rest of the structure. Like the motel before it, the house was a firestorm just waiting to happen, and so before anything could be done to redirect the foam equipment, the house was completely engulfed.

I for one was not the least bit sad to see it go. Yes, it was once an icon of movie history, but for me, that evening, all it had been was a horrifying prison, ready to beat me down and destroy me with its malevolence. The structure rapidly began to collapse in on itself and I reveled in the heat of the inferno brushing against my face, the sparks flying, filling the night, swirling in space like a bunch of fireflies working their way homeward. Anne stared intently as well, the two of us remembering our adventure, and our intimate brush with death.

It really was time for me to go home.

"I have to go to the hospital," Anne informed me. "There's a ride I've arranged leaving in a few minutes." she looked at me and her dirty but still very pretty face, illuminated but the raging fires, offered an invitation I couldn't resist, "You're free to come join me if you want. I think you, more than anyone, deserves to be told the whole story. Come on," and she gestured me away from the fire's ugly sight, "the car's right over there."

We walked towards a battered grey, unmarked police cruiser as the mansion burnt itself to the ground, the fire crews still struggling to get the foam cannons moved and aimed where they were needed most. As we moved away from the diminishing flames, we saw the first spray of the white soapy material, as a silhouette through the rear windshield, finally strike the mostly collapsed structure, sending billowing steam hissing into the night sky. Goodbye, Psycho House, welcome to hell.

The patrol car took us quickly to the hospital, and when we arrived, we were immediately escorted by a contingent of officers to an isolation ward on the 3rd floor. Christine had already received treatment, blood work, a large transfusion and a temporary synthy flesh repair of her leg, or so she was told. I found out from Anne that there was no intention to make the crude repair any better than temporary and that Christine, whatever fate had in for her afterwards, would have to live with the scars for the rest of her days.

She was still asleep in a specially secured room, when we arrived and so Anne and I made our way over to the cafeteria for a drink. The hospital appeared as any medical facility might have in my time, linoleum floors, light green walls and patients in beds in the hallways, due to overload. Quite a normal site. The cafeteria was large, but the offering typical hospital food, soft, tepid and tasteless. Thankfully, we were only there for the café.

"So, quite an evening we've had." I said rather bluntly.

"You sure know how to show a girl a good time!" Anne replied, smiling cheekily for the first time since the chase. "Man, what a night!"

"Well, looks like were even."

"In what way?" she asked curious.

"Well, you saved my skin with your football tackle down at the motel, and I used my baseball skills to take care of the bomb up at the house." I moved my hands to represent my throw, "So, were even!"

"Ah yes, I see." she agreed, a confused look on her face "While not understanding your odd references one bit, I think I got the point. It's good to know neither of us owe each other anything." adding sassily, "Otherwise, it might have meant we were bound to one another in some way."

"Not like that would be a bad thing," I returned to equal the playful banter.

"I agree, but I just don't think it would work out between us."

"Oh, and why is that?"

"That easy, because you're an actor," she smiled broadly, having the last laugh, "and the last actor I knew, I just left handcuffed to a hospital bed. And of course, everyone knows you're all the same."

We both chuckled together, enjoying the time alone and were sipping the last of our café when one of the other officers showed up at our table.

"Detective Mendez?"

"Yes? That's me."

"She's awake ma'am and wants to see you." the officer stated, simply.

"Lead on then, Officer," and the two of us rose from our seats, the luke-warm dregs of our drinks forgotten.

We arrived at Christine's room, moving through the door past the guard on post. She was sitting on the bed; the mattress having been raised so that she could see. The broken woman was looking sharply at us, through her one good eye, as we entered.

Christine was in a pitiful state, an IV was attached to one arm and the other tied up in a sling. The wounded shoulder fully bandaged, its wrappings passing round her chest under her light hospital gown. Her damaged leg was also heavily bound and lay in an elevated position, hanging by some wires from the ceiling, with a tube and drain running down to a cylinder mounted on the floor. Possibly to channel infection away or some such thing.

Her face was the worst, the damaged eye and one of the cuts had been wrapped together, covering it and her skull, so that little of her hair remained visible. The other cut had been roughly sutured and covered with a gauze pad, the adhesive tape covering most of the opposite side of her face. There was an oxygen tube and fitting in her nose, helping her breathe, producing a disturbing gurgling sound emanating from an apparatus beside the bed. About the only part of her head that wasn't covered was one eye and her mouth, luckily enabling her to speak.

Her voice was gravelly and rough, hardly the sweet voice I was used to. "Welcome, Ms. Mendez, and you too, Ryan. Come to gloat, have we?"

"Not exactly," replied Anne now back in her professional role. "We were informed that it was you who actually called us. We were hoping you might shed some light on why you would have perpetrated such heinous crimes."

"You really want to hear it all?" Christine's voice continued to jar me, its tone distorted, but at the same time now reflecting a hint of sadness.

"Yes, if you don't mind. We would like to hear it all, from the beginning. Do you wish a lawyer present?"

"Lawyer? Those bums! I wouldn't give them the time of day! No, I want to get this off my chest now while I still have the guts." she was still angry, as if ready to explode like one of her devious devices.

"Fine, then I must remind you that anything your say, can, and will be held against you in a court of law." getting the Myranda thing properly taken care of.

"Yeah, yeah, do you want to hear this or not?" Christine was impatient to start.

"Do you mind if I record this?" Office Mendez asked.

"No, go right ahead. I'm through anyway."

"Please, then, proceed."

Then Christine related her story.

"As you figured out, or if you need my confirmation, way back in the day I was an actress. A pretty good one if I might add and was doing quite well for myself before the change. That's why I was able to afford my nice clothes, and especially the nice apartment, which I had fully paid off before all this crap happened.

"Everything was real rosy. I had money, fame and a great lifestyle. Then, on my last film, there was an accident," Anne and I stared at each other, as Christine continued. "One of stupid the lighting guys wasn't paying attention and his equipment overheated. Then the fool was reckless enough to knock the lamp over into the set, where it burst into flame. My role at the time happened to be that of an invalid, so I was in a wheelchair. In a futile effort to escape, I fell out of the chair, somehow becoming pinned under it. By now the set was fully ablaze and the staff had rushed to get the foam carts. But, before they could extinguish the flames enough to pull me free, I had already been badly burned. On my face, side and legs." she looked down at her injured leg in its present condition, rather contemplatively. Then her brash manner returned. "I was rushed to the hospital. The last time I was here in fact," then she took a short break.

"Well, they fixed me up as best they could and soon after I went back to my slicer for reconstruction." I rose my eyebrows in question and Christine answered, "Yes, it was Dr. Johansen, the scumbag. You see I was really very lucky. Like most actors in the big leagues, several years before, in order to keep up my mainstream movie star image, I had gone to him for some work, and luckily, he created a full DOTBAM scan of my body. So, after my accident, he was able to use the data base file to reconstruct me." she took another deep breath.

"But even with the data, the synthy flesh treatment had not yet been perfected, and so I was forced to undergo the reconstruction in the old way. The hard way, the painful way. My real flesh was stretched and cut and stretched and cut and cut again. The pain was excruciating, and I had to go through numerous operations, the same cutting and stretching, the same agonizing pain. Especially painful were the repairs to the deep tissue damage. The repairs hurt more than the initial burns." Christine's face cringed as she recalled the pain. "My recuperation was long and hard. I was in an out of treatment for weeks on end and then sitting at home convalescing for many more, only to return yet again for more torturous treatments. It took several operations both on my face and body to get it all right. And, still I was not really perfect. I was never perfect." she sat still for a moment envisaging the memories of her pain.

"Then, when I was finally repaired and about ready to return, all set to call my agent to get me another role. The studio bastards organized the change!" she was mad, no longer contemplative, only steaming mad, "Those heartless scumbags! Just when I was ready to return to the life I knew, they cut off my only source of possible income." Christine remained tense and uncomfortable as she continued.

"But there appeared to be an out for me, an alternative, but only one. You see, back then, the studios liked to use real life models as a basis for their computer-generated characters, said it made them easier to construct, more real. So, right away, with really no other choice, I volunteered to be a model for the computer artists. With my contacts, I was able to secure one of these coveted roles. But there was a catch, there's always a catch. The bastards said I was not perfect enough. Said I needed refinement and that meant more visits to Dr. Johansen." she was not happy, spittle spraying from her mouth, recalling what she had been forced to do.

"I was livid, but with no other choice, I sat through yet another round of operations. The synthy flesh was still in its test phase and so I had to go through more pain and anguish as they reconstructed me to suit their look, their design, their picture of the perfect woman. It was several more months of absolute Hell on earth." she hesitated again, reaching over with her good hand to take a drink of some clear yellow liquid, sitting on her food tray.

"But it all paid off. I made it in as their stupid model, and they used my look for their first female computer lead. I was now known as Cindy Charmed, and my persona was used in over 5 more motion pictures. But that was before things got even more sophisticated, the graphic artists got better, and the technology improved. Thus, allowing the characters to be fully created in the machines without the use of expensive models. Once more the scum, not thinking of me, eliminated my only job, putting me back on the street." a dry throat making her take another drink of the foul looking fluid.

"All that was left was Motion Capture. I tried to sign up as a MC model but was told I was too petite. I tried to get on as a voice actress, but was told my voice was too sweet, not husky enough." Well, it was certainly husky and grainy now!

"There was nothing I could do. The bastards had eliminated all angles, any potential for me to stay in the business. My career in the movies was over!" she took a final sip, finishing the clear yellow swill.

"So, it was Denny's for me after that. All I retained was my apartment, and I was lucky at that. Most of the other owners in the uppity building wanted to throw me out. They believed they were above having a mere waitress living with them. But as I owned it, they had no choice, but I still had to fight tooth and nail to stay. Everything else however, was gone for good. I could not afford any luxuries on a Denny's waitress salary!" her anger had returned, "Oh, I hated those bastards, I hated the studios, I hated the slicers, I hated them all."

"And so, now you know, Ms. Mendez why I began the first set of attacks many years ago. To get revenge. Revenge on all those scumbags who ruined my life, those bastards who put me through Hell on earth and then took everything from me." she looked at Anne with a burning in her eyes, a fire that could not be quenched.

"Eventually, however, after all of your investigations, it was getting too dangerous to continue, and I remember once you almost caught me." Anne nodded, "After that, I gave up for a while laying low, working at Denny's, waiting for another chance to exact further revenge." Christine became quieter again, "I had almost given up. Almost decided to stop planning and move on with my life."

It looked as if she had finished, but I knew there was more. It was impossible to be anything but on the edge of my seat, listening intently to Christine's narrative as it slowly unwound. Even though I did not agree with her methods, I was beginning to understand a little about her motivations and reasoning, but still not liking or accepting it. It was what my mother always used to say; if life throws you lemons, make lemonade.

"But that all changed when I found out about Evans!" Christine was boiling over again, "Yes, that son of a bitch. Remember I told you about the lighting tech who burned me."

Anne and I looked shocked, suddenly realizing the significance and it showed, "Yes, his name was Evans! Over the years the bastard had worked his way up behind the camera and was now a director! A director, for goodness sake, the bastard!" and then Christine lost it.

"I had thought the bum had quit, but no, the studios had made him a director! That was the last draw. With many years having passed and the trail gone cold, it was time to dust off my plastic explosives and to finally get that son of a bitch once and for all!" and she actually giggled with glee, "I had it all planned. I studied his movements, his time in and out of the studio, everything. Eventually, under the guise of the voice actor change, I made my move. But then you came along!" and she looked right at me, her eyes glazed in resentment.

"I was supposed to set a charge that first day we went to the museum. I knew the motion capture sound stage was on the tour and I was all prepared. But when we went into the MC studio, you Ryan," and she stared at me again, "you spoiled any attempt I might have made that evening. Oh, I was furious with you, but decided I would bide my time."

"Then, after you told me where and when you would be working, I rethought it through and decided to take advantage of the situation, dropping you off and then hanging back that day. Entering the studio through the rear fence, I set the charge, marking a time when I was sure the only person left in the soundstage would be him. But your delayed filming in the pool tank studio spoiled all that."

"You killed an innocent woman that day. My friend, Marcia." I was hurt when I remembered it.

"I know, but she was collateral damage, I just wanted to get that bastard, Evans."

No remorse, no regret. Collateral damage indeed.

"What about the day at the slicers? Why the bomb there?" this question came from Anne.

"Well that one was a little different. That day was on a whim. You see, even though I had been the first computer generated lead, nobody ever wanted to be Cindy Charmed. There were no young teenage girls, or boys for that matter, who ever wanted to look like me. I suppose because synthy flesh was not yet viable, but what did that matter! I was jealous of all those kids wanting to be Danny Dunn and Suzie Shine! Why not me, Cindy Charmed. And then my doctor, my torturer was now selling specials to those same kids! Feeling rejected, I was angry, upset. So, on the spur of the moment, I decided to leave our tour and set the charges, teach that doctor idiot a lesson. Pay him back for all he did to me. Again, I was after Dr. Johansen for not only hurting me physically, but mentally as well. It was as good a time as any."

"But this time you knew I was there, what was I to you? Just more of your collateral damage?" it was time for me to be angry.

"No! You moron!" she screamed, "I knew he would take you to his office. I knew he would instruct you to stay in the room a few minutes while he got ready, so that you could watch. I knew, because that was exactly what he did to me the first time he showed me the synthy flesh process. I blew the charge when he was in the operating room and you were safe in the office." she looked at me with I don't care look, but still added. "I knew the size of his door. It was like a bunker. I knew you'd be safe, but I did not count on the girl or your foolish heroics."

This time the look appeared to have some concern, "At the time I was genuinely upset when you eventually got out of there! Because, I really didn't want to see you hurt!" then she stopped, breathing hard, reconsidering, changing her tune almost instantly, "But if I could do it all again, and you were hurt, it would have all been worth it just to see that bastard dead!"

And that stung, it really stung. That's when I really began to dislike this Christine. She had changed and all I was to her was cannon fodder!

"Okay, that explains it." now it was my turn to look at her with malevolent eyes, "So, I suppose I was just another side casualty of your attack on the screening room? I was there too, as you recall, and nearly lost my life there!"

225

"If it makes you feel any better, and quite frankly I don't really care if it does, but Evans NEVER invited anyone else to dailies viewing before! Of course, I knew the projectionist would have to suffer, but again there was no specific intent to hurt you. It was only Evans."

She stalled before continuing, "But nothing went right that day. Evans left just before the explosion and two more unfortunates were killed in his place." again, I had failed, but was determined to continue my plans. But then you two found out! After that, the only way I was going to be able to get Evans was to get rid of you first! And of course, you know the rest!"

"I blame you for my failures. It was because of you he is still alive." and at that she began babbling again, losing her cool, her frustration and anger building once again. This time directed at us.

"I've heard enough!" Anne stated, rising from her seat, getting up to leave, then just before the door, turning to Christine. "When you are well enough to be moved, you will be reprimanded in custody and transferred away from here for immediate processing. Have a good evening!" and with a partial salute, she left the room storming past the guard on watch.

That left Christine and I alone, but one item remained unanswered, "One question," I asked her, curious, "why do you think Evans used your image for his mermaid?"

"I don't know," she almost yelled, "How am I supposed to know?" then added rather schemingly as an afterthought, "Perhaps it was a joke," then she cackled, enjoying herself, "or perhaps, he once had a crush on me and it was one of his ultimate fantasies, the scumbag!" the last part stated with such vindictiveness, it was downright scary.

As I got up to go, Christine grabbed my arm, suddenly changed again. "I really didn't mean to hurt you, you know. But you got in my way."

I looked right into her eyes and replied evenly, my voice deathly flat, "I know and I'm glad I did. Because you happened to have killed two of my good friends in the process. I only wish I could have done more."

Now I was upset, ready to leave, "You know, I don't know what's to come from this processing thing, but I hope you get what you truly deserve."

And then I too left the room. And never looked back.

Chapter Nineteen – The Slicer's New Digs – What is Wrong with this Crazy World?

.

Out of the blue, Dr. Johansen contacted me that evening to say he was extremely thankful for all that I had done for him and his team, but more specifically for what I had done for young Sondra. He was most pleased to say that he would not have to suffer any impending lawsuits stemming from the incident. Apparently, the young lady had been so delighted with her rescue, she had put it down to a once in a lifetime experience, one to be remembered forever, and not to be spoiled by any potentially ugly litigation. He did not appreciate, however, how he had permanently lost one of his clients, but he shrugged it off, 'some people' was all he said. Needless to say, he still sounded quite put out over the com unit.

Then continuing, his mood now much improved, he was good enough to mention, after all that I had gone through, and our resulting adventures of that day, that I had missed witnessing the actual slicing procedure itself. As he was now fully recovered from his ordeal, and he had safely set up another slicing shop in some temporary digs across the street from his demolished office, he wanted me to come down and witness one of the operations for myself. He assured me he would work through, or reading between the lines, he would ignore, any legal issues that might apply for his 'Hero.'

With all of the trauma experienced over the last several days, the distraction might be worth the effort. And as there was still some time before the funeral, I promptly agreed to come down the following day. There might also be a chance to talk with him about Christine, to complete the puzzle, as there are always two sides to any story.

As usual, like clockwork, the sun was up again the next morning and also extremely hot as I looked through the windows of my Robi-car transport at the massive slicing complex coming into view. Although the A/C was on full blast and the main cabin temperature was very comfortable, when moving my head closer to the windscreen for a better look, just like in the California desert, I could feel the burning heat making its way through the shaded glass into the passenger cabin. This forced me to sit back, as the car came to a stop outside of one of the new towers across from the square.

The huge fountain stood, where I remembered it, still sparkling brightly, the falling alcohol droplets making rainbows in the air. The doctor's old building also remained, the black hole in the façade now covered with plywood sheeting, repairs well underway. It was weird to be returning to this location so soon. I had really not expected to come back at all, viewing it as only something to do to fill the time, learn more about Christine, and take my mind off the upcoming somber burial proceedings.

Entering the building, it was immediately evident that it was set up in a very similar way to the doctor's other tower, various greys and silvers welcoming its guests into the lobby. Thankfully absent, however, was the grumpy attendant and the line of screaming youngsters waiting for their 'specials'. The elevator was waiting as had happened previously, barely having to even touch the controls, before it began to move as if sensing where I wanted to go. This time the Doc was on the 45th level, much higher than before, with many more floors to travel. As before, however, the elevator opened almost instantly, depositing me safely at that morning's destination.

The reception area was also much the same as his previous one, its utilitarian design very familiar. Behind the desk was the same cute, freckle faced, green haired receptionist, a wide welcome smile beaming on her Suzie Shine face. She still had a small bandage on one side of her cheek, as I headed right up to the desk, placing one hand on the cold stone countertop.

"Well hello, Mr. Hero," she stated, the greeting very chipper and authentic, meaning every word, but this time with a slightly provocative edge. "Welcome back. The doctor is expecting you. Just head right on down that corridor." then she gestured with her arm, "His office is last door on the left."

As I was about to turn away, she suddenly grabbed my hand, her soft touch, warm and inviting. Acting, as if nervous and having just made a last-minute decision, her false pretty face going pink with embarrassment, she quickly but sheepishly added, "Hey, I get off at 3. Would you like to go for a café somewhere? I know a nice place?" then sat heavily back in her chair, as if she was glad to have gotten that over with.

"Well, my dear, while I'm extremely flattered, and find you very attractive, and I can also see how hard it was for you to get up the courage to ask, I must still respectfully, decline. You see, unfortunately, I will not be in town beyond tomorrow. It was very nice of you, however, to consider asking," and I smiled broadly at the young girl, reaching down and patting her lightly on the hand. She released a deep breath, then pouted slightly, clearly put out at my rebuff after all of her efforts.

"Have a great day." I said, smiling, as I wandered past the desk and down the hall.

The layout of the treatment rooms was very similar, however, there were not as many large view ports and the main operating theater was not in sight, anywhere. Perhaps it was on another floor, or behind one of the blank doorways. The corridor was a pleasant colour, extremely bright and smelled clean, with a just hint of medicinal antiseptic. With no distractions to slow me down, I quickly reached the doctor's office, a temporary tag of his name having been rather crudely installed on the steel entry. There was only a small side light of fogged glass on one side of the door which prevented me from seeing inside. So, I knocked.

Almost as soon as doing so, a shadow appeared, and the door opened, revealing Doctor Johansen with a big smile on his face, begging for me to come in.

"Come in, come in, and welcome, Mr. Hero! It is so nice to have you here." he swept his long white coated arm around the room. "These facilities are not nearly as nice as my last ones but are very sufficient for my proposes at the moment. Yes, very sufficient."

Entering the office, inwardly I agreed with the doctor's initial statement. The room was much sparser than his last office, with a plain, speckled medium blue linoleum floor, white walls and very industrial looking furnishings. His desk consisted of a plain sheet of thick, green tinted glass mounted on two polished steel tripods. The chairs were chrome steel frames with barely any cushion and there was not one piece of art, or any books, in sight, save for a heavy iron sculpture on one end of the transparent tabletop. Quite a marked difference from his last, very opulent office set-up.

"Come in and sit, Mr. Scott," the doctor gesturing almost wildly to the nearest chair. It was shaped to my body and had a black leatherette surface but, just as I had predicted, was not very comfortable. "Thanks, so much for coming. I am so very excited. I have a very special treat for you today, and I can't wait to show you."

As he said this, he rubbed his hands together as if to warm them up, reminding me of a greedy miser counting his money.

"Hey, thanks for having me back. After such a disaster during my previous visit. Really, I didn't think we would ever see each other again," crossing then re-crossing my legs, making myself as comfortable as I could.

"Well, you are in for a real treat. You see, we are doing a whole-body transformation today, a full on personal translational slicing. Or PTS as I refer to it. You know how last time I showed you the dTBM machine and how it can save facial structures."

"Yes." showing only feigned interest.

"Well, as I also mentioned, it retains the added ability to save the patients entire body structure as well. So, as you might expect, we therefore possess the ability to translate that body into something else entirely." he was very excited, "I'm sure you've seen the multi-armed waitresses at some of the high-end restaurants in town?"

"Indeed, I have," remembering the gold tinted, six-armed beauty from the first night Christine and I went out.

"Well, with this process we go one step further, with a PTS, we can change male to female or female to male as the case may be. I just happen to have a young gent in for therapy today who wishes to be Sally Storm, isn't that great!" he smiled ear to ear like a Cheshire cat, "and I'm just delighted to be able to show you the procedure!" and once more he rubbed his hands together.

"Ah, I'm sure that's great doc, but I really want to have a word with you about Christine."

"Yes, indeed. I heard about her." he stated a bit unsure, "Tragic."

"Yes, well I really want to know about her first visits with you. Right after the accident. Can you tell me about it?"

"Indeed, my boy, a most unfortunate story, truly most unfortunate." he had calmed down considerably, and you could tell he was reliving it all in his mind, "That was a few years ago now, but I remember it well. Poor girl was brought in here with massive burns, many of them deep tissue burns, many very scarred. We were lucky to have just recently completed her full body DOTBAM. It saved her.

"I was able to program the system to reconstruct her back to exactly how she was before the accident. Such a beauty." and he stared up towards the ceiling.

"Yes, doc but apparently, at the time of her accident, the synthy flesh was not yet ready, correct?"

"Right you are again. Yes, the synthy flesh process was still in its test phases and so was unavailable for us slicers to use at the time. I had to treat her the old-fashioned way, by rebuilding her own flesh, pulling bits from here, putting it there. A very painful process. Wouldn't want to go through it myself. Wouldn't wish it on anyone for that matter. But she was a trooper, we got it done and almost had her back to normal."

"Then a few weeks later the girl was back here with a series of computer sketches wanting to be re-sliced. I couldn't believe it! She had just been through months and months of therapy, very painful therapy, and had survived. Now she wanted to change it all again. I was shocked. But in the end, I agreed. She paid for it of course! And eventually she got what she wanted; 10 years younger!"

"10 years!" I shouted, flabbergasted.

"Yes... but I thought you knew," he stopped realizing his error, "You didn't know, did you? She didn't tell you?"

I shook my head, negatively.

"Then she couldn't have told you she had a synthy flesh refit, several years ago, either. Oh, boy." he hesitated, "Well I don't know how to put this, so I'll just tell you. Mr. Scott, when the accident occurred, Christine was in her mid-30's. Right now, she's almost 50 years old!"

Not knowing what to say, I was completely shocked with what I was hearing. It was amazing! Christine's initial transformation from mid-thirties back to 20 years old and then her subsequent, much more recent 'refit' turning a near 50-year-old back into a young 30. It was incredible! I could not believe it.

"Of course, the original operation would have been much easier with the synthy flesh. We can use it for all sorts of transformations these days and the healing process is tremendously fast and relatively painless. It's a shame we didn't have it for her 17 years ago." he said it almost as if he cared.

"I assume you use your synthy flesh for this PTS conversion process of yours?" I asked tentatively, beginning to feel slightly uncomfortable with this whole slicing thing, the rapid changes with no waiting, finally beginning to see Christine's distorted point of view of the entire process.

"Indeed, my friend, indeed." The doctor continued to smile, quite excited about telling me the ins and outs of the entire PTS transformation process, "It's quite straight forward really. You see I have a talented group of sculptors and artisans presently under my employ. Using their artistic and creative genius, we fabricate the necessary body parts ahead of time using the synthy flesh and then, after proper preparation and scanning in the DOTBAM, it's out with the old and in with the new!" he stated this so unconcernedly, very proud of his creations, not seeing the potential damage he was promoting with these full scale bodily changes.

But he continued, "All the parts are of course completely functional, and 100 percent guaranteed. Except the deep internals of course," he stated the last part at a lower tone and then bent over his desk, wanting to get closer to me, whispering, "we can't go that far I'm afraid." then he laughed softly, "Wouldn't want any of our boys trying it out getting pregnant now would we?" raising his voice once again, as if the unpleasantness was over, "But everything else is exactly as nature intended it to be!"

The callousness of his speech was unbelievable. This man was talking about changing people's lives for goodness sake! Back and forth in gender like a roller coaster. All for fun and the almighty buck. For the first time, even I began to detest this man and his unnatural works.

But there was more, "The most fantastic part about the whole conversion process," the doctor continued, "is that, thanks to the DOTBAM, we now have the patient's original image on file, as it were, stored right there in our data bank. If the patient doesn't like their conversion, then we can put them right back the way they used to be." and he smiled wickedly, "For an additional fee of course!" then added as an afterthought, "Of course we lost all of our most recent files in that nasty explosion. So unfortunately, those poor souls will be out of luck. Unless then want to go back to looking like Danny Dunn or Suzie Shine instead!"

I was disgusted, but asked anyway, "Do both men and women seek these reassignments?"

"Of course, they do. Some even want half and half, but that's where I draw the line." he was quite adamant, literally drawing a line in the air over his desk with his hand, "it's one or the other for me. They can go to some other slicer for the in-between!" I rolled my eyes at his stupidity and deformed moral compass.

"This latest patient, the one we'll see later, just happens to be one of my male patients, at least for now!" he added and then winked at me, "But everyone try's this. We get almost an equal number of both men and women interested in this form of treatment." adding, "Truthfully though, changing a young man into Suzie Shine, or Sally Storm is a lot easier than altering a pretty girl into Donny Dare or Danny Dunn. It takes much more time and a lot more pre work, if you understand my meaning," and he winked at me for the second time.

"I think I do," now completely losing interest, thinking this man detestable, wanting to leave.

"But that's the nature of this game." and he rambled on, enjoying having an audience, "Some folks they want a permanent change, a new way of life. Sometimes to get a specific job, to do something they presently just can't or, incredibly enough, because their partners demand it."

He took a breath before continuing, "The majority, on the other hand, just want to try it on for size, you know, see how the other half lives. I've had many repeat customers, some who have come in so frequently, mind you, without their image in the data base, I would have forgotten what they originally looked like!" and he chuckled again. "That's the beauty of the DOTBAM system for you, completely unlimited. It can do what you want when you want it and how often you want it. And you can always go back, provided the data base stays intact. And you have the money of course!" the doctor was on a role confirming his motivations, his drive. All for the almighty buck.

Then he got a bit too detailed, and I really began to feel sickened, "We're also careful to keep the existing parts around for at least a year, just in case our patients don't like their 'new' self. Our cryogenic storage is after all, only so big." and then he laughed again, "Of course my previous storage no longer exists thanks to Christine, the troubled girl. I'll have to make a note to source a new one," and he wrote something down on his floating screen.

"Now where was I, Ah, yes. Well for the ladies it's not so bad, everything has to be created from synthy flesh mostly, not much to keep from the ladies who participate, as there's not much to remove, just adding on mostly," and he laughed again, this time quite loud.

Then he told a rather personal story, and as he did, I felt I was truly intruding, now looking for any excuse to leave. But that didn't stop the doctor, who ignorantly had not yet recognized my complete condemnation about the whole slicer mockery.

"You know it's funny, I once had a rich university student who came in here and wanted the transformation just for Spring Break! Spring Break, can you believe it! And so, he left here as a fully functional, anatomically correct rendition of Suzie Shine. He came back two weeks later, and we had him swiftly returned to his former self for the start of term. Quite fascinating!"

"Now mind you," and he looked contemplative for a moment, "Although, we retained the young man's original parts, we had to use a lot of synthy flesh for the other reconstructions, legs, shoulders and so on. You know of course gentlemen are so much larger in body mass than the ladies. Not exactly the same but 99% percent effective. Trouble was, the reversion occurred so soon after his initial change, that his real flesh hadn't yet had time to fully heal. This made the conversion back that much more difficult, but we managed." he concluded his story content, "All in a day's work. Quite the thing to see. Ah, well you get all kinds, all kinds."

Original parts! This sounded like an automobile collision repair shop! Where was the door!

Then Dr. Johansen turned red and began to laugh, hysterically.

"What is it?" I asked, now thoroughly disgusted at this inhuman and demented freak show, denying the very laws of nature.

"It just dawned on me, and I remember it to this day," and he continued laughing, spittle spraying out of his thin lips, "It all happened so fast. You see when we had finished up and sent him home, he still had the suntan lines left over from his itsy-bitsy bikini. Hilarious!"

Hilarious indeed!

I had had enough! The doctor's callousness was outright disturbing, his careless disregard for his patients, their minds and their lives was unacceptable, and it was quite clear the only thing that mattered to this man was the money he made from his slicing conversions! Even in the case of poor twisted Christine it had always been about the almighty dollar! It finally showed me how distorted and deformed this new society had become and only re-confirmed that it was time to go. Go away from here and go home! Reset the clock on this plastic surgery nightmare!

Unhesitatingly, using the break in his monologue, I stood up to leave, "Well, thank you very much doctor, I've heard... and seen enough."

"But you haven't even seen the operation yet?" his smile vanishing in an instant.

"Maybe some other... time," and then it was my turn to laugh.

I turned and exited the room, not looking back, leaving the doctor with an open mouth and a very surprised look on his face.

"But..."

"Goodbye, Doctor," and then I left, happy to be out of there, chuckling all the way back to the awaiting elevator.

Chapter Twenty – The Funeral

et rain fogged the windows of my Robi-car as I headed towards the Hollywood cemetery the next morning, the day of the burial. As it moved steadily through the streets, the constant wash of water on the windshield of the public transport was therapeutic, the sounds of the dropping water somewhat relaxing. The way the rain fell, splashed, then remaining for just a moment, only to be smeared away by the wiper blades, gave me something to concentrate on. Very fitting for the occasion and rather appropriately, mother nature had decided to share in the gloom of the day. The normally sunny Southern California daybreak distinctly absent, the overcast sky's deciding to share in our sorrows, weeping steadily along with the rest of the of the service's attendees.

Making sure to be a bit early, I was able to wander, undisturbed, over to the burial site to convey my own personal respects. With the rapidly falling rain the air was cool, but it smelled fresh, earthy and despite the day, alive. Easily spotting the three coffins located over their respective pits, each one humbly poised and ready for their final reverential lowering into the moist soil, I headed over in that direction. The grass was wet, but had been dry for so long, the ground was still firm, making the walk to the gravesite tolerable, considering my recently acquired limp and other injuries.

The first, smaller coffin held the fully intact body of Marcia, which only a few days previously I had removed from a burning building with the vain hope of resurrection, receiving only negative results. The casket was made of a very beautiful pink toned hard wood, picked out by the victim's Asian parents. There were cherry blossoms dutifully engraved on its surface, very fine delicate woodwork; the kind of detail from a lost time. Various Chinese characters also adorned its exterior having been carved in the middle of the coffins lid, presumably offering Marcia safe travels into the netherworld, there to provide her constant company for her onward voyage.

The second casket was much larger in size and a glossy, jet black, shining like a magnificent grand piano, very suitable for the grandiose, fun loving person that now resided within. Although, unfortunately, the impressive sarcophagus only contained a small selection of charred bones and a skull, representing the sum total of the very meager number of recovered remains of Angelo's body that had been found amongst the burnt rubble and shattered remnants of Screening Room One. A sad excuse of an end for such a lively, caring individual.

The third coffin, was a very humble and basic, light yellow pine affair, also happening to house only partial remains of Christine's last victim, the final casualty of the concluding explosion. The poor young female projectionist who, I found out later, had been a university student fulfilling a part time summer position at the studio.

As it turned out, Angelo and the projectionist were the only ones killed in the incident. Director Evans apparently having exited the building temporarily on an important errand, had managed to avoid the brunt of the blast. He had just left by the main doors at the time of the explosion and had been knocked over by the force of its initial detonation as he stood outside awaiting his driver. He sustained only minor cuts and bruises, and despite his massive headache, was raring to continue, upset not about the loss of his people, but of the daily footage that had been consumed in the blaze.

My opinion of the man altered considerably after the incident and before leaving, had managed to tell him that not only was his callousness not welcome, it was inhuman. The only thing I received, in exchange, was a stifled grunt. Perhaps poor confused Christine knew a little of what she was talking about.

The falling water droplets flowed evenly over the three caskets, coagulating with their other companions, before dribbling over the side, creating individual minute waterfalls descending into the deep pits below. Each coffin was equipped with several polished brass handles that reflected the gloomy mood of the burial's attendees. Small reflections barely visible, many of them distorted due to the accumulations of fluid dripping from each of the cold metallic grips. I stared for a moment at my inaccurate reflection in one of the handlebars on Marcia's casket, thinking the deformed, gargoyle like visage suited my feelings and thoughts very appropriately.

Using an outstretched thumb, I touched the top of each box, gently, making the sign of the cross on its surface, displacing the collected drops of fallen water beneath my fingers, then pressing my wet hand to my lips in prayer. The resulting flow only served to create a new set of micro-waterfalls cascading into the pit, absorbing at once into the drenched soil at its dark bottom.

There was simply no denying that after this, I was leaving Hollywood of 2065, forever.

Looking around at the crowds as they arrived, revealed many carrying their very strange umbrellas, but all wearing the required black silk sash over their multi-coloured outfits, crossed from right to left around their torsos. I too wore mine, prominently displayed over top of my more conservative, navy suit that I had managed to find for the occasion. According to local protocol, I discovered, once the burial was complete, we were all to remove the sash and replace it left to right, almost like some kind of macabre graduation ceremony. It was hard to get used to the differences of this very odd, and often very confusing, future time.

Included in the funeral attendees were of course Marcia's parents, who apparently lived close by, the young projectionist's mother and her sister, as well as Angelo's friends and relatives. If Angelo's mother and father were present, they laid very low and were therefore difficult to discern amongst the large crowd. Marcia's mother, however, was petite like her daughter, her father not much taller. The two looked as expected, extremely upset, Marcia's Mum crying into her husband's shoulder, her father wiping his eyes and nose with a multicoloured handkerchief. There were also a few studio execs, and my new friend, Gordon Flichette, who stood there more reverently than most, clearly very upset about the whole ordeal, the rainwater dribbling off his perfectly cleft chin.

"Thanks for coming," I said politely, as I patted him lightly on his wet shoulder.

"No issues, Ryan. It was least I could do." then he looked straight at me. It was a very sad look, but one full of care and concern, "Hey, you take care of yourself."

"You too. And good luck at the studio." was all I could offer.

Notably absent was Director Evans, who undoubtedly had some dailies to view or a gala premier to attend. Remembering back fondly of how it gave me the greatest of pleasures to tell that bastard to take his job and shove it. I will never forget the shocked and surprised look on his snotty, self-righteous face as I did it, but it was worth every penny.

The service was reverent but quick, over almost before it had begun. Luckily, the rain had subsided, but only just a little, as the cemetery workers began to lower the three caskets, all at the same time, into the awaiting graves. There were many tears shed that afternoon, mine included. Just looking at Marcia's Mum and Dad as they threw some moist soil onto the lowered box of their daughter, would tear at the heartstrings of anyone with even one ounce of feeling.

As I eventually turned away from the depressing scene, I spotted Detective Mendez in the rear, standing under the protection of an oak tree, staying out of the rain and away from the immediate families mourning by the graveside. I wandered over, the trickles of water still flowing down my neck and into my soaking wet collar, my hair plastered smoothly against my head. In the light wind, I picked up the scent of her floral body fragrance as I approached.

"It's nice to see you here," I said quietly, "I'm sure the families appreciated it."

"I'm sure they didn't even notice," she stated directly. "I thought it best that I stay out of the way. Helps avoid dragging up any more bad memories," Anne was nonetheless genuinely mournful, but also clearly expressed the look of someone wanting to talk.

"Well, I appreciate it. And I'm sure Marcia and Angelo do too." I mused, as the water continued to dribble down my face. "They were good people. It's a real shame how things came to this. I just can't believe it; it seems so unreal."

When she just nodded silently in reply, I asked a question to get her back in the conversation, "So, what will happen to Christine?"

"Ah, that's already been taken care of," the Detective informed me, "She has already been tried and convicted of endless counts of willful property damage, attempted murder and both first and second-degree murder. Both from the recent incidents and most of the cold case ones, from over 15 years ago. She'll be sent to the prisoner holding facility at Barstow for processing and assessment and then ultimately... terminated."

"Boy, you guys don't mess around, do you?"

"Nope. We like to keep things quick and simple as possible. Makes things much easier."

Another uncomfortable silence, with us just looking at one another. Deciding to break the awkward peace, just to hear her voice once more.

"Hey, before I go, I have another question that's been bugging me for almost a week now.

"Shoot, what is it?" smiling broadly, welcoming the question.

"Well, why do they call all those self-driving public transports Robi-cars?"

"Ah that easy," and she gently laughed, "it's a local term, only used here. Decades and decades ago, there was a science fiction film, I can't remember the name now, it was way before the change. Anyway, there was a robot character called Robi the Robot. So, when the cars were invented someone started using the term and it stuck."

"It was 'Lost in Space' and it was Robbie the Robot!" chuckling, stating it in full agreement.

"Wow, you must be a real movie buff to have remembered that one! That film's well over 60 years old now." Anne was impressed.

And that only the remake, I thought to myself, "Nah, it may be old to you, but it's just like yesterday for me!"

Anne didn't look like she knew what to say, not quite understanding my curious comment, a slightly odd look visible on her pretty face.

"Well," I said, breaking the momentary silence, hesitating. Knowing now there was not much left to say. I held out my wet hand, "It's been nice knowing you." Anne's hand was warm, against my cold skin.

"Hey, Ryan," she said, softly, "I want to thank you again for helping out these last few days. It was… fun."

"Yes, it was. If you can call getting almost blown to bits three times, fun." laughing nervously.

"You did enjoy my AirLift driving though, admit it?" smiling shyly as she said it.

"Okay, that part really was fun, come to think of it."

We were both quiet again for a few moments.

"Can I give you a ride somewhere?" she asked, hopeful, a slight sparkle in her eyes.

"No. That's alright. I'll just find a public ride around here... sorry a Robi-car, and head back to where I came from. I know how to work them now." Anne laughed at my attempt at humor, "This movie business is, unfortunately, just not the life for me." then adding just to be sure, "And don't get me going about those slicers, disgusting people."

"I understand, all too well. Because I agree with you. One hundred per cent!" a little more cheerful, "There are some things that you just don't fuss with."

And at that we both smiled, before she continued. "Well, you have my appreciation, and my friendship. Thanks again for all of your help. And, hey! Take care of yourself." then she touched my arm, all serious, "Also, one last thing, Ryan. Do me a favour?"

"What's that?" I asked sheepishly.

"Don't run into any more burning buildings, okay!"

With those parting words, Anne smiled. A warm friendly smile, one to take all the cares and worries of the last week and melt them away, just like that.

"I'll try not to," I returned, feeling so much better, "but you know me, Mr. Hero."

"Goodbye then, Mr. Hero."

"Goodbye, Anne."

And then I turned away, back into the pouring rain.

Epilogue – Home Again

It did not take long to catch an automated drive back up into the hills on Mt. Lee. I just told the Robi-car to take me to the Hollywood sign and off it went. Apparently, even though the ancient landmark had been neglected over the intervening years, people still remembered its uniqueness and importance, making the pilgrimage up the mountain drive once in a while. The auto-drive vehicle pulled to the curb at the entrance to the trail, coming to a smooth stop on the still wet pavement. The rain had abated by then and for the first time that day, the sun was finally beginning to peak through the dark grey clouds. Stepping free of the vehicle, I could see the steaming vapours swirling off the quickly warming pavement.

The air was fresh and inviting, and the temperature still sufficiently cool, so that the hike up the trail was easy, comfortable and enjoyable for my last hour here in 2065. It was not difficult to find the location where I had stored my machine and upon arrival, I gently bent down to sweep away most of the accumulated dirt and debris that I had used almost a week previously as camouflage. It had remained undisturbed there on the hill for the entire time I had been away and was in fine shape. Just a little moist from the recent rains.

Repositioning it slightly to insure it would open correctly, I reached down onto the base, activating the opening mechanism. As the upper and lower sections split apart like a spring flower in the morning, I watched as the residue rain droplets dribbled off the rising shell, running down the magnet risers and pooling on the bottom of the dark steel transport plate.

The control panel blipped once, and the lights flashed, the time machine's system powering up and going through the start-up sequence and maintenance diagnostic. I watched as the numerals representing my safe return date, formed in the glowing overhead display.

After verifying all was in order, I turned around, staring intently down the hill once more at Los Angeles 2065. The clouds had now mostly cleared to reveal a gorgeous spring afternoon, the downtown city center sparkling in the crystal-clear atmosphere. Further, to the right of these soaring pinnacles, closer to the undulating waves of the Pacific, were the not quite so tall buildings of the Beverly Hills Medical Complex, the home of the slicers. Squinting, in the gently intensifying afternoon light, I could just barely make out the gaping hole so recently repaired, on the side of the third tower from the left. The stain of the recent explosion like an unwashed blemish on an otherwise perfect face.

One slight turn and I was looking north, up the hill, revealing for the last time, a view of the still poor looking excuse for a historical landmark. The old Hollywood sign's massive letters still broken and misused. The vision made me think back to my experience and adventures of the last week, and for the first time, really began to understand its sorry, neglected and unmaintained existence.

For me, the decrepit sign's condition represented the state of the present society now wildly in motion, in this not too distant future. One that contained an equally rundown, uncaring human populace, where people sliced themselves into someone else just for a holiday, while they watched movies made entirely of non-existent people. It was a society where movie directors and plastic surgeons, cared for nothing, nor anything but themselves, the almighty dollar, and where the next job was coming from. A lifestyle of vending machine shopping, robotic cars and six-armed waitresses. A world where Hawaii was encased in plastic, and marine life virtually nonexistent. A culture that would make a 50-year-old woman, want to terrorize and murder innocents just to seek a pent-up revenge, caused only by suffering and hate. But worse of all, it was a demented civilization where the downtrodden could take up sports like chute less skydiving or cordless bungee jumping, hoping to solve their problems by ending them, permanently.

Granted, this extremely lackluster world did have its minor saving graces, with people like Marcia, Angelo, Gordon and Anne. Just a few of the individuals that had cared enough to help a stranger in need. Little good it did the first two.

They say one truly good person can eliminate the bad deeds of a thousand, so in the end, perhaps this depraved, corrupt and degenerate world was not all lost. The only thing I knew for sure was that I had had enough, and it was definitely time to go home.

I stepped between the static magnetic bars onto the transport pad and activated the time travelling mechanism. As the rails began their circular acceleration, first becoming blurry and then almost invisible, I had my last look at the world of Hollywood 2065.

As the bars slowed to become motionless once again, I was at last greeted by a more familiar downtown LA, bathed in the deep orange sunlight of the late afternoon, the bright white letters of the perfectly maintained Hollywood sign towering above. And around it all, the shadowy mist of a red tinted smog shimmering in the distance.

I had a dinner date with my brother, my nephews and my son later that night and so I was right where I wanted to be. I was home.

Afterward – Author's Notes

I really enjoyed writing this tale of a future Hollywood. I have always loved the movies, the writing, the acting, the music and the special effects. I remember when I was a teenager, seeing Star Wars ten times in that hot summer of 1977. Then skipping school on a Friday afternoon in 1981 to see the first show of The Empire Strikes Back and hear Darth Vader tell Luke that he was his father. I can still feel the chills those immortal words sent down my spine.

For those of you who've read the first story of The Time Chronicles, The Kanusan Legacy, I paid homage to that movie in revealing the villain of the story to be our time traveler, Ryan Scott's own son.

I have paid further homage to many films in my books, particularly, one of my favorite time travelling yarns, the Back to The Future series. While this series of films is riddled with what I dislike most about most time travel stories, the paradox, the quintessential humour, classic comedy, excellent writing, story, music and acting are second to none. And that DeLorean! Wow!

It is a great trilogy, my favorite second only to the original Star Wars trilogy. If you have read some of my other novels you will notice I have also paid this great work tribute in the names of some of my characters; Claire BAINES, Nurse TANNEN, and of course DOC.

Another love of mine is holidaying in California, especially driving there. The first chapter of this book describes a road trip to the golden state that I have taken many times with my family, and all of the locations are real and may be visited. Crater Lake, Mt. Shasta, the Redwood Forest, Napa and of course my favourite city in the US, San Francisco and its glorious architecture and streets! I hope I have done them all justice, but I encourage you all to visit these fabled places yourselves. You will not be disappointed.

But I also love LA, Disneyland and Hollywood. And for this novel, I wanted to center my story around one of my favourite places, Universal Studios. As a small boy, I recall travelling around on one of the old, orange painted trams encircling the backlot, with the well-dressed tour guide and poor sound system, passing over the Collapsing Bridge and through the parting of the Red Sea. It's absolutely amazing that the Flash Flood attraction is still in operation today, as I remember first experiencing it almost 45 years ago!

All of the set pieces for the theme park are described as I have personally seen them, both in my youth and most recently in 2019, when Jurassic World opened to replace the Jurassic Park attraction. I have taken some liberty in the sequencing and positioning of the attractions for my story, but if you travel there today you can see everything I have described, particularly the amazing Wizarding World of Harry Potter, which is truly a sight to see! Unfortunately, the clock tower from the Back to the Future days is no more, but I decided to resurrect it in my novel, just for the fun of it.

I do hope, however, my rather drastic vision of the future does not come true for this great park, and that it will continue to run into the next century, constantly improving and thrilling moviegoers with its magic. I certainly never, ever want to see a Universal Studios Museum!

It was also very thrilling to have the chance to conclude my story at the most famous landmark of all, the Psycho House. Quite certainly the most famous movie house, the world has ever known. It too, still stands there rather forebodingly on the hill in the Universal Studios property and is still included in every backlot tour. I always get a shiver every time I see it.

That being said, I just love Alfred Hitchcock and all he did for Hollywood in the early days and even later, especially what he did for the suspense drama genre. Everyone thinks he made horror films, but Mr. Hitchcock wrote and directed, *Suspense Films*. A big difference. The scene in the classic, The Birds, while Tipi Hedron sits on a bench near the school playground, and slowly, ever so slowly, the monkey bars fill with crows behind her. It is just unforgettable!

I chose the location of my novel's finale in the most famous basement of them all, in homage to this classic film director. Thanks, for all of your great movies, Alfred!

One last thing about this story that I am most thrilled with, in case you did not pick up the significance, is the tribute I have paid to a great story writer from the early part of the 20th century, Mr. Gaston Leroux. He is most famous for his thrilling tale of the Phantom of the Opera, that we all know is a tale set in Paris, France at the turn of the century, where a man, deformed from birth, terrorizes the local Opera house. One of the key characters in that delightful story is the heroine, Christine, with whom the Phantom falls deeply in love. My character of Christine is therefore, rather aptly named as my own disfigured antagonist who sets upon terrorizing Hollywood, in this story of the not too distant future.

Anyway, I hope you have enjoyed the personal chronicles of the trials and tribulations of my time travelling hero, Ryan Scott. After four adventures, I am now on to something new and totally different. Please look out for my next novel, the Knave of Hearts, written in third person, which is my own take on the fabled medieval story of robbing from the rich to help the poor.

So, while we leave Ryan Scott with his time machine safely locked away in his garage for now, perhaps one day, he may return in yet another adventure into the unknown future.

Other Books by this Author

The Time Chronicles

The further adventures of Ryan Scott and his future experiences can be found in the next book of the series:

The adventure begins with:

The Kanusan Legacy

Book 2 – An Artificial Utopia

Book 3 – Repeating Mistakes

And coming soon, a completely different kind of adventure

The Knave of Hearts

Printed in Great Britain
by Amazon

44749249R00161